Turnstiles

Andrea McKenzie Raine

*Scan this QR Code
to learn more about
this title*

Raine, Andrea McKenzie.
    Turnstiles / by Andrea McKenzie Raine.
    pages cm
    LCCN 2013949317
    ISBN 978-1-62901-012-0 (pbk.)
    ISBN 978-1-62901-013-7 (Kindle)

    1. Homeless persons--Fiction. 2. Rich people--Fiction. 3. Prostitutes--Fiction. 4. London (England)--Fiction. 5. Psychological fiction. I. Title.

    PS3618.A3932T87 2013   813'.6
                    QBI13-600201

Publisher: Inkwater Press | www.inkwaterpress.com

Paperback ISBN-13 978-1-62901-012-0 | ISBN-10 1-62901-012-X

Kindle ISBN-13 978-1-62901-013-7 | ISBN-10 1-62901-013-8

Printed in the U.S.A.
All paper is acid free and meets all ANSI standards for archival quality paper.

3 5 7 9 10 8 6 4

For Connor and Joel, my beautiful boys.

Acknowledgments

I wish to acknowledge the insights and musings of Friedrich Nietzsche in his work *Beyond Good and Evil* and the selected poems of Emily Dickinson on exploring the human condition.

On a personal note, my heartfelt gratitude to my mother who read the early chapters and encouraged me to "keep going," my husband who read the later drafts and allowed me the time to enter my other world, and to my third grade teacher who nurtured and celebrated the writer in me with a life-altering prediction that one day I would become an author.

Chapter 1

MARTIN

Martin opened his eyes. He squinted between his zippered lashes, stuck together with sleep. A small army of shoes marched past his face, which was half-hidden inside a dingy blue sleeping bag. His first instinct was to place a limp, protective hand on his red knapsack. He was inside a short tunnel that lay beneath a busy London street beside Hyde Park. He didn't look up. He knew what their faces would convey, their cowardly faces. He was experiencing the real Europe, instead of peering out at it through heated hotel windows or hostel bunk beds or tour buses. He didn't have to pay anyone for his space of concrete bedding. He was free. He closed his eyes. Martin was free.

He ignored his growling stomach as he smelled the subtle waft of fries from the nearby Hard Rock Café. *Tourists*, he thought. They were all missing the local colour. Except Joe the hotdog vendor, who was from the north, a Scot, an outsider. Hot dogs in London were a foreign idea, but it seemed to catch on like every other

American phenomenon. London was a metropolis with people from every race sounding their thick British accents. It didn't really matter who you were or what you were, only where you happened to become that person. Still, people could tell if you were from somewhere else, and Martin stuck out like a wounded hitch-hiker's thumb. He had a quiet bond with Joe the Outsider and, on most occasions, received his hotdogs for free. Then he would usually lie under a tree in the park and watch tourists get charged two pounds by security for using the lawn chairs. The grass was free. Martin felt as though mindless sheep surrounded him. He had it all figured out.

A year before he had bought a cheap ticket to London and decided to depend on the day to see him through. Martin cherished every consequence. He held on to every face that examined him with curiosity or disgust. He always kept a plain expression. He had no reason to indulge anyone with his emotions. In fact, he barely spoke. Except to people like Joe.

When he opened his eyes again, a different army of shoes were marching past. The tunnel was never quiet, and he had long been used to the intrusion of echoing sounds and rustling pavement. It was a small sacrifice. He wriggled out of his bed and began to pack up. He would return later that night. Martin had become a familiar sight, and some of the locals knew this tunnel was his home. So did some of the other shoestring backpackers. Martin marched alongside the army and out of the tunnel. The sun was out, and again, he squinted. He ran a hand over his stubbled head and rubbed his eyes. He turned left.

The sun was already seated royally in the sky as Martin strolled down the wide, crowded sidewalk. He could see the faint shape of an umbrella a few blocks away, and as he came closer, he recognized Joe. Martin's stomach began to growl again.

"Get your hotdogs here! Hello, sir, what a gorgeous day. Would you like a hotdog? Get your hotdogs here! Good day, love! Can I get you a hotdog? Would you like the works?" Joe called to the passing public all day long. He set up his stand on the same corner every day, and everyone who frequented that spot knew him. Some just by his ruddy, round face, and others knew him well enough to have a word or two. Martin felt he could relate to Joe, because it seemed they were both stuck in London making a living on the sidewalks, and most of the people bustling by chose to ignore them.

"Hey, Joe." Martin showed a couple of teeth and then retracted his smile. Even though he liked Joe, he was still careful not to let anyone get too close. "Catering to the North American public, eh? It's amazing you are able to sell hotdogs here. I guess if you had your way, you'd be selling cans of haggis."

"Marty, my boy!" Joe's face opened wide with good-natured eyes. "How was your night? Those bloody bed bugs didn't bite ya, aye, lad?" he boomed in his rich, Scottish accent, completely disregarding Martin's offhand remarks.

"Nah, Joe. No rats, neither. Just the bloody tourists waking me up in the morning." Martin grimaced.

"Bloody tourists?" Joe raised his eyebrows so high they looked comical. "You better button your tongue, Marty. If there were no tourists, there'd be no hotdogs! Besides, what the devil do you think you are … a member of the general voting public? You're the worst kind of tourist, Marty. You don't pay taxes and you don't leave!" Joe chuckled and flung a hotdog with ketchup and mustard into Martin's waiting hand.

"See ya tomorrow, Joe," said Martin without looking at his friend, and he began to walk away.

"See ya, Marty," Joe said quietly and to himself, because Martin was already out of earshot. And they both knew they meant it. Tomorrow. Chances were they would find themselves in the same skin and doing the same thing. The two of them were like hamsters trapped in transparent, plastic balls looking out at the world, unable to break free of their bubbles and constantly bumping into walls.

WILLIS

The radio alarm clock began to hum in Willis Hancocks' hotel room, which he rented in downtown London. He groaned, rolled over, and slapped his hand on the off button without looking. He rolled back and stared groggily at the dented pillow beside him. She was already gone, and he was trying to recollect the night before. He rolled his eyes towards the dresser. There was his wallet, open and most likely empty. His pants lay crumpled beside the dresser. He rubbed his hands over his face and gave a self-deprecating chuckle. Then he began to rise. He was anything but happy. She had definitely served her purpose, but the others had been more professional, and much more discreet. When this happened, he usually didn't realize he had been robbed until hours later, when he found himself at a store counter fumbling for his credit cards.

"You cheeky little bitch," Willis mumbled to himself as he flipped through his wallet. She hadn't been discreet, but she had been thorough. Even his lucky franc coin from his trip to Paris was gone. It must have caught her eye. Ignorant street kid.

"She'll never use it," he mumbled. "Never in a million years." And, suddenly, he felt vulnerable without it. He was used to having small charms in his pockets. They were little reminders that there was some luck in the universe, good or bad. Later that morning he was going to the courthouse to hear his father's will. His father. He sure as hell had never been a dad. He hadn't earned the title. Dads taught you how to play cricket on summer days. Fathers called from foreign cities to say, again, that they wouldn't make it to the biggest day of your life.

Willis was tempted to throw the wallet in the wastebasket, but he gently placed it back on the dresser with an air of defeat.

An hour later, he was showered, sharply dressed, and hurriedly locking the hotel room behind him. He strolled with purpose through the chic lobby and out onto the pavement. He was not rushing to his appointment with excitement or even mild anticipation. He was rushing to get it all over with. He desired the whole matter to be dead and buried. There was a shameful question repeating itself over and over again in his head, and he tried desperately to ignore it ... *What did the bastard leave me? His only son. What did the bastard leave me? Bastard ... bastard ... bast—* He began walking faster.

As he rounded the corner, the large, impersonal, grey building loomed before him, with its long, stone steps. He vaguely imagined guillotines. Willis couldn't remember the streets he had walked, as though something else had brought him to this place without his knowing or consent. In many ways, it had. He did not want this part of his life to exist. Where was Occam's razor for moments like these? How wonderful it would be to splice out all the undesirable bits.

Willis threw these encroaching thoughts from his mind and scurried up the stone steps. The engraved wooden doors looked large and imposing, but were surprisingly light and swung open with ease. Willis couldn't help thinking that perhaps these doors were much like his father. If only he had taken the time to turn the doorknob. Once again he banished his useless mind chatter. None of it could be helped now. His father's barrister, and friend, was waiting for him, perched on one of the many benches placed along the sides of the grand hallway. The white marble floor was immaculate. Almost so that, if he desired, he could see his reflection near his feet, but few dared to look at themselves in a courthouse.

The man rose to meet Willis. Willis knew this man well—too well. Sometimes the disappointing calls from his father would be telegrammed through this man's voice.

"I'm sorry, son ..." the voice would say, "your father has been held up in a meeting." Even this man knew his father well enough to know he was only that. A father. A sperm donor. An absent male figure. The dictionary was far too generous with the word. Father. A male parent. God. One who originates, makes possible, or inspires something. The word dad was merely listed as a colloquial term or a shortcut for father. It was all so backwards.

"Hello, Willis," the man said as he extended his hand, which was taken without hesitation. However, Willis shook hands limply. He was still overwhelmed by this place and these people and papers and things. They were all just things. Was he grieving? He didn't know. It was all packed somewhere inside his big toe. Everything would take a very long time to reach his mouth and then his brain.

"Hi, Sam," he answered in a voice that was barely audible. Sam motioned him into another room nearby. There were too many thresholds that day. The room was small and dimly lit. The blinds were down and the large desk and tall bookshelves seemed to judge Willis from their standpoints. Willis loosened his tie, feeling the musty tone of the heavy, dark brown books and neglected carpets. It was a furnished closet where many unsaid things happened.

"Would you like some coffee?" Sam offered. Willis thought he could use something a bit stronger, but he politely raised his hand in decline. Sam poured himself a cup and settled in behind the large oak desk. He folded and unfolded his hands and then laid them flat before him. There was no real sense of sorrow in the room, but the situation was delicate and Sam wasn't sure where to begin. He didn't want to touch a raw nerve.

"I have your father's papers," he began. He pulled an envelope out of a large, squeaky drawer in his desk and deftly handed it over. Willis didn't make any move to accept it.

"Shouldn't mother be here?" Willis stalled.

"Your mother conveyed point-blank that she isn't interested in what he had to say."

Willis nodded solemnly. She was still his widow, but he had been less than a husband to her. She had known the truth behind his unscheduled business trips years ago. However, she had kept quiet and continued to pack his lunch every morning and make pork chops every Tuesday night. It had been a different era then, and she probably made herself believe there was nowhere else for her to go. Maybe it would have been easier if he had run off and left her for good. Besides, she had to stay. She had Willis to think about. And now Hancocks Sr. was dead. The freedom of it was suffocating.

"Heart attack, was it?" Willis asked. He tried to sound casual. Sam didn't answer right away. Instead, he let out a long sigh through his nostrils.

"Yes, I believe his heart simply gave out. Strange that it wasn't his lungs instead. He certainly liked his tobacco, didn't he?" Sam attempted to be warm, almost nostalgic. Willis squirmed in his seat. He felt his own heart tense.

Sam noticed his anxiety and decided to move things along. He was starting to feel uncomfortable too. He jerked the envelope impatiently towards Willis. The younger man glanced at him sharply, warily, as though he'd been wakened from a deep sleep. He didn't want anything from his father. Not like this. Feeling cornered, he accepted the envelope and toyed with the seal.

"Do I have to open this now?" he asked, sounding like a child who didn't want to do a chore. "Here?"

"I must be a witness to make sure you understand all the implications of your father's last wishes," Sam answered in a distant voice. Willis began to peel open the seal. The package felt quite heavy to be from a man who had been so empty. He pulled out a stack of papers attached with a clip. There was too much print— large blocks of ink that Willis didn't want to swim through. He passed the document back to Sam with a plea in his eyes for some comprehension. Sam put his reading glasses on with an air of formality and began to read:

"Here states the last will and testament of myself, Willis Hancocks Sr., to be read upon my time of death. To my faithful wife I leave my property estate ..." *Faithful! How the bastard could even constitute the word and never know the meaning.* Willis felt his innards turn and was relieved about his mother's absence in this obscene mockery.

"... and to my only son I leave a portion of myself that I hope will fill the gaps I have left behind. ..." The remainder of the document contained instructions for the dividing of his assets, including a generous portion granted to Sam for both his personal and professional services through the years. Willis barely heard the rest of it.

"How much?" he interrupted. Sam stopped in midsentence and removed the ominous glasses. His dusty blue eyes were small and beady. His lukewarm glance took on a cooler slant.

Sam had been a dutiful friend, even when it had gone against his better judgment. He was trying to be discreet, even now, by sounding vague and assuming his authoritative business voice, but the younger man knew him too well. Sam's voice began to trail off, losing its facade.

"It's quite a sum, Willis," he replied in a serious tone.

"How much?"

"Your father wasn't very good with his feelings. He didn't really know how to express—"

"How much?" Willis was becoming irritable.

"Fifty million pounds, son." His voice was like a dull thud in the room. Then he added, "Your father set up a trust fund for you when he found out he was dying from his clogged arteries. I've already taken the liberty of depositing the funds directly into your account."

Willis felt immobilized in his chair. The cushion on the chair had suddenly become quicksand. He was a millionaire, just like his father. Just like his father. Willis wanted no part of his father's impersonal, hard cash world.

His father was made of money, it seemed; still, he couldn't take it with him.

"What about my mother, Sam? What did she get?"

"Your father made sure she would be comfortable. Hopefully, your mother was also given some closure." Sam seemed uncomfortable and avoided eye contact.

"What if I don't accept?" Willis said, but he thought, *brilliant.*

"Then the money will be given to the city," Sam said with urgency. His loyalty still lay with his friend, and the last thing Hancocks Sr. ever wanted was to invest one cent in the government. He never trusted the politicians to do the right thing with their liberties.

If Willis had known, he would have marched down to City

Hall and delivered the boodle himself, but the unreturned affections he carried for his father lay like silt in his stomach. He also didn't want his father's money to go into a new McDonald's or a city parking lot. The two men stood up abruptly and shook hands. Willis just wanted to escape. When he emerged from the ominous courthouse doors, he took a long pause on the entrance steps. He drew everything in, and the world looked stranger. Even the clouds appeared to be moving faster across an otherwise pleasant sky. The voices around him slowed down. The tempo in the atmosphere was out of step. The mechanics in his brain had been reduced to a hamster in a wheel, overworked. What had just happened?

⤞◄●◗●►⤝

MARTIN

Martin had been wandering the streets all morning. The sidewalks were wide and crowded. The streets had a smaller ratio of traffic, and he was tempted to walk along the painted dotted lines in the middle of the road and dodge the cars. At least he would get paid if some careless driver bumped into him. The mob on the sidewalk lived by the rule of every man for himself. He unsuccessfully tried to avoid the shoving and gave it back where he could without making eye contact. He had grown sour and didn't want to admit his thoughts, even to himself. The truth was that he was young and ready to accept his creature comforts again. He began to miss pillows, basic warmth, and friendly conversation. The problem was, he had delved so deep into his notions of the world being dictated by the evils of money, politics, and fads that he didn't know how to slip back into the norm undetected. His rebellious nature had won him a reputation in the spreading vicinity of his tunnel life.

His thoughts pushed behind his eyes as he walked recklessly. What could he do now? He had no money. Suddenly, the colourful printed paper and accumulative clinking coins he once detested seemed essential. He kicked the pavement in defeat. There was no use fighting the greedy gods. Could he work? Would anyone hire him? Here? His appearance was almost frightening. He prayed for rain on the days between using the public showers, which cost two pounds. Martin didn't want to admit that he had failed in his attempts to move against the grain, to not be a sheep. He always returned to his home in the underground walkway. After all, home was a place you could escape to after your legs grew weary and your head swelled with the pressure of people and words and laborious tasks, wasn't it? Perhaps Martin's home didn't provide the best comfort, but it did provide him with shelter and a place to submerge from the busy streets. The hum of cars and shoes clanking on the grates above him provided company in the night when only a few stray souls, also hiding from the moonlight or police car beams, might join him or pass through, stealth-like. Martin wandered the streets of London by day and hid from them in the late, dark hours.

As he headed back to Hyde Park, he would often see the homeless people cluster together in alleys. They were prohibited from seeking soft grass beds in the parks, even in the warmer season. So, in alleys, they lit each other's cigarettes and spat on the sidewalks. They swayed from the drink and huddled together to keep warm and upright. They cajoled with each other and laughed with smoker's lungs. Martin didn't know them, and he avoided them. Whatever choices those poor, fading souls had ever made in their lives, they had not chosen to live on the streets with every door closed against them. At least, he was sure the choice had not been a conscious one. How the warmly lit windows in every flat on every block must have appeared to them.

Martin was painfully aware of his free will. Still, he wasn't ready to surrender. He had chosen the broadness of the streets over being confined in those brightly lit boxes of windows, looking down. Now his smug feelings had slowly turned to jealousy. He suddenly hated the working locals and carefree tourists, brushing by him cheerfully with their groceries and Harrods bags, for a different reason. They had something he didn't have. They were free.

Martin sat down and occupied a piece of concrete.

WILLIS

As Willis rounded the corner, he almost tripped over a grungy looking young man sitting on the pavement. The man looked as though he had walked across the continent. The blue of his startled eyes as he glanced up looked lost and old. The young man's expectant hand emerged from his jacket sheepishly and wavered open before him. Willis hesitated for half a second and then pulled out an executive-looking leather booklet from his inside pocket. He then pulled a pen out of his shirt pocket and began scribbling furiously inside the booklet.

"Here, chap, here's a big fat cheque, and all you have to do is authorize it. I hand you the keys to my palace," Willis said. He roughly stuffed the piece of paper into the other man's waiting hand and hurried off, jamming both of his empty hands into deep pockets.

Chapter 2

MARTIN

As soon as Martin had sat down on the sidewalk, a man came around the corner at a rapid pace. He stopped short and caught himself from stumbling over Martin's hunched frame. The moment was confused; Martin was rarely surprised these days, but the look in the man's eyes was stricken and tormented. Martin thought he knew his own suffering until then. By habit, he already had his hand out and he suddenly felt ashamed. The other man looked agitated, and then he asked, "What is your name?"

"Mart— Martin."

"Martin. Martin what? What is your last name?"

"Sourdough." Martin coughed.

The man smiled a strange little smile at him, with his eyes full of fire, and then he took a rectangular book and a black pen out of his jacket and wrote something down. Impatiently, the man grabbed Martin's wrist and shoved the rectangular paper into his open palm, saying something about a cheque and the keys to a palace.

The offering was so abrupt, somewhere in the back of Martin's mind, he wondered if it was a curse. And then the man was gone, disappearing into the crowd and covering ground with long strides. After a minute, Martin slowly uncoiled his fingers and stared at the piece of paper, a loosely crumpled ball nestled in his palm. He began to delicately pull at the corners, as though recovering some ancient artefact, to free the item from its condensed shape. Then he stared longer in disbelief. The implications of the treasure in his hand registered rapidly. Okay, it was a cheque. He could barely get past all the zeros. His fingers trembled as he held the thin paper. His hands did not dare to grasp the paper and pull at the corners more, as though trying to stretch more zeros out of it. His hands were not so confident. Instead, he held the cheque as someone might examine the feather of a long extinct bird. His name stared back at him in the "pay to" field. The man's signature was in the lower corner. Both names were written in ink. The greedy gods had shown some mercy. Martin quickly folded the paper and shoved it deep into his pocket.

He did not move. He sat for a long time with his hands clasped around his tucked-in knees, in an upright foetal position, while wrestling with his inner voice. As harsh words ping-ponged between his ears, his own self-deprecating words, he wanted more than anything to feel comforted. He had seen the name printed on the cheque. Willis Hancocks Jr. Even the name sounded like money. He smirked at his runaway thought and then caught himself with a strange wave of guilt. Even in this humble moment, Martin could not lose his zeal for sarcasm. Perhaps he was still trying to shake the tormented look he saw in the stranger's eyes. His train of thought turned. The entire episode was ridiculous. For over a year he hadn't had to juggle more than a twenty pound note for a week of living, and that was a good week. The only thing he had to do now was endorse the cheque, stand up and claim it. Fortunately, he would not have to forge the signature. Willis Hancocks Jr.? Hell, Martin didn't look like anyone's junior. Some people even gossiped in low tones that he didn't have parents. Perhaps they also thought he had been left in the London tunnel. Martin smirked to himself again.

He was not a malicious man. He knew that. He hadn't put out his hand for charity until the thread became too thin and he could barely scrounge enough to eat. He hadn't asked for this, had he? He wanted to run after the man and throw it back at him. If the man didn't want it, then why didn't he just give it to a charity or an orphanage or a fancy university? Why did *Martin* have to accept this ... this gift? Why couldn't he just call it a blessing and be thankful? Martin wasn't sure about the workings of fate. He admitted to himself how he had brought on his own failures, and consequently, he was faced with a "no exit" sign. It was everything he had said he wanted, once. To be his own master and treat his experience on earth as being no more than a human body occupying space and living day to day, just as people had done before government and laws and technology. Martin hadn't expected a dead end to come so soon. And now there was an opening folded neatly in his pocket. But it wasn't really his opening. It was a door or a portal that haunted, hasty man had closed.

Martin crouched on the pavement for the remainder of the day, and as the sun began to set, he slowly rose to his feet and started trudging back towards the tunnel. Home was only the distance of one foot in front of the other. He deliberately kept his hands out of his shallow tweed pockets until later, when, forgetting his reasons why, he habitually shoved his chapped, closed knuckles into them. The corners of the folded paper brushed against his startled fingers, and instead of rapidly jerking out his hand as though it would get bitten, he retrieved the cheque and toyed with it for a few minutes. He walked slower and with a small grimace on his face. He placed the cheque back in his pocket and walked past the tunnel at Hyde Park. He always returned to the tunnel. He considered it his home, but not that night. He vaguely knew that he couldn't go back there anymore.

Martin aimlessly covered the streets of London for the better part of the night, and eventually found his sleep on a park bench. The morning came earlier than he was used to, since being in the tunnel he was sheltered from the sun's dawning beams, which now pierced him like swords. He opened one confused eye to witness a familiar sight. Only, this time, he saw briefcases, flouncing skirts, and wristwatches marching past him. He didn't really care to know what hour it was. Filling the hours that day would not be an uncertainty. It had a purpose. He sat upright and stretched his neck about to determine what part of London he had landed. Greenwich. He hadn't ventured so far in weeks. Already he was beginning to stretch his boundaries, and now there was nowhere to go except farther. He had tried not to think too much about the cheque in his pocket as he concentrated on the sound of the worn soles of his shoes scuffing the old cobblestones the night before. Everything seemed to echo at night, without the buffer of bodies crowding the narrow backstreets. He had been able to hear his thoughts in the rhythm ... scuffle, scuff ... scuffle, scuff ... move ahead, move ahead.

Martin's eyes had adjusted to the sunlight, and for the first time in ages, he genuinely smiled to himself, mostly because the border between yesterday and today was ironically faded. Pray for rain and one might get hit by lightning. He noticed that the passersby in Greenwich didn't notice him, and he was quietly relieved. Sadly, he could not have smiled to himself so easily in Hyde Park. He was finally abandoning an identity that had created its own villain. Martin was shedding an old and useless skin.

He spotted a barbershop on the opposite side of the street, reached into his other pocket, and pulled out five pounds. As he waited for a break in the traffic and jogged easily between the slowing cars, he was struck by another humorous thought: Only the day before, he would have wished for a car to hit him so that he could claim injury. Despite Martin's growing lightness of heart at the change of events, when he reached the barbershop's door, he did not bounce through it like a normal person with a moderate weight on his shoulders. None of this was routine for Martin, and the reality of it smacked him in the face. For a moment, he suddenly felt like a criminal or subhuman as he lingered outside the establishment. He opened the door slowly and went inside, but not without a few bewildered looks from the handful of customers sitting in a row with their coffees and magazines. Even the barber, who was doing a routine beard trim, raised one eyebrow.

Most of the barber's customers were regulars, and he had never laid eyes on Martin before. At first glance, the young man looked grubby and moth-eaten. His hands and face were dirty and his tweed jacket and jeans had hanging threads and discernible holes. His stubbly head was growing in dark roots. The most he required to look presentable was a bath, new clothes, and a clean shave. But as long as he could pay, the barber didn't care what he looked like.

"Hey, look what the cat dragged in!" exclaimed one of the younger men waiting, but he had no supporters.

"Shut yer pie hole, Danny," mumbled an older man seated beside the boy. Danny gave the man and Martin a cutting look and poked his nose back in the daily paper he was reading. Martin's first instinct was to thump him, but he felt he was out of his league in this joint. He was the stranger.

"Take a number, lad," the barber shouted to Martin from his chair. He also gave Danny a disapproving glance. "I'll be with you in two shakes." Martin picked up a magazine and settled into the only empty chair left. He tried not to notice the men as they examined him.

The older man piped up again, "Leave 'im alone, boys. Yer no' bein' very subtle!"

With his back turned, the barber smiled to himself.

Martin remained unmoved until his number was called. When he was finally called to sit in the chair, he noticed the barber made no enquiring looks towards him.

"What'll it be today?" he asked in a friendly tone.

"I … I guess I just need a cleanup," Martin muttered. He felt small in the chair. He wasn't used to having anyone take care of him in any fashion. Now he was at the mercy of this man's razor. Martin had lost his own rusted razor two weeks before; he usually ducked into open washrooms in the mornings to quickly drag the razor across his head and face.

"I agree; you haven't got much to take off the top ... but you do look a bit grizzly," the barber jabbered on, "I mean no offense!"

"None taken."

"Alright." Then he kept on jabbering. Barbers were like bartenders. As a customer, you felt an obligation to tell them everything because they were being intimate with either your beard or your beer.

"So, where did you roll in from?" the barber asked easily.

"Hyde Park."

"No, no ... I mean, where are you from?"

Martin wasn't sure how to answer and kept silent a moment. Then he uttered again, as if he was afraid it were the wrong answer "... Hyde Park." The barber was silent as he shaved Martin's beard and moustache. There seemed to be a shift in the air, and Martin felt sorry for it. He was more different than he realized, and it was becoming rapidly apparent. How was he ever going to fit in again? It was a nightmare. The barber wheeled Martin around to face the mirror.

"There you are, Mr. Hyde Park ... like a new man!" he exclaimed.

❖

WILLIS

Willis had begun to move with the crowd and then quickly ducked into a familiar pub a block away. That day there was a new face behind the bar, possibly the bartender's son. He gave Willis a passing glance as he cleaned the mugs. Willis was thankful to not see a familiar face. He didn't feel like shooting the breeze. He approached the young bartender and ordered a pint of Scottish ale, the darker the better. He proceeded to order the same for the rest of the afternoon, trying to clear away the murky waters he found himself drowning in. Eventually, the man behind the bar, who he now didn't recognize at all, asked him to leave.

"I think you've had enough drink for today, sir."

"What? Oh shut up and pour me another."

"I can't do that, sir."

"Well, then I'll get behind there and do it myself," Willis shot back as he attempted to clamber over the bar. He felt a strong grip on the back of his shirt, and he knew it couldn't be the young bartender, because he was square in front of him, looking very bewildered.

"Hasn't anyone ever told you it's rude to go helping yourself?" the deep voice from behind growled, and the next thing Willis knew, he was standing out on the curb with a trail of jeers and laughter behind him. He wobbled for a second and leaned his hand against the wall. His arms and legs were like spaghetti.

"Bastards," he muttered. He lifted his head to see a sea of people moving towards him, and in his drunken state, he laid himself flat up against the building in fear of being trampled.

"Whoa, there, where's the fire?" he exclaimed. The only response he received was the disgusted grimaces on the faces of the passersby. Willis began to move slowly against the crowd. He clung to the wall like a first-time ice skater. Then he saw him, and he remembered. That crouched, sorry figure was still squatting on the concrete. Willis' eyes narrowed. He stood only a block away from the remains of his life, one block away from what could have been his future. He knew that either way he would have still felt hollow. He had exorcised all of his ghosts by relieving himself of that cheque—that gift or burden. Hadn't he? Or had he invited more demons? He stood and watched and felt perilous. His form was highly conspicuous in contrast to the bustling sidewalk. So was this strange beggar's form. Neither of them seemed to fit, and somehow, they were connected. Anyone watching from a distance would have taken note of this blocked interaction;

the watcher being watched. The beggar never glanced in Willis' direction. He seemed to remain naïve to the entire scene, staring ahead. Meanwhile, Willis battled with his spiralling thoughts, like demons trying to ascend back into heaven.

The sun went down behind the buildings and Willis, still in a drunken stupor, was leaning lifeless against the wall. He had not moved an inch in an hour, and his eyes were still fixed on the crouched figure, until it began to stir. The figure leaned forward and stretched into a tall, animated being, which then disappeared around the far corner of the street. Willis caught his breath; he had to remind his legs to move until they transitioned into an awkward trot. He followed the stranger, keeping a calculated distance. Part of him wanted to reach out his hands and grab him, apologize, and scour his pockets. Mostly, he felt obsessed about the man to whom he had given his destiny. Suddenly, the cheque was not just a symbol of the money that had replaced his father's affection. Willis had been irrational. He saw that now. And there was still a chance to make it right. If only to see where this man went ... like a mother giving away her baby ... simply wanting to know if the right choice was made. Willis was not in the right state of mind, and he had no real intention of doing anything. He followed the stranger all night, all the way across London, just to watch him fall asleep on a park bench in Greenwich. And he waited until morning on a different park bench.

When Willis awoke, he met more grimacing faces. He had once been one of those faces, thinking to himself, *Damn bum.* However, these faces were mixed with puzzlement at the way he was dressed. Willis appeared to be nothing more than a crumpled gentleman, except for the fact he still reeked of beer. He glanced across the street and farther down to find that the park bench the young beggar fell asleep on was empty. He reeled around frantically, startling those around him with his wild, jerky movements. Then he spotted his target, entering a barbershop. Willis was willing to wait, but a bobby approached him.

"No loitering here, move along. There's a hostel down the road. You can clean yerself up there." Willis stalled for a moment and made a motion to tie his shoe, but he felt the swift pat of the bobby's stick. Willis gave him a wary look before slinking away down the sidewalk.

"Get movin', man," the bobby growled. He stood in an authoritative stance, surrounded by happy-faced, law-abiding citizens, and watched Willis leave.

———

Willis felt something gnawing inside of him, a driving force that he didn't agree with and yet one he couldn't ignore. He was obsessed with the loss of his father, which led back to his childhood. Willis hated his desire to be near him and to have a piece of him. He had thrown away his father's final gift into the hands of a stranger, a stranger who was, seemingly, also leading a less than ideal life. Perhaps his father's gift would bring this man happiness, if not love. There was such a bitter irony to it all. Still, Willis returned to the barbershop a few hours later, after he had sobered up with a cup of coffee.

When he reached the entrance, he lingered outside for a moment. The shop was empty except for the barber, who was sweeping the hair on the floor into a pile, which began to resemble a small, furry animal.

The barber looked up and saw an agitated-looking man loitering outside his shop. The man did not look like respectable clientele, so he decided to confront the stranger. A little bell sounded in the doorway as the barber poked his head outside, startling the stranger.

"Can I help you with something?" He sized up the stranger, and a funny vibe told him that he was not in danger of offending a potential customer.

"Uh, yeah … yes," Willis stammered. "I'm looking for someone who might have come into your shop earlier."

"This morning has been very busy ..."

"A tall fellow, tweed jacket, a little on the scruffy side?"

His eyes visibly scrutinized Willis. He couldn't explain why, but a protective inkling came over him.

"I vaguely remember a chap like that ..." He tried to sound evasive.

"Any idea which direction he might have gone?"

"Oh, I don't know ..."

"Think." Willis was growing impatient, and then he realized how he was behaving, and internally, he kicked himself. He saw the suspicion in the barber's face. "I mean, well, it's important. If you can remember anything at all ..."

"You could try Hyde Park."

"Hyde Park?"

"That's all I remember, chap." The barber was growing irritable. "Now, if you'll excuse me."

"Right ... thanks." Willis moved on down the street, not sure if he wanted to traipse back across London.

The barber stood in his modest doorway, watching him go, and wondering what he had done. "Hope you don't find him," he said under his breath.

Chapter 3

WILLIS

Instead of taking the barber's advice and heading towards Hyde Park, Willis found another pub, had a few more drinks, and then went back to his hotel room. He sat in a chair near the window, with his head tilted back, not bothering to put a light on. Eventually, he went to bed. The next morning, after a sleepless night, his alarm clock sounded as usual. He rubbed his forehead, trying to soothe his hangover from the day before. It wasn't working. His back ached from a night spent on a park bench, and he wondered how the street people managed. They had no choice, of course. At the time, he felt he didn't either. His father was gone, every part of him that had been there or not. The possibility of him was gone, which rattled Willis most of all.

He tried to rub out the truth and moved off his bed in the rumpled suit he had been too drunk and tired to take off. He shed his suit onto the ground and stepped out of the bedroom, naked, and into the shower. The steady pulse of water felt like a gift. Warm water cleansing him; a bar of soap—he was rich. He stood there, eyes closed, wanting to stay there and feeling the weight of the water rubbing on his skin. Still, he knew he couldn't stay, which kept his insides cold. He turned off the tap abruptly, like ripping off a Band-Aid. *Okay, get on with it,* he thought. He towel-dried himself and put on a new suit, the same dark-blue colour as the one he'd taken off.

The traffic seemed more chaotic than usual. The day before, he had shut out everything except his duty to his father, and then his failed pursuit. He forgot there were other people living in the world and making daily decisions, clambering over each other for some greater happiness. Where were they all going? He hailed a taxicab.

"Where to, mate?" the taxicab driver asked, half-interested. It was his job to know where people were going.

"Hancocks and Associates Law Firm. Earl's Court Square."

"Law firm? Are you a barrister?"

"Yes."

"What kind of barrister? My brother-in-law is a small claims barrister." *Taxicab drivers always wanted to talk,* Willis sighed in his head. They drove around in their hard shells all day, disconnected from the world, but seeming to know everything about it through the sources they found in their customers or through the car radio.

"A criminal defense barrister," Willis answered tersely.

"Oh, ho! You're one of them big barristers. Big cases, I bet. Are you 'andling the case of that murder that 'appened in downtown London last week?"

Which one? Willis thought cynically.

Instead, he answered, "Possibly. There are a few recent murders that are being investigated." He was tempted to add, "No trials, yet," but that was privileged information. The police only had the victims' stories and no suspects. The newspapers were chomping at the bit, and he was glad he didn't have to answer their phone calls yet. Instead, he was trapped in a moving vehicle and being questioned by this chap, a roadway philosopher.

"You know, people can say wha' they like—but I don't think they all need to go to jail."

"No?" Willis mused, "You'd rather have them 'anging around your neighbourhood then? Jolly good."

"No, that's no' wha' I mean, exactly. I mean, they 'ave to go somewhere where they can't 'urt anyone, including themselves."

"We're still just talking about the murderers, then?"

The taxicab driver was silent for a moment, as though he was being challenged.

"No, no' exactly ..." he started off, slow and careful. "Anyone who 'ad done any kind of 'arm to another 'uman being—couldn't they do something more useful to pay for that crime, rather than just rot in a jail? I mean, does anybody learn from that?"

"Most people don't care if they learn," Willis answered more thoughtfully. It was a question he sometimes caught himself asking.

"'Ow does it ever get better, then?"

"Sometimes it doesn't. People either want to see those criminals die or they don't want to see them at all, ever again. They don't want to know that those people still exist and that they are being sheltered and fed."

"But, *you* try and get them off ..." The taxicab driver let his thought hang out, somewhere near the windshield, still inside the car.

"Yes, I do."

"Why's that, then?"

"That's my job, to try and make sure the wrong people don't go to jail."

"'Ow do you know?"

Willis didn't answer right away. It was too early in the day to question his existence as a barrister—his life, his career. For some reason, he was supposed to have this conversation. There, then. Something was stopping him in this taxicab to give an answer, or something close to it, for his choices.

"I don't always know. I try to have faith in people's stories or find some explanation for their guilty actions. I guess I try to show that people aren't always bad just because they may do bad things."

"No offense, mate, but I'm glad I don't 'ave *your* job."

For a second, Willis desperately wished that he was in the taxicab driver's seat.

Chapter 4

MARTIN

Martin moved through Victoria station and found himself immersed in another swarm of bodies. The only difference now was that he didn't feel so removed from them. Instead, he felt swept up in their energy—the happiness and anxiety of crossing over foreign boundaries. At the bank, he cashed a hefty portion of his cheque and opened an account with his passport ID to keep the rest of his newfound fortune, all the while trying to conceal his knees shaking. Afterwards, he smiled to himself all the way to his next destination, with the money in his red knapsack flung easily over one shoulder. He had no idea where he was headed, and that alone enthralled him. Martin felt as though he was approaching the very edge of the earth, and after that he could only pray for his parachute to open.

The queue inched forward, person by person, going over the edge. Martin shuffled down the human conveyor belt until he had to state his destination too and was then handed a ticket. This rectangular piece of paper, which could be torn so easily, was his passport to a new life or an extension of his old life. Even though his daily regimen in Hyde Park had been tethered and desolate, it was a familiar place. More than twice that day, Martin had questioned himself about what he was doing and why he was doing it. Oddly enough, there were no solid answers, and he could no longer justify his doubts.

"Track seventeen," the man in the conductor's hat announced sharply from behind the counter. When asked about his destination, Martin had squeaked, "Paris." Not because he ever had the desire to stroll through the streets of Paris, but because it would not be a far journey, geographically, and he was taking baby steps. He didn't speak French, but he knew how to be silent and still make his way.

Martin sat on one of the rickety benches that lined the platform on track seventeen. They were planted like telephone poles until they miniaturized and disappeared. He hugged his red knapsack against his chest. He looked to his left and realized he was at the end of the track, or the beginning. *Those seated at the far end perhaps believed the same thing*, he mused. An elderly couple seated on the bench next to him acknowledged his youth and smiled. He wondered if they were marvelling at him, thinking, *It must be wonderful to be young and free*, and remembering, even though they were headed towards the same destination. He smiled back, not really understanding what he was smiling about. The train he was waiting for could be taking him to the end of the earth.

After an hour of waiting, a train pulled in to the dead-end tunnel. Martin watched people tumble out of the passenger car with luggage and kids in tow. A small percentage of them almost tripped over him as they bustled by speaking English and other garbled languages. Then the platform was silent and empty again, much like him. The excitement was beginning to wear off, and now the only tingling he felt was spreading in his feet and his rear end.

The train became a ghost waiting patiently in track seventeen and seemed to be growing faint cobwebs. The escalator that had been transporting invisible patrons up and down for the past hour suddenly carried a waterfall of people. Where had they all come from? The upper lobby must have overflowed, and these were the pitiful remnants cast from the upstairs world of changing billboards, shops, restaurants, and expectant travellers. The billboards displaying departure and arrival times of various destinations vaguely reminded Martin of a stock market. The signs spun around so quickly unseasoned travellers may feel they were gambling on what train to take. Put your money down and spin the wheel again.

His attention moved back to the flow of bodies about to reach the track platform. Everyone seemed to meet the bottom of the escalator with an easy bounce and without any signs of hesitation, then making a beeline for the train. Once again, there was a mad dash of women, kids, luggage, and husbands or boyfriends in tow. Martin didn't take much notice of the men. All he could see were painted lips and high heels. He forgot how scruffy he still looked in his punchy tweed jacket and sole-worn shoes. He felt a slight rise in his pants and clasped his hands in his lap.

As the crowd began to thin out, Martin stood up, ironed the tail of his jacket nervously with his hands, and joined the procession moving towards the train. Once he was inside, he manoeuvered his way along the narrow hallway and slid into one of the first coaches he spied. He slid the door shut behind him, slowly, and sat down. The upholstery was lush and the contours of his back and shoulders melded easily with the fabric. Martin looked out the window, as though he was intensely interested in the view of the dried grass beside the track. He was wrapped up in the anticipation of what he would see outside that window. Much like a first-time flyer, eagerly watching the men on the ground stuff the luggage in the underneath compartments and wave their arms around, having no inclination of soaring through the clouds above.

The metallic beast began to move, first with a squeal and a grunt and then with a strange, determined rhythm. The grass began to blur. Martin closed his eyes and listened to the wheels. The door slid open abruptly with the sound of metal grinding against metal, which startled Martin out of his meditation with the music of the track. He opened his eyes and pushed himself back into his seat as the whirlwind of a girl flew into the coach. At first she didn't even acknowledge him being only inches away from her long, untamed legs. She pulled a cigarette out of her purse, lit it, sucked back, glanced out at the scenery whipping by, and exhausted the smoke from her neon pink lips. Then she collapsed in the chair farthest away from the window and surmised her surroundings. Martin could feel her eyes on him, moving up and down his lanky frame, but without much interest. Even when the intrusive eyes of pass-ersby in London had scrutinized him, he had never felt so taken in and tossed aside, all with one glance. She was beautiful. Martin looked out the window.

"What do you see out there?" she blurted out impatiently. Her voice was sultry. Perhaps it was just the smoke in her lungs. Martin didn't answer at first. He turned to look at her and then looked out at the world again.

"I'm not sure. ... I see the world slipping by, I guess." It seemed like a silly answer, but the blend of nature flying past his eyes somehow made it sound sane. His heartbeat was in rhythm with the pulsing train. He had never moved so fast.

"Huh," the girl grunted. "I tell you what I see ... trees. That's all I see." Martin moved away from the window and nestled back in his seat. He suddenly felt foolish. *I see too much*, he thought. He looked over at her, wanting to say more, but her head was back in her purse. She was too busy rummaging for things. Then she looked up when she sensed his eyes on her.

"What are you gawking at?" she snapped. Martin motioned his

hand towards his collar. Her eyes squinted, not comprehending, and she warily brought her hand up to her own collar. The tag was sticking out of the front of her shirt.

"Oh crap." She toyed with the tag in disbelief. "I got dressed in such a goddamn hurry." And without a second of hesitation, she pulled the fabric over her head, exposing her black lacy bra—barely restraining her full breasts—pulled the fabric through as though she were wrestling with a pillow case, turned the collar around, and squeezed herself back through. Then she collapsed into the back of her seat with angry exhaustion. She pulled out another cigarette.

"Thanks." Her eyes gravitated towards Martin momentarily, and with a strange gratitude. He was frozen. He had never seen the female form before, and he had never imagined he would witness it under such nonchalant, brash, and unnerving terms. He didn't know where to look. He didn't answer. He turned his face to the windowpane, feeling the sensation of his hot cheeks, and stared at the trees.

"Hey." Her voice was softer. She leaned over and offered him a cigarette. He took it without a word and let her ignite the end. He puffed silently and exhaled a thin cloud of smoke. She smiled as she dropped the lighter back into her purse. He never mentioned how many cigarette butts he had picked up off the London sidewalks. She put her butt out on the floor, stretched out the length of her body on the seat, stuffed her jacket under her head, and closed her eyes. Martin watched her, thinking how much she resembled a little girl sleeping there. Everyone looked so vulnerable when they were sleeping. A few moments later, as they slowly became submerged in the Chunnel, he closed the curtains and then his eyes.

An undetermined amount of time had passed by when the sliding door slammed open, abruptly waking them both. Martin, who had been disturbed by the door for a second time, blinked at the intruder and grimaced.

"Come on, get out here," he barked at the girl. "There's someone who wants to meet you." The man was older, with salt and pepper hair, and he had a British accent.

"Now?" She sounded groggy.

"Oh, excuse me, your highness … is now inconvenient for you?"

She sighed heavily, "I'm coming … I'm coming." She dragged herself into a sitting position and reached down to grab her purse, then, suddenly, he yanked her arm and pulled her to her feet.

"Now means now, you lazy slut!" He shot Martin a threatening look as he forced her out of the coach.

Martin wasn't sure what to do, so he decided it was not his problem and tried to fall back asleep. Strangely, he couldn't. When had he ever cared about someone else's bad luck before? *Stupid girl*, he thought. But he couldn't convince himself of it. A short time later, he heard her sneak back in. She reached over deftly and drew the curtains open, even though they were still in the Chunnel. He watched her trying to resume her old sleeping position. It was impossible to settle in the exact same spot twice.

He was awake long before she was, and he watched her in between gazing out the window and resting his eyelids. They were now on French soil, but the trees looked the same. Eventually, she opened her eyes and looked at him as though she didn't recognize him. He watched her as she pulled herself up and brushed her hair with her hands. Maybe he had watched her too long, because she looked up at him with eyes that told him to mind his own business. He shifted in his seat.

"What?" she said, finally. He raised an eyebrow. He was feeling a little braver with this girl.

"That your friend?"

"Yeah." She stifled a laugh. "Guess you could call him that."

"Hmm."

"What?"

"Nothing."

"Look, times are rough, okay, and all that other shit." She pulled out another cigarette. She seemed more agitated. Martin kept silent. He had no right to get involved in this girl's problems, and she didn't look like she wanted to be saved from anything. She went through cigarettes the way a grieving woman went through Kleenex, and it fascinated him. She was so rigid and despondent. He couldn't help wondering if she was screaming beneath those layers of barbed wire. She wasn't looking at him anymore, and he felt that, to her, he was no longer even there.

"Just mind your own damn business," she said flatly, and she averted her eyes.

They spent the rest of the train ride in silence. Eventually, the train began slowing down, and the relentless, hypnotic message in the click-clacking of the wheels could almost be deciphered. Martin stood up to leave the coach and was tempted to walk out without a word. Something stopped him, and he stood in front of her long enough to become visible again. She looked up at him as though he were about to make a toast.

"I hope your road gets smoother," he said. Then he slipped out the door. In some way, he had made a small toast to her. He was struck by how she seemed to perceive him as someone who didn't understand how rough life could be. Then he realized the importance of not assuming anything about anyone.

Chapter 5

WILLIS

When Willis walked into the law firm office, he felt like an impostor. The young girls smiled up at him with their pretty faces, combed hair, and fresh makeup, greeting him from their desks. "Hello, Mr. Hancocks! Good morning, Mr. Hancocks!" they said as he barrelled down the hall, and his male colleagues lifted their eyes to him in passing, maybe with a word or two, a cordial, yet distracted acknowledgment peeling them away from their thick documents. This was the daily agenda: meeting clients, reviewing case files, drinking endless cups of coffee, and weighing personal judgments and career decisions. Who could really tell the truth? Criminals could be crafty poker players. Witnesses could lie and jury members could see what they wanted to see. What divine judge could always tell the difference? What barrister had never spun the story to help his client? Once you were in, you were in. You made your bed, unless there were conflicts of interest or outstanding circumstances of guilt. What barrister didn't want to win? Still, what barrister wanted to be notoriously known for setting a criminal free? What if the whole system was a farce? How did any of them know, beyond the textbook?

He didn't feel well. Still, he smiled back and made steady eye contact with his colleagues. This was his profession. The ladies in the office were paid to smile at him, say good morning, and organize his day.

By the time he reached the end of the hall and turned in to his own office space, he had been pummelled with bright teeth, red lipstick, near coffee spills, messages, meeting agendas, and case files. He closed his door, loosened his tie, and breathed deeply. He prepared himself for another day of attempted justice. He was the head of the law firm now. Almost overnight, Hancocks and Son had become Hancocks and Associates, with no junior. The phone on his desk buzzed.

"Yes, Cynthia?"

"May I come in, sir?"

"Yes." A moment later a willowy girl poked her head in his office and then entered with fresh confidence. She held a small stack of files against her chest.

"Sir, I just wanted to extend my sympathy to you in the wake of your father's passing. He was a great man."

"No, he wasn't," Willis blurted out. He hadn't meant to be so candid or abrupt, but he was still reeling from his unpleasant experience the day before. He looked at her then, and saw a confused, embarrassed look pass over her face. "It's alright, Cynthia. I appreciate your condolences. I'm just processing all of it. He was a great businessman—he built this law firm and gave me a position." *Only problem is, now I don't know what to do with it*, he thought.

"You earned your position, sir. You were a team." She gave him an earnest look, imploring him to believe in something he wasn't sure of.

"Thank you, Cynthia. What is on the table for today?" He eyed the files she was clutching. She had momentarily forgotten them and then, flustered, began handing them over to him with descriptions of each case. He stopped her at the mention of a couple of names.

"I thought those cases belonged to Brown?" Stephen Brown was a junior associate who had recently joined the firm.

"They did, sir," she hesitated. "Stephen— Er, Mr. Brown felt they might be a tinge out of his league. He's still working on softer cases, testing the waters and gaining experience in the courtroom. Besides, he wanted you to stay in the saddle." She liked Stephen Brown, it was evident. Willis gave her a half smile.

"Stay in the saddle?"

"Well, after everything. He felt this wasn't the time to try and prove himself and then risk having you come in and pick up the loose threads."

"Mr. Brown needs a lesson in self-confidence. I've seen him execute a few of his cases in the courtroom with both passion and integrity—he knows what he's doing. Tell you what, I'll take these on and employ his skills as a research assistant. I want him to work with me on these."

Cynthia smiled. "I'll let him know." She ducked back out of his office hurriedly, reminding him of a lunch date. He watched her go, admiring the small, round shape of her ass in her tapered, knee-length skirt. He then turned and looked out his window, high above the city, and vaguely imagined a more industrial time. In his mind's eye, he saw church steeples and large factory chimneys blowing smoke. His sight then returned to the present time, witnessing tall, glass buildings—the modern day factories putting men in their graves early—obscuring the church steeples, the ones still standing.

He turned to the stack of files on his desk and began to flip through them. One case in particular caught his interest: a man accused of murdering his wife one year before. It wasn't unheard of, or terribly sensational, but the circumstances seemed odd. Throughout the pretrial investigation, the man had not made any attempt at claiming his innocence. He also admitted that his wife had not been cheating on him and he had not been cheating on his wife. There were no large insurance claims or inheritances to act as a motive. Although the accused had been told that he had the right to remain silent, the man apparently would not stop telling the police his reasons for murdering his wife. "She was too domineering in our relationship," was his persistent argument—his plea to the police to understand him. Of course, his plea fell on deaf ears. This man was clearly guilty, but Willis was fascinated with his reasoning. The police report stated that he seemed to have had a psychotic episode, and other than this incident, denting his wife's skull with a remote control, there was no prior record of any domestic problems. Neighbours said the accused and his wife were quiet and appeared to be a happy, young couple. No kids—though the wife had apparently expressed to neighbours a wish for having them.

Willis shook his head. He looked at the name on the file—MICHAEL HARRIS. Willis pressed the buzzer on his desk. Cynthia poked her head in.

"Cynthia. What do you know of this Harris case?"

"I hope I don't sound too unprofessional when I say it's just bizarre," she said, then she added, "Mr. Brown has been taking care of the pretrial work for Mr. Harris."

"I'd like to meet with Mr. Harris."

"Are you thinking of taking him on?"

"I don't know yet—I have to talk with him first."

"You mean—"

"I mean Mr. Harris." Willis smiled at her.

"Of course, sir." She was about to leave, but turned back around in the doorway. "Sir, I'd think hard about this one."

"Thank you, Cynthia. Can you arrange a meeting?"

"I'll call correctional services. He's being held at Wandsworth Prison."

Willis thumbed through the file. "Ah, yes, says so here."

Cynthia began to close the door gently. "Wait," Willis called out, "don't tell Brown, yet. Not until I make a decision."

"No, sir." She closed the wood door.

Chapter 6

MARTIN

The Gare du Nord Station was buzzing with people hugging and hurrying to their platforms. The scenery was the same as the London station, but the confusion was heightened by the foreign sounds. French was a language that barely came up for air, and one of pleasing resonance to the ear. Martin happily drowned in this new ignorance until he found himself lost. He hadn't thought about where to go once the train was done carrying him. There was a large sign swaying above a small desk with a large lowercase letter "i" painted on it. He was reluctant to approach, wondering if this particular "i" stood for anything in the English language.

"Ah, *monsieur, comment puis-je vous aider?*" the man asked. Martin stood rigid, staring at the man through small pupils. "How may I help you, sir?" The man smiled politely, after realizing the dilemma.

"Where is the subway?" Martin asked.

"Where are you going?"

"I don't know," Martin replied, taken aback by the question.

"Where do you think I should go?" The man gave an exasperated sigh and pulled out a transit map from a wire map holder on the counter.

"Is this your first time in ..." Then the man caught himself and continued with finesse, "Yes, I can see that it is." Martin shifted in his shoes. Then the man asked, "What do you know of Paris?"

Martin thought for a long moment. "The Eiffel Tower?"

"Yes, good. The Eiffel Tower. You will be able to see all of Paris from the most spectacular tower in the world. A wonderful choice."

Martin smiled as though he had just passed this man's test. He had made a wonderful choice.

"Okay, this is how you go to get to the Eiffel Tower. ..." The man plucked the cap off a red pen and proceeded to doodle on the map. "Catch this train, going in this direction, then get off here, then cross over to this track, then get off at this stop ..."

By the time the man was finished explaining, Martin was left with a map covered with x's and o's. To him, it looked like a football strategy. He walked away in a bigger daze, barely knowing how to leave the maze of train travellers. One friendly traveller, whom Martin asked further directions from, noticed how lost he looked and offered him her subway ticket.

"*Merci*," he stammered. She smiled and responded with a clear and careful, "You are welcome."

The subway train came quickly and the doors pushed open, much like a long series of mouths opening to project a mob of people coming out and swallow the ones going in. There was a limited amount of time to do either, and the mob pushed forwards and backwards. Martin was swept inside and found there was nowhere to sit. He stood hanging on to a pole for the length of four stops, until a few people left their seats. He was counting the dots on the wall, representing the stations, waiting for his stop, because he could barely comprehend the muffled voice recording calling out the name of each station. Martin took a seat near the window and, absentmindedly, held his red knapsack close. As he watched the world go by, he felt he was once again becoming part of it.

The train stopped again, and the mob was thinning. This time only a handful of people came aboard. One passenger was dressed in the stereotypical Parisian attire. He wore a black beret, a red scarf, a red and white striped shirt, and black slacks. He carried an accordion strapped around his chest. He began playing almost immediately, strolling up one side of the subway car and down the other. Martin noticed that hardly anyone paid attention to him; their faces were tired and stern, with tight lips and fixed eyes. The accordion player approached Martin and Martin smiled. The man looked perturbed and carried on. Martin had not realized he was looking for handouts. He immediately felt foolish and waved the man back.

"I only have British currency," he explained sheepishly. The accordion player looked at him blankly. Martin handed him two pounds, and the man's face grimaced even more. He shook his hand at Martin in decline and carried on playing.

At the next stop, Martin climbed the underground steps to street level. He felt as though he was coming out of a manhole in the middle of a circus ground, as the cars roaring by honked and dodged each other, with fists flying, and people on the sidewalk were yelling, talking, and laughing. He found a currency exchange booth and handed over a modest, yet sufficient amount of money from his knapsack. Afterwards, he couldn't place his bearings and stopped a woman strolling along the sidewalk. He remembered what he learned in his high school French classes.

"*Excusez-moi, ou est Eiffel Tower?*" He didn't even attempt to hide his Canadian accent, and the woman smiled at him knowingly.

"Ah, welcome to Paris. You see zat road?" She pointed in front of them. "You are very close. Follow zis road and you will see ze Eiffel Tower."

"*Merci.*"

"I see young travellers like you all ze time. *Au revoir.*"

Martin followed the narrow street until he stumbled upon a large park. He entered, treading on freshly cut grass and a nearly immaculate gravel path. There was barely a fistful of stray dirt on the grass. Then he looked up. The Eiffel Tower loomed before him, and on the lawn there were bodies lying entwined and singular and in bliss under the warmth of summer. He needed no translation for this.

Martin paid his fare and began to hike up the flights of steel stairs. He felt exhilarated; he didn't attribute his lack of breath to the exertion of the climb. When he reached the first tier, he stood by the railing for a long time. There were people crowding together like cattle to board the elevator that would propel them to the top of the world. Martin felt he was already there. He secretly feared he would pass out from lack of oxygen if he tried to beat those heights. He felt his blood pumping. He gazed out over Paris, breathing it in and quietly serenading the city with his thoughts of freedom. Free in his mind and in the world. He looked out at the twilight settling over the vast city, mingling with the architecture and history and clouds.

⟞●◗◗●⟝

Afterwards, Martin wandered aimlessly. He loved the feeling of being lost in another place. It had become depressing to circle around and around the London streets, knowing every lamppost and building he passed, only to circle back to the tunnel at Hyde Park. They were large circles, but they were predictable and endless. They didn't lead to new places. Paris was much like London in the way it stayed awake long past the sun. People clung to daylight in small outdoor cafes, lighting candles on tables and playing music. The stars themselves were company for the lovers strolling along the Seine and under the streetlights, which were shedding their light like old friends. Martin walked alone, but he did not feel alone. He leaned against the bridge crossing, watching the ripples in the moonlit water. The night reflection made the river seem less deep than it was dark. He strolled along the Seine River, following in the footsteps of the lovers hiding in shadows beneath the bridge and never falling asleep.

Martin watched the sunrise. His eyes adjusted to the light and he gazed at the new day arriving as though it were his first. He wandered slowly to street level, meeting the odd passerby with a curt, yet cheerful, *"Bon jour,"* and carrying on his way. For the most part, he had the streets to himself.

He found another subway opening in the sidewalk. Martin hopped on the first train that came along, and without knowing what direction it was going. He closed his eyes while sitting inside, his head against the window. He may have looked asleep, but his ears absorbed everything. He became lost in the whirring of the track and the metallic scraping of the automated doors. He eventually opened his eyes. A few minutes can feel like hours when you are not listening to the world with your sight. This made Martin feel confident, like manoeuvring his way through a dream blindfolded and not able to predict the outcome, only having the sensation that it would all turn out brilliantly. He exited the train.

When he climbed to street level again, like a mole, he squinted at another exquisite site. The majestic Académie Nationale de Musique loomed above him with all of its faded antique charm. The grand pillars suggested an elegance of another time. He scurried across the busy traffic and climbed the stone steps of the entrance, not knowing what place he would enter.

He was relieved the staff didn't ask him to leave his red knapsack at the front desk. He began wandering the grand halls. There were no words to express this place. Beauty, space, and time spiralled around the pillars and up the numerous slides of staircases. They sang like tripping piano keys, up and down the scales. Martin's heart could hear them. He wondered if he was alone. His eyes flew past the banisters and far up to the dome ceilings. Something beyond those ceilings seemed to hover over him and follow him as he wound his way through the hallways, rich with ivory and gold, glass and marble. He came into a small room filled with enormous mirrors. Each mirror embossed on the concrete walls stood an equal distance apart from the next, and he felt ambushed by them. He caught himself in the second one that he passed, and he stood fixed in his own reflection. At first these mirrors seemed to mock him, as they threw back in his face all he had either shunned or neglected for so long—himself and the world. How could he have forgotten the beauty of a humanity that created something like this? And yet, this was a piece of work built for the sheer amusement and pleasure of a spoiled monarchy. Martin knew that, but he didn't see that anymore. Instead, he saw the creative genius of one man, a man who built this magnificent place for himself. Maybe he knew it would bring him fame and fortune. It didn't matter. In the end, when the Opera House was finally completed, it must have brought him peace.

The longer Martin looked at himself in the mirrors, the more he felt ashamed for his stupidity in disregarding all the materials of the world. His ignorance swelled in him. Martin abhorred this grotesque display of his own image after being witness to so many beautiful things. Things. No, they were far beyond being things. This place had been one man's vision brought to existence. *What a beautiful mind he had*, Martin thought. He then thought, *My presence has ruined this place.* But how could it if it sparked such an inspiration in him? Especially where there had been no inspiration before. Perhaps he was the one person coming through these grand halls to fully take in the purity, appreciate every detail of craftsmanship, and hear the staircases sing. But that would be vain. At any rate, he had entered this place for a reason, and not just because it was one of Paris's top ten picks of famous tourist attractions. He passed a few more mirrors, not failing to recognize the beauty of their craftsmanship as well, but appreciating more the transitional beauty of his own image. He had finally awoken to something larger than his own naïve ideals, which had served to do nothing more than isolate him.

There was something else strange about this place, which

Martin took careful note of. As he analyzed his own image in the mirrors, he caught a glimpse of the couples walking behind him. They merged and separated into whole and separate beings. Somehow, they appeared to be more whole when they were not linking hands. It was a common phenomenon that Martin had witnessed before, but rarely in such a peculiar light. Couples were strange. They seemed to come together instinctively, holding hands and gazing at a majestic waterfall or a breathtaking sunset, the kind of sunset that tells you there is a God, blending earth into sky, so you don't know which side of heaven you exist in anymore. Any act of nature seemed to bring people together because of the universal beauty two people could enjoy in the same magnitude. Any creation of man had a polarizing effect. Couples tended to drift away from each other in order to appreciate the beauty or inspiration of anything manmade. The Opera House had faint whispers in the walls, from centuries past, whispers one had to strain to hear.

The same was true in museums and art galleries and all abstract environments where couples enter, separate, wander, and, afterwards, reunite to compare their individual experiences. Much like in real life, as art aims to mirror real life. Holding hands in these places was a distraction from the senses. Each person must be allowed to breathe and not be encumbered by the presence or opinions of their partners when viewing what is abstract. Since any man's genius is abstract, as it comes from imagination, the poor soul viewing it is left to his or her own interpretation and a journey of decisions he or she is forced to make alone.

There were the age-old questions about why there was life and religion and why catastrophes and miracles happened, but people put it down to faith and turn to their good books. When a man creates something that others can't fathom or explain, but that has the ability to make them think and feel, they have no references to turn to and are left to wonder without a sure reason. The answers weren't there and Martin didn't feel so alone in his journey through those halls. For once, wandering souls surrounded him. Being in this place, it was okay to be alone. There was nothing else to do there except absorb, dissect, ingest, and, finally, leave the place the way it was discovered, undigested. Martin followed suit.

There was also a formality to ingesting this artwork, an art in itself, as those around him walked a step or two slower and, periodically, tucked their hands behind their backs. Martin accordingly clasped one palm gently in the other, behind his back, and strolled thoughtfully past the mirrors. He surrendered to this place and began believing he might belong.

Chapter 7

WILLIS

Willis' taxicab stopped outside the gates at Wandsworth Prison, one of the oldest prisons in London. The tall and murky towers painted a scene that could have come from Dickens, with their worn, black stone and bleak windows. There was no hope inside those walls. The buildings were a city within the city, and a gloomy reminder to not test the laws. Willis wondered about the people outside who had to pass this fortress each day. Did they spit on the ground, or did they walk by with heavy hearts for the doomed souls inside? This prison was maximum security; this was no slap on the wrist or a place for "easy time." This was a place for lives that had come to an end, for no more than the price of ignorance, violent upbringings, and bad choices. The prison wasn't a symbol for society's safety; it was a symbol for its downfall. Too many men lost.

Willis was led by the guard into Mr. Harris' cell and with a curt, "Visitor for you," as an introduction to the inmate. Before leaving, the guard raised his eyebrow at Willis with a silent message that said, "Your funeral, mate. Any trouble and you holler!" Willis gave back a small smile of understanding. Mr. Harris sat upright on his cot, which was suspended on the concrete wall by a long chain.

"I requested that we meet in your cell so that we might have a more private chat," Willis started. "I hope that's alright."

"Any company is alright," Mr. Harris replied. He looked well-rested, which was surprising to Willis. He didn't think himself capable of lasting two minutes in a place like that. "Are you my barrister?" Mr. Harris burst him from his thoughts. The look in the inmate's eyes was both hopeful and skeptical.

"Er, let's talk first," Willis began again. "I'd like to know your story."

"My story?" Mr. Harris slouched on his cot. "Oh ... you mean the story I told the police."

"Yeah, that one." Willis eyed the other man cautiously. "How did you come to murder your wife?"

"I did it."

"So you said, and since you said it, I'm not sure now how I can save you from spending the rest of your life in prison." Willis refrained from telling him he could also be given a death sentence. The man let his head fall forward, more from exasperation than remorse or worry.

"I loved her, you know. I really loved her. She just never let me ..." He broke off as though there were no words that could finish his sentence, and Willis wasn't armed with the right words, either.

"Never let you what?"

"She never let me be the man."

"What?"

"You know—you get married, you become man and wife. *Man* and wife. Not husband and husband—you're not supposed to be the same!"

"She wore the pants, you mean?" Willis tried to understand and to keep him talking.

"I really loved her." Mr. Harris' voice was quieter. "She just wouldn't let me play the role I was supposed to. She made all the decisions ... Where we went, who we saw, what TV shows we watched, what we ate for dinner ..." He faltered, his hands grasping helplessly at some invisible answer.

"What did you do?" Willis quietly asked.

"Whatever she wanted to do."

"Why?"

"Because I loved her, and I wanted her to be happy—but I knew inside that I wasn't happy."

"Couldn't you talk to her?"

"Whenever I tried to say something about it, she just burst into tears. I couldn't bear to see her like that. But, you know, part of me did like it. It was only then that I felt like I had some control, but I didn't really want to make her cry. She didn't make any sense when she cried and that drove me crazy."

"Women," Willis found himself saying out loud.

"They can't help it," Mr. Harris reasoned with him. "They're weaker than us, aren't they? I mean, that's what I've always been told. My father always told me I had to be the stronger one and that I had to set the rules. She wouldn't let me, though. She wouldn't follow any rules."

"Couldn't you have left the marriage? Or had an affair?"

"An affair?" Mr. Harris looked at Willis as though he were the devil dressed in a suit and sitting in his cell.

"Well, maybe not an affair—that would have been too complicated."

"And wrong," the inmate added.

Right, Willis mused in his head. "Okay, there are prostitutes around, you know," Willis suggested. "Just to let off steam—to get it out of your system." He couldn't believe he was giving this kind of advice to someone who was already convicted and in prison. Besides, it was reasoning after the fact.

"Do you know how many diseases there are out there?"

"Right." Willis suddenly remembered a doctor's appointment.

"Besides, it wasn't about sex. It was about my need to gain some respect in that house, in our marriage, and for us to be partners. It was about making everything the way marriage should be."

"You could have divorced her," Willis said finally.

"I vowed to keep her and love her—until *death* do us part." Mr. Harris raised his head and looked Willis straight in the eye.

"That you did, Mr. Harris."

Chapter 8

WILLIS

The day turned out to be sunny. Willis and his mother stood by the grave, not speaking and not crying. The minister's words bounced off the tiny drums in Willis' ears. They weren't real enough to stick, but the sound of death, the finality of it, vibrated in him. It wasn't that he wanted to hold his father or say something useless and phony, like, "I love you, Dad," because he didn't. He was past wanting to hear it, too. More than anything, he wanted to have that man in the ground back to hear him out. He wanted to talk out the stored feelings of betrayal. He wanted to strangle his limp neck and pound on his dead heart.

The setting was picturesque and out in the country, as his father had wished to be buried with his ancestors. It was a small cemetery near Willis' father's family land. There was no room for mother; no arrangements had been made for her.

Sam stood nearby with a stiff lip. He looked older, even since the week before. He didn't look over at them. He seemed uncomfortable in their presence, this man who held most of his father's secrets. Willis wanted to turn him upside down and shake them all out of him. Instead, he looked into the dirt hole below their feet, with the box in it, and knew there was a whole secret life being buried. Perhaps an entire life even Sam could only guess at. The three of them and the minister were strangers to this man, and yet they were the only people at his funeral. It was almost like a practice run, and Willis waited for his father to pop out of his earth-dusted coffin and say, "That was okay, but couldn't any of you say something more?" No, they couldn't. They had to let the minister throw down their goodbyes for them, as inadequate and inappropriate as it was. The minister knew his father even less, his father who had never set foot in a church. The whole thing was a joke.

Willis reached into his jacket and pulled out a silver mickey. His mother jabbed him in the arm as soon as she saw the sunlight hit the flask, but he wasn't deterred. He unscrewed the cap, took a long swig, and screwed the top back on, ignoring the glares from both Sam and the minister as he solemnly tucked the bottle back in his inside coat pocket.

"How rude of me," he said, interrupting the minister. "Would anyone else like a taste?" The other three silently grimaced, until Sam motioned for the minister to continue. Willis took the general decline of his offer and bowed his head in mockery. The service wasn't long, and in the end, they each took a handful of dirt and scattered it on the coffin, and Willis thought, *We're burying you, Father. Don't try and come back.*

"Do you want to come back for tea?" his mother asked. Her tone was flat, and he realized she was asking him more out of a sense of duty and decorum than genuinely wanting to spend time with him.

"No, thank you, Mother," he answered politely. "I have a client to see."

He had lied to his mother on a day when she maybe needed him most. He couldn't tell anymore what she was thinking or feeling;

he only saw a curtain drawn behind her eyes. She'd had that look in her eyes for as long as he could remember. He chose not to think about it as he kissed her cheek and helped ease her into the back-seat of the limousine.

"Aren't you at least going to drive into town with us?" she asked. She sounded a little indignant, and Willis couldn't understand why. He wasn't coming over to visit her, so what did it matter?

"No, Mother, I've got my own transportation," he lied, again.

"You've been drinking," she said accusingly. "Where are you parked? We can drive you to your car."

"I'm fine; go on," he insisted. She screwed her lips up tightly and sat back in the leather seat. The window closed with a faint whirring noise as she muttered, "I hate limousines."

Willis waited for the car to drive out of view, and then he went into the main office of the burial grounds to call for a taxicab. He was going back to the office. He wanted to spend some time with the Harris file and get his head around his prospective client. He sensed he may take the case, but he wasn't definite about it yet. There was a small part of him that sympathized with this man, and that part was growing. He almost felt guilty himself, because he didn't know how he could be feeling such an empathetic bond with an accused murderer. He had never murdered anyone—how could he begin to know what might drive someone to such a ghastly act?

The man talked as though he had committed murder in self-de-fense, protecting himself from being emasculated by his wife. Women were cunning animals, and there was a movement that had been building for decades, a shift in the gender roles. Wives didn't stay in the kitchen anymore, raising their children and taking care of their working men. They were out there, becoming bosses and buying takeout dinners. They were driving cars with their husbands in the passenger seats. Some women were insulted by men who opened doors for them, as if it was a message that a woman was physically unable to open her own damn door. What were the men supposed to do now? The men kept quiet, stopped having opinions, made dinner, and gave up the remote control. They picked up their kids from school and waited for their wives to come home.

His mother had been a housewife; she had raised him sin-gle-handedly so that his father wouldn't have to worry about "one more thing." In the end, for the most part, Willis had raised himself, because he knew that lonely women, not women who are alone, found it difficult to raise children. He understood that. He also understood why he didn't want children in his life. He didn't understand why his father kept his distance from them, why he left his mother in every way, slowly and painfully. She never fought him for the remote control. She couldn't—he was never home to watch television. She never watched television either. "It makes my head hurt," she had once told him as she sat at the kitchen table drinking a glass of wine, her tired shape half-hidden from the living room. Willis lived inside the television set where fathers lifted their sons onto their laps to tell them about how life worked. He wished he knew the answer his father might have given him.

A taxicab slowed down against the curb and Willis slid into the backseat, giving the driver the address to his office.

⊰•◊•⊱

Willis returned to the office after hours, as his assistant was for-warding her phone to the answering service and getting ready to leave. She was startled when she saw him. Not that she was unac-customed to him working late, but she knew he had been at his father's funeral and hadn't expected him to come in that day. She asked if he needed her to assist him with anything. Willis patted her on the shoulder. "Go home, Cynthia. Your husband is going to come down here and beat me up if I keep you working late."

She smiled, "There's no one waiting for me except my cat. He won't be impressed, but he won't starve either."

"I guess I don't ask you much about your personal life, do I?"

"That's okay. Have a good night."

"Thanks," he called after her. She was already near the elevator doors that opened into the office reception area. He wanted to tell her that he had decided to take the Harris case, but he wanted to be sure. He still needed to look through the rest of the file, and he could tell her his decision in the morning. She was a sweet girl, and his relationship with her was most likely the only female relationship in his life that felt normal and uncomplicated. At times he could feel a flirtatious vibe from her. She didn't know who he was or wasn't, what he was capable of or not, and when he was in the office, he was in command of himself. He turned his desk lamp on and flipped open Mr. Harris' file.

Mr. Michael Harris had no previous record of illegal activity. He was as clean as a whistle, with no history of violence. Mr. Harris was a librarian. What was it that went through his head while he was sorting books? The stacks were a quiet place, and there was a lot of time to think while shelving and retrieving titles for patrons. Still, did the nature of his job mean that he was automatically guilty of having premeditated thoughts of killing his wife in the slow hours of his work shift? He had been married for seven years. No kids. His wife was an elementary school teacher. Did they try to have kids? Did Mr. Harris want kids, and was he opposed by his wife—or the other way around? Were there any financial troubles? These were questions that Willis needed to have answered; the only way to know would be for him to talk with Mr. Harris again.

Willis took a bottle of rum and a highball glass out of the top drawer of his desk and poured two fingers. He looked at Michael's mug shot. His hair was a bit mussed up, as though he had been dragged out of bed to have his picture taken. He looked like a librarian, serious and with glasses. He didn't look menacing. He looked defeated and like someone who had already reconciled to his fate. Willis looked at the photos taken of Mrs. Harris at the crime scene. He took a healthy swig of his drink and positioned the photographs side by side on his desk. Every photograph showed a side profile of the injury to her head. He couldn't tell how she would have looked alive. She was evidence, cold flesh, and nothing more. Willis finished his drink and resigned to meet with his client in the morning. If he didn't take this case, he wouldn't find the answers. He didn't know yet if he even wanted Mr. Harris to be innocent or guilty. He was too far into this puzzle, and not finishing it would keep him awake at night.

———⟫•◊•⟪———

ELLIE

Ellie Hancocks returned from the cemetery in her husband's limousine, dressed in a black suit, and wearing black satin gloves. She climbed the stairs to her flat and, in the front hallway, frowned at her reflection in the mirror. She took a nude-coloured lipstick from her purse and applied it to her aging lips. She then took a large, white napkin out of her hand purse, her hand shaking. The napkin was the only item left to her by her husband. She had read the napkin over and over since the morning when she had received it from Sam. She unfolded the napkin and read again the block letters in black ink:

DEAREST ELLIE—
I WAS NEVER FAIR TO YOU. FORGIVE ME.

She was told the napkin was found beside him, his final note. Ellie pressed her lips together on a corner of the napkin, visibly disturbed. She looked at the wastebasket, but folded the napkin carefully and placed it back in her purse. She closed the clasp smartly.

Chapter 9

WILLIS HANCOCKS SR.

Willis Hancocks Sr. sat at a desk in a dark room. Next to him was a small bottle of medication for his heart and a glass of whisky. He pulled a black executive pen from inside his jacket and proceeded to write on a large white napkin. Then he folded the napkin in half and slipped it into an envelope. Next, he reached for the small bottle, unscrewed the cap and poured half the pills into his palm. He held them there for a moment, contemplating them. Then he casually scooped the pills into his mouth and chased them down with a long swig of whisky. He laid his head on the table and closed his eyes, anticipating a long and painless sleep.

Chapter 10

WILLIS

The prison guard was surprised to see Willis at the gate. Cynthia, however, had not been surprised when he told her his decision to take on the Harris case. She asked if he still wanted the new barrister, Mr. Brown, to help with the research. Willis told her that he wouldn't need assistance on this particular case and assigned to Mr. Brown a few of the other files stacked on his desk. He thought he may have to give over those files entirely to the new, young barrister, depending on his involvement with Mr. Harris.

Willis nodded to the prison guard and said, "Good morning," as he passed through the gate and routine security check. The guard didn't make any small talk; he simply led him to Mr. Harris' cell. Willis had the impression the guard had no time for murderers and probably thought Willis was insane to even bother listening to this prisoner. Mr. Harris gave Willis a much warmer welcome.

"Hello, Mr. Hancocks. I'm glad to see you again. May I ask, does this visit mean that you are going to be my barrister?"

"Yes, Mr. Harris, I think it does. I need to ask you more questions, though. We have to start preparing for your court date." Mr. Harris was scheduled to appear in court in one month. There wasn't much time. "I've looked through your file to get a better picture of you and your wife, and your relationship. First of all, I understand you are a librarian."

"Yes, I was a librarian," Mr. Harris corrected him. "I love books. I believe the written word is the greatest accomplishment of the human race."

"Well, we eventually had to write something down to communicate, didn't we? I mean, we can't all remember everything."

"They used to remember. Bards used to memorize their stories—important stories about their cultures and histories—and travel like nomads from village to village, relaying their stories in repetitive poems or songs, and the people would remember their words and pass them down."

"People used to have more patience."

"People weren't so informed then."

"We have to prepare the story we need to tell," Willis said. He mostly wanted to get them back on track, talking about the trial. *Hopefully, the jury will be patient*, he thought. Michael moved to the edge of his cot and leaned forward, balancing his forearms on his knees, indicating his willingness to get down to business.

"Was your wife a full-time teacher?" Willis asked.

"Yes, she loved kids. She loved teaching."

"Did she love kids as much as you, Michael?"

"What do you mean?" Michael shot him a hurt look.

"Did you want kids?"

Michael didn't answer right away. Then he said, "She said that she was happy enough with the kids she taught."

"That's not the same as having your own."

"She had a stressful job. A baby would have been too much work ... too expensive and time consuming."

"For who? Please, Michael, answer my question. Did you want kids?"

"Yes, I told her I wanted a baby."

"And she fought you on that point in your marriage?"

"Yes."

"Your wife told your neighbours that she wanted to have kids."

"What? She never expressed those thoughts to me."

"Perhaps she was put on the spot."

"That is possible. Our neighbours are older, retired. They are a different generation. They may have thought she was strange if she said she didn't want kids. She may have been afraid that they wouldn't talk to her—or worse, they might have tried to change her mind."

The cell felt smaller. Michael began to fidget. Willis decided to move on. "Did you fantazise at all about not being with your wife—not being married to her?" Willis asked.

"I told you, I loved her. I can't imagine not being married to her."

"You're not married to her now."

"I'm still married."

Willis could see that the argument was useless. "These are questions that the prosecution will bring up, Michael. You have to be ready to answer them. Everything I tell them will be to emphasize your unhappiness and your sense of being trapped in your marriage. This is an abuse case, and we are going to submit a plea that you acted in self-defense or experienced temporary insanity, whichever you prefer. We can call it a crime of passion."

"No, I'm not insane."

"Did you think of killing your wife before you murdered her? I mean, at work or anywhere else you would have had the time to make such a plan?"

"Plan? I didn't try to hide anything. I'm telling you the truth. I've been telling the truth since she died."

Willis noted that he didn't say "since I killed her."

"I believe your truth, but I also believe that you felt controlled by your wife."

"I may have had thoughts, but they weren't serious. I didn't wake up that morning and think that I was going to kill her."

"Then it was not premeditated murder."

"I loved my wife."

Willis wasn't sure if he should advise his client to not say that phrase over and over in the courtroom. It seemed to be a moot point in the circumstances of her death. He sounded pathetic, and Willis was worried that it would create a contrary effect on the jury, something opposite to sympathy. No one had held a gun to this man's head.

Willis visited Michael's cell once a week until the trial date and coached him for the time he would spend on the witness stand. By the time they went to trial, Michael had a better understanding of what to expect from the prosecution, but neither of them could predict the thoughts of the jury members. He trusted Willis to state his case fairly and honestly. There were no strings. Surprisingly, after the time Willis had spent with his client, he wanted to see this man claim his innocence, or at least receive a light sentence. He knew there were gaps that the prosecution would tear wide open. Willis had not been able to help his client with the alternative options he may have had to killing his wife; his approach was morbid and stoic. Mr. Harris insisted that she was his wife and he couldn't dishonour her or upset her; he either had to live with her or end her time with him. He couldn't hurt her by leaving, and he couldn't break their wedding vows. In his twisted mind—a mind he argued was perfectly clear—there was no other way.

Any other barrister probably would have walked away from the case, but Willis sympathized with him. There was some part of him that also felt women should not have the upper hand. If there was to be equality, women couldn't rise up and assume a greater power over men. The balance of power had shifted and it unnerved him. The evidence was in this man's desperate act to regain his manhood.

He doubted the jury would see the repression and desperation he saw in the case of Mr. Harris; this revolutionary view—the advocacy for the abused husband—was not popular. Society sided with the female power, the unearthing of strength seemingly covered by the insecurity of men for centuries. No one wanted to hear about the emotionally-battered male. Nobody believed it was possible.

Chapter 11

WILLIS

The courtroom was just as Willis had expected. There were few spectators in attendance as he walked down the aisle to take his seat at the front table. Michael wore a charcoal suit and looked grim. He held his composure when he was asked to stand and greet the judge and later cried openly at the mention of "the deceased." He pleaded guilty, against advisement from Willis. As his counsel, Willis caused a brief verbal scuffle in the court proceedings, in an attempt to change his client's answer, but he was unsuccessful. Willis watched as the jury came into the room: a few middle-aged professional men, a couple of senior citizens, a handful of younger professionals, and a sprinkling of housewives. Willis sucked in his breath and looked at his client, much like a sergeant looking at one of his soldiers before battle. The odds of victory were against them.

In Willis' opening statement, he recognized that his client had made a guilty plea because he was aware that he did commit this horrible act. However, what would be revealed to the court was that Mr. Harris also acted in self-defense, to uphold the rights of his person. Willis gave examples from his client's marriage where he had been cut down, ignored, and undermined by his wife on a daily basis. There were no witnesses who came forth in his defense; no one was put on the stand to validate Michael's character, except Michael. He was a quiet man who kept to himself, with no close friends. He only had his late wife's friends, once upon a time.

Willis never understood why the benches in the courtroom looked like pews. *They should have bleachers in here*, he thought. After all, this was an arena for inquisitions—not a place for hope. The seats were half-filled with immediate family, media vultures, and a few supporters or morbidly curious spectators. There were no witnesses to this crime, only the hard evidence: a body, a weapon, and a man pleading guilty. Willis casually looked around the room at the small gathering of stern, tired faces. He spotted Michael's parents. It was easy to tell who they were—sitting in the back row looking sombre and slouching down in their seats, clutching each other's hands. Another older woman, the late Mrs. Harris' mother, was sitting near the front and turned around once, glaring in the couple's direction. There was no hint of sympathy, no bonding in their misunderstanding of this tragedy. No love lost, it seemed. This was their sentence, too. Michael never turned around to make eye contact. Willis found that odd, as well. He thought his client would at least try to show some sign of being human, looking for the support of his family. Instead, he acted as though he were the only person in the room. This was his judgment, and he was already alone in it.

Willis felt his body form to the wooden chair and his hands were surprisingly dry. He was in the passenger seat, as he knew Michael would not budge in his own conviction. There was nothing more he could do to advise his client; he could only support Michael in the way he wanted to handle his own trial. Willis didn't even really need to be there, except to be a body standing beside Michael. He had wrestled with the rights and wrongs and hadn't been able to make any conclusive, black and white judgments either for or against his client. He wasn't sure what drove a man to such extremes, but clearly it was something beyond any reasonable control. The way he saw it, Michael had been a prisoner for years. Would the jury convict a slave that lashed out against his captor?

The first day of the trial was tedious, and the judge tried to look impartial but kept glancing at Michael as though he carried some disease or might break out in some mad fit. Willis toyed with the latches on his briefcase, agitated. The prosecutor was young, probably a few years out of law school, and his fangs were dripping. He was biting into this case like it was a big, juicy steak, and he had a lineup of the victim's close friends and family members to avenge her past person and character. Michael had no one.

The prosecutor also had the good sense not to drag Mrs. Harris' mother up on the stand. She sat rigid in the bench, looking indignant and broken. She nodded vigorously and pulled in her quivering lips when anything positive was said about her daughter. Her mother looked fierce. For some strange reason, Willis wanted to hear her speak. He wanted to hear how she sounded, even if she yelled and screamed and cried in the courtroom—he wanted to know. He wanted someone in that room to say something humane, something that made sense and started the healing. The courtroom seemed to shrink around him so that he was uncomfortably aware of the jurors looking pensive in their box. They were the audience that mattered. Willis thought about the responsibility that weighed down on their shoulders, determining the fate of a man's life. It was no surprise that no one volunteered for jury duty. Instead, it was a dreaded piece of unexpected mail that arrived like a draft letter. Whatever the jury decided, he didn't envy them and he didn't blame them.

Still, he felt that he wasn't doing all he could to prevent the inevitable, but that was how his client wanted his fate to play out. Michael didn't want to slip out of the noose because he had a barrister with an easy charm and golden tongue. Instead, he sought honesty and willingly laid his head on the block.

The sister of the deceased was asked to take the stand first. She was tall and willowy and wore a light-coloured, knee-length dress with a slim belt. Her hair was pulled back into a loose bun. She looked as though she hadn't slept for a week. She probably hadn't. She stated her name and swore to tell the truth.

"I want to say that my sister was a giver," she blurted out before any questions were asked. She was reminded, gently, by the judge to not speak until she was asked a question. She sat in the witness stand like a caged rabbit, her eyes darting from the judge to the barristers and jury members. She averted her eyes from Michael, as though even looking at him would do harm to her sister's honour.

The prosecutor stood up and came slowly around the table to the front of the room. "Did your sister ever speak to you about any abuse in her marriage?"

"No, never," the young woman answered, looking warily at Michael out of the corner of her eye. She seemed unnerved by Mr. Harris' direct stare. Willis also noticed how he watched her: unabashed and with an open interest, but without malice. His stare was unwavering, almost inviting her to say whatever she needed to. He watched her like he would a wounded bird, not an insect trapped in a turned over glass.

"In the time you have known Mr. Harris as your brother-in-law, has he ever seemed negative or argumentative?"

"No, not really," she answered again, sounding doubtful. "He has always been fairly quiet."

"Ah, watch out for the quiet ones, as they say," the prosecutor said flippantly.

"Objection!" Willis stood up, pushing back his chair with unnecessary force. "The prosecutor should not make unfounded comments that may sway the jury."

"Sustained," said the judge without emotion. "I would advise counsel to watch his comments."

"I retract my comment," replied the young prosecutor, unmoved. Willis often wondered how the jury was expected to erase from their minds a comment they had heard quite clearly and possibly already assessed as part of their opinion. As a seasoned barrister, Willis could almost see the workings of the prosecutor's line of questions taking a swift sidestep and moving in another strategic direction. It was like watching a rugby match in play. Grab the ball and run; drop the ball and go back to the huddle and emerge with a new game plan. The witness waited patiently, readying herself to catch the next ball that hurled through the air.

"Okay, so he was quiet. Did your sister ever seem uncomfortable around him?" The prosecutor continued.

"Oh no, she was a very bubbly person, the life of the party. She socialized enough for the both of them. Everyone loved her."

Willis noticed that Michael tended to look down, bowing his head, when she mentioned her sister, his wife.

"So, do you think the imbalance of their personalities could have caused a rift in their marriage?"

Finally, Willis thought—a question that could implicate both husband *and* wife.

"There was a problem. She would complain that he didn't talk to her about different issues in their relationship. If she felt frustrated about something, he would simply leave the room and not bother to stay and try to sort out the problem. She hated that," the woman answered, focusing intently on the prosecutor. "In the end, she felt as though she had to do everything and make every decision for them. He would never tell her what he wanted."

"No further questions, your honour." The prosecutor moved back to his table. The judge asked Willis if he wanted to cross examine.

Willis looked at his client, who promptly shook his head. "Not at this time, your honour," Willis replied. It was clear that his client didn't want to put her, or himself, in a hard position. There was no question she wanted to talk, but she was a poor witness. She had recently lost her sister and any opinions or observations she had would be clouded by her emotions. It did not mean she would not tell the truth, only that she would tell *her* truth, a truth that came by hearsay from her late sister. There were no ghosts speaking in the courtroom that day. The judge told the woman to step down. She looked bewildered, her mouth moving with no words. The question was still hanging in the air—*how did this happen?*

Day after day, Michael was led into the silence and fury of the courtroom to face his judgment and to listen to the indisputable evidence: the details of the crime scene, his wife's limp body on the couch with a dent in her head, and pieces of plastic debris from the remote control strewn around her. He listened to the police officers who had arrived at the crime scene retell the grisly details. Michael was made to relive the event again and again, not that he didn't see it every minute he was alone or whenever he closed his eyes. She would always be there. Willis could see that: the sadness. Michael didn't want to get away from her. He listened to her friends talk about how wonderful she was and told Willis later that he couldn't argue with those descriptions. His wife was a force of light, a dynamo, do-it-all, energizer bunny. Maybe she wore him out and made him feel inadequate. Who could stand next to that year after year and not get lost? Maybe he let her. Maybe he chose to be the shadow, the battery, the place she could dive into when she came down off the social highs. Maybe it was all too much for both of them.

On the last day of the trial, as Willis watched Michael take the stand, he remembered the last conversation he'd had with him in the prison.

"I don't expect to win this trial," Michael had said, "but I want to thank you for trying to help me."

"We're not there yet, Michael. It isn't over. Don't think that way."

"I'm not going to play any games. I am going to continue to tell the truth, and people don't always like to hear the truth."

"Our justice system is built on truth," Willis argued feebly. He could barely swallow his own words, which went down sourly.

"You really believe that?" Michael asked. He had looked at Willis as though he was a toddler and believed everything. There was another look of mistrust, almost amusement, in his eyes that showed he didn't believe a word Willis was saying to him.

Now, in the courtroom, the mother of the late Mrs. Harris bristled and shifted uncomfortably in her seat, and Willis heard the old woman mutter, "What the hell has he got to say?" as she dabbed one eye.

Michael raised himself slowly, steadily from the table and approached the witness box. He was the only true witness, and once again, he leaned towards Willis and whispered, "I am going to tell the truth." He intended to tell the court exactly what he had told Willis in his cell. He wasn't looking for absolution, only peace. The judge looked on as Michael swore with his hand on the heavy book. Michael then entered the box and sat down. Willis approached him, and throughout his line of questions, he strove to establish the relationship Michael had with his wife. He focused on Michael's mild-mannered character and his lack of premeditation for murder.

"How did you feel about your wife?" Willis began.

"She was amazing. I loved her very much." The prosecutor tried to argue that the "feelings" the accused held for his wife were irrelevant and further commented that people have been known to murder their spouses out of feelings of "obsessive love." His protest was overruled. Willis thought the judge maybe held some interest in his client's testimony and wanted to see how the trial would play out uninterrupted. This was, after all, his client's only opportunity to speak.

"Were you at home the evening your wife was killed?" Willis lifted an eyebrow. He knew he was walking a dangerous line—one that could even cost him his career. He hoped for the slight chance that Michael had considered creating an alibi. Instead, Michael looked at him strangely.

"Yes, of course I was at home. I told the police everything when they arrived. I killed my wife."

Willis had to restrain from closing his eyes in quiet defeat. He had thrown his client a rope, and his client let it fall ten feet away from him, with no attempt to grab on. So Willis continued, respecting his client's wishes and trying to give him both dignity and a chance to explain.

Willis exhaled softly. "Why did you kill your wife, Mr. Harris?"

"I didn't plan to," Michael began. "I never planned to kill her."

"So, what happened the night she died?" Willis repeated.

"I had been looking forward to a quiet night to stay in with her. I had been working a lot, and there was a movie on the television I wanted to watch. I was going to make us dinner first. I thought we could just relax at home—I had been working in the evenings and she was usually out with her friends. We barely saw each other. I kept trying to make a date for us to be together, but she always had other plans. She was complaining that I didn't pay any attention to her and that I didn't like to go out with her friends. She said I was pretending to work late. I complained that she was never home either. I always came home to an empty house, and I didn't work very late. I never worked past seven in the evening. I felt bad afterwards. So I wanted to make it up to her—to be romantic.

"I was starting dinner—a fish dish with salmon and rice. Then she came home. She came into the kitchen and poured herself a glass of white wine. I had a bottle of red sitting on the counter. I had already poured a glass for her. Then she took a sip of her white wine before I had a chance to fill my own glass. I wanted to clink glasses, but hers was already near empty. 'White wine goes with fish,' she said when she saw the bottle of red. She gulped her wine. Then she looked inside the pot on the stove top and told me the rice was sticking. As I was rescuing the rice, I told her how I wanted us to have a quiet night in and watch a movie.

"'Great,' she said. 'Let's go to the video store.' I told her there was a movie on television that I thought we could watch. She said she didn't like watching movies on television because they cut out all of the good parts. I insisted that we stay in. I don't usually argue with her, but I was really looking forward to the movie on television, and I just wanted to stay in with her. I was checking on the salmon in the broiler, and she marched into the living room with another glass of wine and sat down on the couch in a huff. She started switching channels. I could hear her laughing at the screen. Her laugh was louder than normal.

"I prepared our plates and suggested that we sit at the dining room table, which I had set. There were lit taper candles ... the full monty. We hadn't sat together at the table for a romantic meal in a long time. She insisted she was comfortable on the couch, so I brought the plates over to the coffee table. Then I went back and picked up the candles for us to eat by them. 'Let's watch this show instead,' she said. I argued with her that I didn't want to. 'The movies you choose are always so stupid,' she told me. I was hurt, but for the first time, I wasn't backing down. She became more aggressive and more determined, and so did I; something in me was beginning to snap. I always gave her what she wanted. I was never able to make a decision for both of us. Neither one of us had touched our dinner. I didn't have a glass of wine. I told her *no*, and that I didn't want to watch anything else. I told her I wanted us to enjoy our romantic dinner and watch the movie I had planned for us to watch.

"I didn't want to feel angry, but I did feel pushed. She had a strong mind. She saw that I was serious, and so she did something unnecessary. She grabbed the remote control and held it from me. So I got up to change the channel on the set. Then she screamed and tried to tackle me, yelling that I was an obsessive control freak. She yelled at me that she had cancelled plans with her girlfriends that night and she didn't even want to be at home with me. She yelled that I was boring, that I didn't want to go anywhere. For some reason, I tried to grab the remote control from her. I was crying. I wanted her to be home with me, and happy. When I finally got the remote away from her, I smacked her in the head. I smacked her hard. She had a stunned look on her face, and then she collapsed. I could see the bruised dent in the side of her head, and I checked her pulse. There was nothing. I was numb. I dragged her over to the couch and called the police."

The courtroom was quiet. When the judge asked the prosecutor if he would like to cross-examine the accused, the other barrister shook his head and said "I have no questions, your honour." Mr. Harris was asked to step down. His former mother-in-law shot daggers at him as he returned to his chair. The jury was gravely asked to weigh what they had heard without bias, but with fairness and justice. The judge then announced that the court was adjourned until the following week, during which time the jury would come to a decision. The guards came forth to handcuff Mr. Harris once more and lead him away, back to his cell.

"I know what you were trying to do," he said quietly to Willis.

"I was just— I was trying to—" Willis started, but he couldn't bring himself to say "I was doing my job."

"You were being a friend," Michael said gently. "Thank you. I'll be okay." Then the guards moved him towards the exit.

In the end, Willis' argument didn't wash with the jury or the judge. Michael was asked to stand to hear his sentence, after the jury returned from a week of tiring deliberation. The trial had lasted three weeks, and Michael was convicted of second degree murder, just as he had been telling everyone since the murder, and he was given a life sentence in prison. Before the bailiff clamped the handcuffs on him, Michael turned to Willis and solemnly shook his hand. "Thanks for doing what you could," Michael said. Willis couldn't say anything. He couldn't even say sorry. In many ways, he was shaking a dead man's hand. The world had fallen off its axis.

———◆◆◆◆———

One week later, Willis' office phone rang. The voice on the other end identified himself as the Warden of Wandsworth Prison.

"Mr. Hancocks? We need you to come down here."

"What is the matter?"

"Your client— Er, Mr. Harris committed suicide in his cell last night."

"I'll be right there." He replaced the phone in its cradle with a shaky hand.

When Willis reached the prison, the same guard let him in. This time, the guard's facial expression was a bit softer, more resigned. "I'm sorry," he muttered. Willis nodded. He didn't take him into Michael's cell, but they had to walk past its empty chamber. Something cold slapped Willis in the chest. He was escorted down the long hall and then downstairs.

"How did he—?" Willis asked the guard.

"He hung himself. He got a hold of some rope from one of the inmates. Contraband. Unfortunately, it happens sometimes."

They arrived at the morgue, and the guard left Willis with the attendant there.

"Mr. Harris?"

"Yes."

"Do you want to see him?"

"Yes." He was led to a wall of large drawers. The attendant scanned the wall and then pulled on one of the handles. A body emerged, draped under a light green sheet. *Prison issued*, Willis thought. The attendant pulled back the sheet over the head of the body. Michael lay there, eyes closed, looking peaceful. There was a sharp, red line across his neck. *Where are you*, Willis thought.

"Take all the time you need."

"Thank you. Are there any personal effects?" Willis thought to ask the attendant.

"Not much ... his mother and father picked up his things earlier this morning. He did leave this for you, though. We found it inside his shirt pocket." The attendant handed him a folded piece of paper with *Mr. Hancocks* scratched in ink on the front. Willis opened the note and read.

I knew it would end this way. The justice system can take a long time, and I told my wife I wouldn't be long. Thank you for your friendship.

He refolded the note and tucked it in his own pocket.

Chapter 12

WILLIS

Willis hopped on a double-decker bus, careened through the streets of downtown London, and watched for familiar landmarks while heading to his mother's flat. He had not visited her in weeks and he felt a son's obligation to be with her in the wake of his father's death. He also knew he was not in the best state of mind to see her, and he wondered if he was only destined to do more life-altering damage, especially to this person he revered. How much damage could he do in twenty-four hours? Perhaps he was testing himself; the day was not over yet. *She was a fragile type*, he thought, and this was not an easy time. He should staple his lips shut, but he knew something would inevitably slip out.

When he pressed the buzzer to her flat, no voice welcomed him in return. There was only the sound of a hand picking up the receiver, a faint static sound, and then the abrupt metallic rubbing of the lock unhitching in the front door. He pulled open the door in time and entered. He felt nauseous climbing the stairs to the third floor. The elevator had a sign put out that read *Closed for repairs*. He thought of his aging mother, nearly in her 60s, trapped on the third floor and surrounded by pictures and flowers and, possibly, boxes. Her life was now contained in a one-bedroom flat. He thought of her, alone and broken. He came because he wanted to pity her and be pitied himself, although he would never admit it. Her door was left ajar.

"Mother?" he stepped in and closed the door behind him, bolting the lock. "Mother, you really shouldn't leave your door open. Anyone could waltz in here and take you for all you're worth."

"Ah, and how much am I worth, dear?" Her voice floated down the hall. "What do you think, some little old rogue is going to totter in here and threaten to rape me by holding his walking cane to my head?" Her flat was larger than he had remembered, or perhaps imagined.

"Oh, Mother."

"You're the one who suggested I move to this seniors' building, and that I didn't need the house anymore."

"Would you have liked to stay and clatter about in that old house by yourself?" He was feeling annoyed already, but admired her spite. She came around the corner in a festive blouse and demure knee-length skirt. A sporty scarf was tied hastily around her neck and she wore a flamboyant hat with a large hat pin.

"No. No, you are right, too many memories there."

He stood in the hallway with his shoes still on and stared at her.

"What is it, dear?"

"What are you doing?"

She looked down at herself. "I'm going to Covent Market."

"But dressed like that? I mean, everybody knows, you know, and you look like ..." He hesitated.

"Like what?" she started, mildly annoyed.

"Like you're ready for Mardi Gras!"

"My dear, life goes on. I'm sorry if I don't seem heartbroken. What reason do I have to be?"

"You were his wife. You have an obligation ... not to mention the fact that you only just put him in the bloody ground a month ago!"

"Obligation?" she chortled. "Don't speak to me about obligations. He had an obligation to be with his family. An obligation to honour his wedding vows, an obligation to be a decent human being and be moved by something more than the feel of a crisp pound note. Perhaps if I really were made of money ..." She caught herself. "Well ... life goes on. You need to remember that, too."

"I don't believe you. I came all the way over here to be of some comfort to you. It looks like you don't need any." He stood looking confused and hurt.

"I am surprised, Willis. It would be nice if you would come to visit when it doesn't serve your own purposes to be ... *helpful*. Honestly, I thought you would be the least upset. He was never there for you, either. Don't you remember? He didn't care, Willis; you are more than old enough to realize that now." She shook her head, her face grim, but she was far from tears as she pulled on her gloves with some effort. "I never would have said a harsh word against your father when you were younger. That would not have been right, but he let go of us a very long time ago. I was the one who kept up the front of a stable family. I was the one who suffered most. Well, guess what, I'm finished suffering. Now I am going to live my life." This was not the fragile old woman Willis had anticipated. He had wanted to see her grieve for his father and the missing pieces he had left in both their lives and to help her sweep up those pieces and put them away.

"You were the cause of him not being there," he said calmly. He wanted her to be suffering. He didn't know or care how many nights she had lain shattered, alone in her king size bed, wanting to suffocate herself in the pillows. He wanted her to suffer now. He wanted to see it. Most of all, he didn't want to be alone in his grief.

She stopped tugging on her glove and looked at him, hard. She looked at him as though she didn't recognize him. She simply stood there, her other hand on her glove, not tugging. Then she gave it a sharp, defiant tug, lifting one eyebrow, and reached for her handbag. "Well …" she began, "if I don't get to the market soon, all the best bouquets and loaves of bread will be picked over."

"Mother," he faltered.

"Thanks for dropping by, Willis. Now if you'll excuse me."

"Mother, wait." He sat down in a small antique chair by the door. "Mother, I'm sorry. I've been feeling confused and I wanted to blame you. I know the man my father was and I understand more than you realize. I was only a small boy, but I remember. There was nothing you could have done. And now I think I've turned into him, God help me." He moved from the chair, slumping forward, and walked towards the door as though chains were shackled around his ankles, hindering his stride.

She could see her little boy in his tall, broad-shouldered frame, the illusion of a man. She wanted to reach out and take his arm, but there was some deeper sadness that held her back, and it was not her sadness. He seemed so vulnerable, so she was not prepared when he turned to her as he reached for the doorknob and said, "You weren't a wife, Mother; you were just someone he slept with." In spite of herself, she felt her arm come around to slap him, but he caught her wrist in his hand. He caught her with confidence, but without malice. Instead, he looked her in the eyes sadly and said, "I understand now why you are happy he's not coming back." And with that, he let her wrist fall and quietly exited.

As Willis left his mother's building, he walked considerably slower than when he'd arrived, with his hands shoved deep into the pockets of his overcoat. He wore this coat like a heavy shield to keep out the biting, cold wind, and to keep a little warmth next to his heart. Unfortunately, too much air seemed to steal into the folds and snuff out the little flame. He didn't pay attention to where he was walking. He just needed to walk. Even if he was going in circles or backwards, it didn't matter. Perhaps he needed to go backwards. He wished very much to go back to that place where he had seen a clear path to follow, as well as the one beside it that looked dodgy and overgrown. Which of the paths had he watched his father trundle down without any hesitation, and why did it seem he had the need to follow him, not knowing where it would lead to? Simple, there had been no other man walking up ahead of him.

Willis had recurring dreams of his father. He could see him in his smart fedora hat and grey trench coat, with a cigarette dangling from his mouth and a long-legged filly on each arm, fingering his lapel and kissing his ears. The girls never noticed him trailing behind them, but his father would always turn around and give him an easy look, and without moving his lips, he would say to Willis, "Stay close and look sharp, boy. This is the place you want to go." Every time he awoke, he cursed his wayward and womanizing father. Willis thought of how he could always see his own feet in the dream, one stepping dutifully in front of the other. There was nothing else to identify himself in the dream, only his feet.

Chapter 13

MARTIN

Martin had strolled through the Vancouver International Airport with his boarding pass in hand. None of his family members had come to see him off, because they didn't know he was leaving. They didn't know anything about him. It wasn't their fault. He would send a postcard. He pushed back the thought and grabbed a burger from a McDonald's kiosk. He paid for his burger, knowing that he would probably *pay for it* again or be even hungrier later on. Martin had two more hours to kill and a one hundred dollar bill in his pocket. Besides McDonald's, the airport terminal boasted only a snack bar with coffee and watery hot chocolate that tasted like the Styrofoam cup it came in.

He thought about how many things he had been killing lately: his night-shift job at the gas station and his dreams of doing something important with his life. After high school, Martin flunked his college upgrading courses because his job didn't allow him time to study. He had wanted to become an artist. He was fascinated by people's expressions and the way everything seemed to turn into a choreographed dance. Even the people in the terminal, the way they swerved around each other. He knew he lived in a different world. He took out his sketchbook, and sketched the faces of the travellers. He wasn't so concerned with the minute details; he wanted to capture their movement.

As he sketched the crowd, he thought of how his friends had disappeared into their university lives. They had all moved on, moved towards something, while he had kept his crappy job at the gas station and let everything eat away at him piece by piece. He sketched furiously, trying to freeze time. He was envious; he wanted to think they were all working hard towards their eventual unhappiness. One day, each of them would wake up in their beds in a cold sweat, realizing that happiness is not a product of money. There had to be something more.

His family was also wrapped up in their own concerns, their own paths; still, he was a grown man—why should they all be expected to pay attention to his pitfalls and pipe dreams? He needed to get away from his life. He didn't really care about what would happen to him next. Sure, he could have abandoned everything and roamed the streets in his home city, but there would be too many people to see him struggling. They would try to pull him out of himself when all he really wanted was to sit in his own amniotic fluid for a few months and start over. It wasn't their fault, leaving him behind; in his mind, it was the only way to find what he needed.

The woman at the check-in counter had eyed him suspiciously when she asked about his luggage and he held up a tattered plastic Sears bag with a small book, a pair of jeans, and a couple of t-shirts folded inside. "It's all I need right now," he had said. "I'll buy more when I get there." He had the money to fly, so what was the problem? Why should this lady care about how many personal items he was taking? He had himself, and for now, that was enough. The woman told him he could take his plastic bag on the plane as "carry-on … luggage." She grappled with the word. She wasn't laughing at him;

she was confused. He had smiled politely, said thank you, and left the counter with his boarding pass in hand. He was handsome, even though he didn't spend much time grooming himself. Martin was tall and lean, with engaging blue eyes, mid-length brown hair, and a scruffy dog look about him. The woman had smiled back—she appeared to be in her mid- to late 20s, like him, so maybe she secretly understood. Maybe she even admired him. He wasn't wild or rebellious; he was just tired of it all—the whole game. Martin was not yet thirty years old and he was tired.

He began to search the shops in the airport terminal for items that might amuse him. In the duty-free store, he found a Scooby-Doo PEZ dispenser. He opened the package, loaded the candy into Scooby-Doo's head, and popped the candy one by one as he paid for it at the counter.

Martin was leaving the small duty-free store when he spotted a red knapsack hanging on the far wall. He had a closer look and found that it was a durable, nylon material. There was no expensive brand name sewn on. He took it off the hook and adjusted the straps to fit snugly around his shoulders and underarms. The knapsack wasn't too large, either. It was a student knapsack with one large compartment meant for books and packed lunches. He read the price tag: twenty dollars. He placed his Sears bag inside the compartment and brought it over to the same counter.

"This too." He smiled. The clerk rang up the purchase and he zipped his supplies safely inside the knapsack. He had seventy-five dollars left in his pocket. He would eat on the plane, and whatever tomorrow brought didn't matter. He had a few personal belongings; he had luggage. Now he was prepared.

Chapter 14

MARTIN

In Paris, the sun cooked the sidewalks and the warm, sickly smell of poodle droppings became noticeable to even the most seasoned Parisians walking by on their afternoon strolls. For six weeks, while finding refuge in a hostel, Martin had wandered over two-thirds of the city. He had seen everything from the Louvre to the Basilique du Sacré Cœur, always in a state of disorientation and wonderment. Now he found himself in the hub of downtown Paris, without even knowing it. The bustle of people and cars kept turning him around like a toy train in a rotating tunnel. He strolled down the Avenue des Champs-Élysées; the long straight line gave him a secure sense of direction.

He came up to where there was a roundabout in the road that crossed over the traffic to the Arc de Triomphe. Across the heavy, chaotic traffic, he noticed a tall girl standing against a building. Somehow, in his perception, he wasn't sure if the building was holding her up or if it was the other way around. He began to move into the street again, forgetting the traffic, until a car honked aggressively and the driver threw French obscenities at him. Helplessly, he watched the girl from across the river of cars. She didn't see him. At least he didn't think she did. He began to cross the road, walking a little faster as he kept his eyes fastened on her. Soon, he was in front of her.

"Excuse me," he blurted. She turned her eyes towards him. Those eyes. She didn't answer, but waited for more. He took a chance.

"I know you," he said. "The train from London? The Chunnel? We shared a coach."

Her eyes widened, but not with the easy recognition that Martin had anticipated. They widened with fear.

"What are you doing here? Why are you speaking to me?" She looked flustered and her focus flew around as though looking for someone, but not for someone she wanted to find.

"You must go," she said sharply.

"I don't understand. How are you? How do you like Paris? Why don't we have a drink?"

A man with salt and pepper hair came around the corner; the same man from the train.

"Yvonne? Is this man bothering you?"

"I—" Yvonne started, but the man didn't wait for an answer.

"Sir, are you interested in my lovely Yvonne?"

Martin looked at the girl as her eyes dropped. She looked humiliated and mute.

"Because if you are not, I suggest you go to Amsterdam for your window shopping. Yvonne is a real treat. You would be mad to pass her up."

"Yes, I am interested," Martin heard himself say, "very interested."

She looked at Martin with strange, petrified eyes that were undetected by the older man standing close behind her. He was tauntingly tracing one side of her jawbone with a lazy finger. It was as though she knew Martin was not that sort. As if she could already tell so much about him, and most of all, she could tell that he shouldn't be with her.

"Excellent. One thousand francs for an hour." Martin discreetly stuffed six thousand francs worth of notes into the older man's hand and, with one more sweeping motion, took the woman's arm.

At first, the man was ready to protest, but a moment later, he simply leaned back on the building and counted his day's work.

"Thank god he didn't recognize me from the train." Martin had let go of her arm a block and a half later.

"He wouldn't have cared."

"As long as you're getting laid, he's getting happy, is that it? Is that all you care about?"

"Fuck you."

"No thanks." Martin didn't know why he would have found her in any other state. He had been thinking about her in the back of his mind ever since he left her. He hoped that what he witnessed on the train wasn't happening at all.

"Then what the hell do you want with me? A picnic in the park?"

"Maybe ... for starters."

She turned away from him.

"Look, buddy, you paid for me. If there isn't evidence of something happening between us ..."

"I'll look very happy when I send you back, don't worry." She didn't respond. Then he said, "I just wanted to talk to you. Maybe it's no use and maybe it sounds silly, but I was hoping to see you again in Paris."

"You don't even know me." *You don't want to know me*, she thought. They walked in silence for a long time, and then she said, "How about that drink?" It was strange to her. For once, she didn't feel paid for.

They found a little outdoor café, like something straight out of Van Gogh's *Open Air Cafe*. It was midday. She squinted into the sun as she lay back provocatively in the chair. She didn't seem as anxious there as she did on the train. Perhaps shifting between destinations made her nervous and Paris was large enough for her to feel there were no more borders to cross. She had crossed them all. Maybe she felt hidden for a while, sitting there having a drink in the company of someone who demanded nothing from her. And it was true. He was asking nothing except for her to be herself. He wanted desperately to sketch her in this moment.

"I can only imagine what you're thinking of me." She looked straight into his eyes and then turned away again to watch the people passing in the street. She had perfected her hiding. She had a strange, sad smile on her neon pink lips.

"None of my business," he answered shortly. He knew this was the truth as well. There was nothing more to say just then. They ordered their drinks. Martin had a glass of water and she ordered a Martini. When their drinks arrived, she laughed at him and sank her olive in his glass.

"I think your beverage needs a little colour," she said. He loved her laugh. It was sweet and genuine. At least she hadn't left her laugh behind. Martin made a mock grimace, as he swished his water and stared at the olive.

"Thanks," he said flatly. Then he smiled back. She sipped her Martini slowly, the same way she drank in the sunshine. Martin leaned back with his olive water and watched the people go by. He didn't ask her any questions; he had set her free for a short time.

At times she looked a bit reflective, and then she would give him a small smile. Often she closed her eyes and leaned her head back on the chair, which told him she felt safe with him and maybe even trusted him. Martin made some small talk about the passersby, commenting on outfits and hairstyles. Aside from the obvious tourists, Paris was like one gigantic catwalk. She would nod in acknowledgement as she squinted into the street and then closed her eyes again. After a long time, after she took her last swig of gin and vermouth, she leaned forward in her chair and folded her arms smartly on the table.

"I don't even know your name," she said matter-of-factly, as though she were surprised by the anonymity.

"Mart— Marty," he stammered. He could have told her his name was Martin, but somehow he didn't wish to sound so formal. He didn't want to distance himself anymore.

"Are you sure?" she laughed. "Marty," she mused, "I like it. Short for Martin?"

"Yeah, I guess." He was caught off guard by her perceptiveness. "But my friends—some people call me Marty. Yvonne is a pretty name," he added shyly.

"Yeah, I guess," she replied, sounding disinterested.

"You don't like your name?"

There was a long silence.

"It is your name, isn't it?" The thought suddenly occurred to him that her loose profession might require some anonymity of its own.

She was tempted to answer that her name was "anything you want it to be," but she didn't want to hurt or embarrass Marty. And she, too, didn't want to hide behind masks anymore.

"Evelyn," she answered quietly, as though she were ashamed of that name too. He smiled at her. A concrete wall had been levelled between them.

"Nice to meet you, Evelyn," he said just as quietly. She had to fight back a tear and shook her head as though she were trying to shake off more than names.

"So, Marty, you have me for six hours," she said with new confidence. "What are you going to do with me?" Martin's mouth opened slightly in surprise. He was sure she hadn't seen him give her pimp the six thousand francs, never mind having the time to count them. "I take care of myself," she said in answer to his unspoken questions. "Maybe he can take everything else. Maybe they all can, but nobody can have my mind."

"I can see that, my dear." He couldn't understand how she had ended up in such a place. She was intelligent and strong-willed, and yet something inside her allowed such horrific violations on her spirit. She kept a vault inside of her, like the black box on a plane that can't be destroyed and records everything. And nobody had access to it.

Martin and Evelyn spent the afternoon wandering and soon found themselves in a park surrounded by summer flowers in bloom. The iridescent colours used the freshly cut greens as their canvas. It seemed everything in nature used something else to upstage the world, like an attention-craving child, and in return, the world smiled on it. It was a natural given that in order to have beauty, there must be something lacklustre nearby to illuminate the beautiful. Martin felt that Paris, the flowers, and even he were meant to enhance Evelyn's beauty, and she was so unaware of it all. He recalled how she looked in the open-air café. How tiny strands of sunlight entwined in her hair, like fairies of light rushing to frolic for a fading second before she tossed them out with a flippant movement of her head. The sunlight seemed to be enamoured with her. Undaunted, she picked a flower and caressed the tip of her nose and lips with its soft purple petals. Her eyes were far away.

"Why?" she suddenly asked. She had a strange habit of breaking the silence with questions that had no beginning or end. She lived in the middle of things. Either that or she had finished a running dialogue in her head, assuming he had heard every single one of her inner thoughts, and now she was quizzing him.

"Why what?" he mused. He didn't lecture her on the fact he had no idea what her question was or would be. Perhaps she hadn't constructed the question yet. Perhaps the answers were too large. There were many questions and more to come.

"Why are you doing this for me?"

"Taking you for a walk in the park?"

She didn't answer; she wasn't sure if that was her question. She started to forget what she was asking.

Martin could sense that, and he partly understood what was rolling around in her mind. "You seem lost," he said. "I know what it's like to be lost."

"So you decided to find me?" She wasn't hostile anymore. She was too busy soaking up the flowers.

"You look like you're beginning to find yourself."

"This is just a walk in the park," she sighed. "This doesn't last."

"Why not?"

She was silent again. He hated making her silent, but she didn't seem to be closing off. She was collecting her thoughts, choosing her words carefully. The only random thing she had done that day was pick a purple flower.

"My life isn't this simple."

"And why not?" *God, she is infuriating*, he thought. She insisted on giving him only snippets of herself. It was like watching someone slowly shred a napkin and save each piece.

"What are you, a three-year-old, for Chrissake? Why? Why? Why? You don't know a goddamn thing!"

Now he was silent. He was silent for a long time.

"You don't have to be this person," he said, finally. "Be somebody else. Like today, okay? Be somebody else ... with me, okay?" He didn't look at her as he spoke, he watched as his shoes covered the patches of concrete beneath him, step by step. She hadn't said anything, so he looked up. She had stopped walking. She was staring at him like he was a madman. She was also staring at him like it was all she could do, like there were no words anymore.

"Don't say that shit!" A tear came into her eye, and he wanted desperately to stop it from falling, as though it were a bomb, something catastrophic. If it hit the ground the world would end. But she caught it with her eyelash. She knew how to dry quickly. "You don't understand. It's all fantasy talk. What the hell do you want me to do? Just run away with you somewhere? He'd kill me! Do you understand?"

"Kill you?" Martin was so innocent. He'd lived on the streets, but he had only looked out for number one. He couldn't imagine anyone holding a gun over his head.

"Yeah, and that isn't just a figure of speech, either. You don't know him. You don't know Frank. I'm bought and paid for. ... You understand now?"

"I know ... I didn't mean ..." A wave of guilt washed over him, because he realized he had paid for her, too.

"Six thousand francs, Marty." She read his thoughts. "You're just as bad as he is. You're just as bad as all of them."

"Now, hold on a minute." He was getting angry. The flowers around them had lost their brightness and the whole day was shifting. "Have I even laid a finger on you?"

"No, which makes me wonder—are you queer or something, you jackass? Who the hell pays six thousand francs for a fucking martini and a walk in the park? What the hell is this, anyway? What the hell do you want?"

"Something you're not ready to do," he spat back.

"Yeah, well what sick proposition do you have in mind?"

He stared at her, hard, right into her blue irises, and it scared her a little. She didn't feel the same kind of fear she did when Frank came into her face like that, staring right into her core. She was usually smacked without warning after a stare like that, seconds later. Marty's stare was more like an angry, concerned father trying to drill something into his kid; to protect her from some far greater danger. He was trying to scare her enough to smack out the attitude.

"Walk away," he said simply, but each syllable was like a hammer driving into a nail. "You are like a caged animal. Just because there are bars in front of you, you think there's no way out. Those bars may be made of steel or straw, it doesn't matter. They are still bars and you can't get past them. You've forgotten your own strength, but you haven't lost it."

"You don't know me." The bombs in her eyes started falling. The world came crashing down. But her world needed destroying—to make room for something else.

"Yes, I do," he said adamantly. "I am you."

Chapter 15

MARTIN

"We need to find a watering hole." Martin avoided Evelyn's perplexed eyes.

"Wait a second, what did you mean by saying that—that you're *me*? That's a strange thing to say, you know. How the hell do you know anything about it? How dare you belittle me! How dare you make fun ..."

"Where is the closest pub: do you know?" He stood firm. "C'mon, I'll tell you as soon as I've got a beer in my hand."

"Can't tell the truth without a little alcohol?" she jeered.

He wasn't listening. At least, he pretended not to listen.

"Down that way there's a bar," she relented. She had been in Paris long enough to know where the surrounding liquor joints were and to know all the losers in them. It made her tired thinking of it.

"We were just at a restaurant where you could have had a drink," she added. He ignored her.

The bar was almost empty, save for two men seated on the shoddy stools. They eyed the strangers with more than a hint of curiosity. Not many strangers waltzed into their pub on a sunny afternoon. Evelyn and Martin noticed the abrupt silence as soon as they entered ... the sudden break in a man's story, his voice teetering like his balance at the bar. "And then the guy says to me ..." And that was the sudden conclusion or punch line. The words were in French, but Martin silently injected his own dialogue into the rhythm of the other man's voice. He'd heard that tone of voice a million times before. All drunks were storytellers. Martin ordered a 1664 Kronenbourg and found a small rickety table in the back corner.

"*Mademoiselle?*" the bartender inquired hopefully. He was an aging fellow who looked as though he never drank a drop. Sober as the bright stars on a clear night.

"*Non, merci.*" Evelyn spoke quietly and apologetically with a small wrinkle in her nose. The twitchy, obtrusive girl on the train was dissipating into something less sure, but more open. Martin picked up the tone in her voice, and he remained silent. The easiest way to scare off anything was to bring some attention to it. People are all most brazen when they believe no one is really watching. Once they catch the watcher, sketching their fragile selves into their mental sketchpads, they see how vulnerable they really are.

"You aren't having a drink?" He sounded surprised, but he wasn't sure why. He just wanted her to remain in a relaxed state. He still visualized how free she looked waving a martini glass in her lazy hand. But there was more sunshine then, and perhaps she found the dim, musty bar more confining.

She hated bars and the eyes of the men at the bar on her. She struggled to place her attention on Marty as she brushed away the cobwebs of drunken men and sticky bar room floors in her mind's eye.

"No ... I want to listen to everything you have to tell me," she confessed. "And I want to remember it." Her small smile and bright apologetic eyes suggested she meant the latter to be a joke, but he only heard the honesty in her voice. He wasn't mistaken.

She couldn't hide truths very well, not even with all her porcupine needles jabbing away at the mistrusted kindness in the world.

She noticed he had stopped talking, really stopped talking. He looked at her as though she had revealed herself to him as his guardian angel, come to take away all his wrongs. It scared her.

Martin didn't think. He only felt a strong connection with this woman. This woman who was willing to listen, and the sad part was how foreign a concept it was to him. He hadn't been used to anyone reaching out for so long, and maybe never. There had been Joe, but he had only been a convenient acquaintance, someone to shoot the breeze with. He never really knew Martin, no more than anyone else. And whose fault was that? Martin felt as though he had been trapped in a steel brace, which now instantaneously burst and freed him. She was another gift.

"You want to listen to me?" he said in half-disbelief. Before he could think, he moved to touch her hand. Her fingers jerked away as though she had been given an electric shock or been bitten. The moment was blurry. In only a short frame of time, he had felt overwhelmed, affectionate, afraid, confused, and then rejected. Mostly, he felt confused, and now his arm lay vulnerable across the table, his hand empty. She sat across from him, looking almost as startled.

She was confused by the moment, as well. She desperately wanted to apologize, but she was frozen.

The incident needed saving, and all Martin could do was start talking. First, to distract them both, he dug into his pocket and pulled out Scooby-Doo. "PEZ?" he offered. She accepted with a funny smile. Then he began by saying, "A year ago I decided to fly to London." He tried to keep his voice casual and steady. "I didn't have any plans. I just wanted to be somewhere else. And then, in London, I wanted to be somewhere else. I think no matter where I am, I will want to be somewhere else."

"And where are you from? There is a starting point ... where is it that you want to be somewhere else the most? Are you from America?" Her voice grew excited, as though America was an exotic place. Like Africa or Asia. Or maybe she had a connection. She had a muddled accent that he couldn't decipher.

"No, I'm from Canada. I'm *Canadian*," he repeated with emphasis. "There *is* a difference. An American will be the first to tell you." He preferred to say *an* American, as opposed to saying *any* American.

"Okay," she replied in a dumb fashion.

She didn't really understand, but she didn't want to interrupt his story.

He did that himself since he became so riled up. "Americans. And Joe said *I* was a lousy tourist." He went into his own world, forgetting his audience. "You know, when I first came to London, I hopped on one of those double-decker tour buses, right?" Evelyn nodded dumbly.

"Poor goddamn bus driver had to take a detour because there was construction on the road. This American tourist had just gotten on the ride with his family. His kid was picking his nose and looking out the window. Anyhow, the audio tour had stopped for the moment until we got back on track, and this loudmouth American gets up and stands right behind the driver, demanding his money back because he paid for an audio tour. Poor goddamn bus driver. There was nothing he could do. Now a *Canadian* would understand and feel sorry for that bus driver; I'm sure of it. A *Canadian* would patiently wait for the bus to get back on track." Martin took a considerable gulp of his beer.

"You know, they come north of the border for a holiday and they can't even relax long enough not to demand their change to be in American currency. Funniest thing in the world, they come up asking for blue Canadian flags, all dressed up in their parkas and expecting to see polar bears. Funniest thing in the whole world!" Then he grew pensive, and his beer was half-gone. "But, you know, I could probably never name all the U.S. states in less than two minutes, so there you go. Seems to me we all know so goddamn little about each other, and yet we're sticking our hands into each other's problems. Trying to save the world, but sometimes, we only make it worse. We're all so ignorant, really." Evelyn started to get up from the table. "Where're you going?" Martin asked, surprised.

"I thought you had something important to say. I'm not going to sit here and listen to you bash the world just because you have some asshole chip on your shoulder."

"You were asking me about where I'm from." Martin tried to erase his self-absorbed trails of thought, which led off into nowhere and had no real foundations to begin with. He was simply regurgitating his observations of the world. He had spent so much time alone. So much time being alone and lost and angry. He forgot she was listening to him.

"Don't ever listen to a B.C. boy, okay? Even the rest of our own country barely listens." He was trying to be funny.

"What did you mean when you said that you were me? That's a pretty strange thing to say, you know." She tried to steer the conversation. To get answers.

"I know," he admitted. "I'm not sure where to begin with that. I guess it's like we're both chained to something that we can't break free of, whether we've been doing it to ourselves, or someone else is waving an invisible gun over our heads."

"Trust me, Frank's gun isn't invisible," she interjected. She thought about all the times he waved it in front of her, threatening all the ways he was going to use it on her if she didn't behave like a "good girl."

"Yeah, but there must have been something in your life that led you to Frank?" he insisted. "I went into my own captivity because I was running away from the world, which I considered to be one giant prostitute."

"Then why aren't you running from me?"

"Because, like me, you are only a victim of yourself." Martin's voice was full of tenderness. "Babe, you're not a prostitute. Not you. For you, it's only a word. It's not who you are. Only to Frank and your own little demons, that's all."

Evelyn lowered her eyes, examining the floor and trying to

absorb what was true and what wasn't. She wasn't sure how much emphasis she should place on a word that defined her or how she could put no meaning into it at all. Would that be freeing her or erasing her? The smallest of words could embody so much.

"I got lost," he continued in a more sober voice. The alcohol hadn't blurred the reality of the past year. "I thought I didn't need people. I ended up alone, and the only reality I found was stone walls.

"I had no money, no one, and nothing." He couldn't bring himself to go into any concrete details yet, the half-smoked cigarette butts he picked off the sidewalk or the weekly showers. He hoped that saying he had "nothing" would paint a vivid enough picture for her. Why relive the grit? It was strange—she was so afraid of her past, and he was offering safe arms for her to collide into. However, he couldn't bring himself to burden her with his selfish life. Perhaps it was because he saw all the stupidity in it now. As much as the world was becoming too power hungry and detached from the human realm, none of it excused him from inflicting a different kind of misery on himself. He had thrust himself out into the cold. How could he ever justify that to someone who never wanted to be out there in the first place? Simple, he couldn't.

She was eyeing his red knapsack, which was hanging on one strap on the back of his chair, and he instinctively secured it closer to him.

She wondered about his knapsack because he never opened it.

"So you decided to hop on a train to Paris?" She didn't conceal the suspicion in her voice, and he didn't chastise her for it.

"The train ticket was— it was a— a gift," he said finally. She observed how he had a strange, unsteady way of grappling with simple words. Not the words themselves, more like the implications behind the words. There were holes in his story that she could sense, but she couldn't quite see where they were and what they were almost exposing.

"And the six thousand francs?" She was not giving up on her interrogation. Part of her almost wanted to find him guilty. "If you were living penniless on the streets, where did you come up with such a large sum of money? Money that you could just throw away on an afternoon with a prostitute?"

"Correction." His eyes became firm again. "You mean, an afternoon with an extraordinarily beautiful, extremely annoying and nosy—I mean, perceptive—young lady?"

"Yeah." She was amused.

"Alright, there you've got me." He thought quickly. "Some guy in London approached me on the street. He was an antsy little guy, and he asked me to deliver his marijuana for him to some guy in Paris. He gave me a ticket and everything. So that's why I came here. To meet some pothead Frenchy."

"I see," she responded casually, a hint of suspicion still lingering in her voice. "How much marijuana?"

"What?"

"How much ..."

"Oh, yeah, okay ... let's see ... I guess about a kilo worth."

"A kilo? For six thousand francs?" He couldn't read from her if that sounded like too much or not enough, so he took a chance.

"Uh, he was a cheap dealer, I guess."

"Uh-huh." She'd done the math, since six thousand francs was roughly equivalent to the amount of twelve hundred American dollars. The usual cost of a kilo of marijuana, the good stuff, was about five hundred American dollars.

"Look, I'm no pothead; how the hell should I know how much that shit goes for?"

"Did I say anything?" She flashed an innocent look. "I'm only curious about one thing."

"What the hell is that?" Martin was getting tired of his own charade, and the holes were beginning to show. He felt irritated.

"Why did the dealer pay you, some random guy on the street, to deliver it? Why didn't he deliver it himself and collect from the guy?" She looked perplexed, as though she were trying to string together clues. She was beginning to sound like Velma from

Scooby-Doo, and it was making him nervous. He could imagine himself with a fishnet over his head, cursing vehemently, "If it wasn't for that damn, meddling kid … !"

She carried on. "I mean, you could have easily just taken off with the weed or the drug money."

He was silent for a minute, then, "Did I say that's what happened?"

"Well, … no. …"

"Did I say it was the dealer who paid me?"

"Well, I thought you said …"

"No, that's not what I said … if you were listening. … I said the dealer bought me the train ticket …"

Evelyn sat with her mouth in a straight line and her eyes fixed on him, intent on listening.

"I met up with the guy yesterday and traded him the goods for the dough. You're right, though—I took the money and ran." Then he added, "I'm not interested in marijuana."

"Alright, it's crystal clear now. So, you screwed this poor, pathetic dealer in London and spent the winnings on one afternoon with me."

"You don't believe me." He tried to sound annoyed and hurt.

"I never said …"

"What part don't you believe? What do I have to explain over again to you?"

"Look, Jesus, I believe you. …" She sounded tired, suddenly. "It's just that I'm bored with the whole story now."

Her averted eyes and change in tone told him to drop it. So he did. He was more annoyed with himself for trying to cover up pieces of his life, and annoyed that he hadn't picked a convincing story. He was feeling tired as well.

"You haven't told me about your life yet."

"I don't want to talk about it now."

"I spilled my beans." He choked on his words, because he knew he had only given her fragments of truth. He didn't know why he should be angry with her for doing the same. He was pounding back his selfish feelings with the remaining beer in his glass.

"You didn't have to."

"I didn't have to, eh? Miss twenty questions?"

"You felt obliged. That's not my fault. Besides, you can see my life."

"I don't believe it has always been this way."

"Believe what you like."

"I believe in you." God, he sounded pathetic. He was thinking dangerously out loud.

"Why don't you go back to your home country?" She wanted to come away from the spotlight, change the subject, and listen to him speak of anything besides her.

"I don't belong there."

"You don't belong at home?"

"I just don't belong." Inwardly, he whittled away at his own character, as though filing a puzzle piece to make it fit. Even if in the end his piece didn't match the completed picture, contrasting his life with the rest of the world, leaving a small gap destined to exist, if only in him.

Evelyn hesitated, and then lightly brushed her palm over his clenched, dormant knuckles.

Chapter 16

WILLIS

Willis was carrying a deep sadness. He felt like a mule toting around his past and everything that was decided for him, including his money and ambitions; he could see his father up front pulling on the reins. Every time Willis slowed down or hesitated about the direction he was heading in, trying to listen to his own voice, there would be a sharp tug on those relentless reins. Why fight it? He had learned no other way to get through life or become anything better. He began remembering his father and all the times he thought he was being a father to him. He remembered when his father stuck a cigar in his inexperienced mouth on his twelfth birthday and congratulated him for being on the brink of manhood. His mother had turned away. She had said something about not wanting him to get sick from smoking, but she never called it filthy or ordered his father to stop. She didn't even bother to take him into the den or outside where the fumes could escape. Willis had worshipped his father then. He hadn't yet seen the danger or the damage. Now he cursed his father.

As these dark thoughts plagued him, Willis found another pub and fell in. The pub was unfamiliar to him, but crowded enough that the regular crowd didn't even lift their eyes to observe him. He was glad. He felt alien enough. Two o'clock in the afternoon and he was ordering a scotch, but that was becoming normal. He thought he could drown himself. The first glass he ordered turned into a bottomless round of glasses. After a few hours, while sitting on the bar stool and making friends with the bartender, he couldn't feel his legs anymore. He liked it that way; it meant he couldn't go anywhere, and for a little while, nobody could tug on his reins. What he didn't see, though, was that his reins were being pulled on harder than ever, and he was being dragged down a steep, treacherous slope.

He looked down the bar and noticed a young woman sitting alone staring into her glass.

"Hey, mate," he said to the bartender, motioning for him to move in closer. "How long has that bird been sitting down there?"

The bartender cast him a sideward glance, "The better part of an hour, I'd say."

"Give her another round of whatever she's drinking."

"I don't think you are in any condition to be making any passes tonight."

"Whaddaya mean? No condition. Bollocks. I'm sparky as ever." Willis made a face and downed the rest of what was in his glass. Then he held the glass out to the bartender.

"Oh, no, you've had enough for one afternoon. Tell you what, how about a coffee on me. Maybe that will at least curb your slurring before you decide to slur all over her."

Willis made another face, "Yeah, alright." He nursed his coffee, served black, until he felt the tingle return to his legs and he could stand and walk over to the woman without falling all over the bar. After a while, the bartender approached the woman with a drink and motioned to Willis who raised his coffee mug with a wink. He slid down to where she was sitting, like a snake approaching a small, unsuspecting prey daydreaming in the grass. She sensed him coming and was cautious. At first she pretended he wasn't there.

"Thanks for the drink," she uttered once she had disengaged her lipstick lips from her small cocktail straw. She said these words into her glass, not turning to him.

"Well, you looked like you may need a refill."

She smiled. "Strange word that, isn't it?"

"What word?"

"Refill." She paused for a long moment. "I think everybody needs to be refilled. Don't you think?" Her eyes lifted to his face for a brief second, but her gaze only reached as high as his nose. It was a trite thing to say, attempting to sound philosophical, and she retracted her gaze as though realizing she had uttered out loud what should never have left the secrecy of her mind. He wished she had not sounded so childlike, turning to him for validation of her thoughts. Why was it that everyone had such a yearning to be agreed with? Why couldn't they all just live by their own convictions and throw the rest aside?

"Sure," he answered, not sure. But he didn't want to let her slip through his fingers or have her think he wasn't interested, and he did feel like he could stand to be refilled. In some ways, she had voiced his own thoughts, but he didn't want to think about that now. Instead of being refilled, he wanted to empty himself into her and maybe, just maybe, get something in return. She finished her drink and looked at her watch.

"Are you leaving?" he asked.

"Soon," she said. "I can't stay here, can I?"

"Would you like to join me? I mean, go somewhere?"

"Where?" She met his eyes now. The last drink had worked. She was talking a little braver.

"I don't know where ... somewhere that's open." He kept her gaze.

"Alright, then." Her eyes became more lucid. "Hey, what's your name?"

"Never mind; is that important to you?"

"No, I guess not. I'm Jodie."

"Let's go, Jodie." He left a handsome tip on the counter, and the bartender shook his head at both of them and continued to wipe the glasses clean.

Chapter 17

MARTIN

Martin woke up in a strange bed in a dimly lit room. It was the middle of the night when he opened his eyes, groggily, and saw the silhouette of a woman hovering near the door. A moment later he realized the woman was Evelyn, or Yvonne, or whatever she wanted to be called. She was barely dressed. He tried to recall exactly how many beers he drank.

"Evelyn?"

"Call me Yvonne."

"Where are we?"

"It doesn't matter, but I want to take you somewhere."

"Where?"

"Somewhere you've never been." Her voice was strange and husky. Martin tried to think of all the places he'd never been. "Lie back." She began crawling over the sheets, like a snake with legs, and then she was on top of him. She was wearing silky, transparent lingerie.

"Wait," he whispered urgently.

"I'm not waiting for anything. Trust me, honey. You'll get your franc's worth."

"Ev— Yvonne. Stop."

"I don't care about the marijuana or the money ..." she persisted. "I just want to be with you. Besides, I know you were lying."

"Please, stop." His voice was so agitated. She stopped.

"What's the problem? Don't you like me?"

"Yes, yes ... I do. Just—not like this," he sighed. "This is my first time, okay? I want it to be right. I don't want to think of you like this."

"How else do you want me?" She looked confused and a little hurt.

"Like this." He hesitated and then touched her face and moved slowly towards her, kissing her gently. "I want you like this." Martin peeled away the lingerie to reveal her unadulterated beauty, and then he caressed her soft skin. He made love to her awkwardly, and she responded to him as though it was her first time as well.

For her, the act of lovemaking had never been so honest. They were like children.

In the morning, Martin opened his eyes to discover he was alone. He propped himself up in the squeaky, double bed, smiling at the squeaking they had caused during the night. He could hear someone whistling in the street below the window, and a woman's voice calling, "Hey, baby!" He scrambled out of bed, realizing it was Yvonne. No, she was no longer Yvonne. She had become Evelyn in the night. Martin jumped into his boxer shorts and ran down the stairs and out onto the street. She was parading herself one step off the curb, beckoning with saucy comments to passing men in cars.

"What are you doing, Evelyn?" At first she was startled to see him outside in his boxers and to hear the sound of her Christian name. She wasn't sure she was ready to return to her forgotten self, and it perturbed her. He was getting too close, somehow. But a part of her warmed instantly to the way he called her.

"What does it look like? You want breakfast, don't you? We're not going to get by on your good looks." He looked at her with misunderstanding in his eyes. What did this all mean? She answered his confused look with three simple words.

"I've run away." She smiled like a little girl. Martin grabbed her arm, gently but firmly.

"Come inside," he said. She followed him with reluctance. She wasn't sure what was happening, and she was a little puzzled by his seeming lack of enthusiasm for her bold announcement. She had decided to stay. Didn't he want her to? He led her upstairs to the room, and sat her on the bed. She sat quietly and obediently, watching him grab his red knapsack and pull back the zipper. She caught her breath as he pulled a large wad of cash out of the compartment.

"Marty." She couldn't say anything else.

"There's plenty more where this came from," he beamed. "Babe, you don't have to show off your thighs or anything else out on the sidewalk ever again." She pulled herself into the middle of the bed, as though there were monsters beneath the mattress, and instinctively clutched a pillow in her lap. She kneaded small dents in it with her fingers, as though looking for something. She looked at him with a strained expression on her face. Her eyes screamed suspicion, confusion, and unspoken joy.

"Where did it come from?" Tears welled up in her mascara eyes and strolled slowly down her pale cheeks.

"Don't be afraid of it," Martin urged gently. "It's clean. It's mine." He knew how he had felt when fortune fell into his tainted hands. She was contracting into a ball, just as he had done, and giving her the space she needed to absorb it all was the most he could do.

"Is someone going to come after it … after us?" she asked in a panicked voice, as though she was looking for reasons to be afraid.

She couldn't believe yet that it was really theirs. It. The money. She could comprehend the money no more than she could comprehend the notion of a baby left outside the door of their hotel room.

"Listen." Martin broke her stream of thought. "Take a deep breath." She obeyed. He was beside himself, wanting to share with her all of his ideas. They had no boundaries. At least, none they could ever dream to cross. Mostly, he didn't want to overwhelm her. He knew she had to embrace it on her own and in her own time, if she embraced it at all. Perhaps that was his main fear: this would be too much for her. Perhaps he was being naïve, thinking he could save her. Still, something made him press on, ignoring his mind chatter. "Just listen. I don't think anyone is coming for the money. Part of what I said was true ... it was a gift." Then he mustered his courage and took her hand gently. "Evelyn," he began, "did you mean what you said before? Are you going to stay?" Her eyes focused on him, and she snapped out of her dreamlike state.

It didn't seem real, but the reality was slowly setting in. "Oh, Marty." Her focus flew away again. "They will come after us. They'll come after me."

"Who? Frank? You mean Frank and his thugs? I won't let them. I'm not concerned about that. I'm asking you, are you going to stay?"

She gave him a small, brave smile and nodded briskly.

"Good," he whispered. He squeezed her hand.

"What are we going to do?"

"Anything. We'll do anything."

She looked stunned at the idea, and he laughed.

"For starters, why don't you come back home with me?"

"Home?"

"Canada."

"I thought you said you don't have a home there anymore."

"I do. I just forgot about it."

"What made you remember?"

He was silent for a long moment. He wanted to tell her it was because he wanted to give her a home. He wanted to tell her it was because she reminded him of the importance of home.

"The fact that we've both been lost for a while reminded me of going home," he replied.

"I can't remember home," she said.

"Well," he leaned forward and held her tight to his chest, "this is what home feels like," he breathed into her ear. She wrapped her arms around his thin body, and they both shut their eyes.

Chapter 18

WILLIS

Willis found a motor lodge a few blocks away and told Jodie to wait around the corner of the building. She sneered at the idea, not liking to be kept in dark corners, but acted obediently. He straightened his shirt and coat, checked his breath, and made a smooth entrance into the lobby.

"I'd like a room for tonight," he told the clerk behind the counter.

"I didn't see you drive in," the man said. He was at least thirty years older than Willis and eyeing him like a suspicious parent.

"That's because I didn't drive in. I'm staying in London for a few days with friends. I've found myself a bit stranded after hours and I could have taken the Tube back, but I lost my extra key to their flat and it is late and I didn't want to wake them up." Willis' face never faltered, and the man reached back for one of the few keys left hanging on the board, murmuring something about how unfortunate for him. He handed Willis the room key, took his name and money, and directed him to the room, a left turn and three doors down from the motor lodge entrance.

When the owner was gone, Willis stepped out of his room, reentered the summer air, and gave a soft whistle toward the side of the building. Jodie appeared from the shadows and scurried inside the doorway of the motel room. Once inside, Willis turned on a lamp and lit a cigarette. He sat on the bed, removed his hat and watched her take her coat off. She was a striking girl, with medium length red hair and full legs. She was shapely and he liked that.

"You shouldn't wear so much makeup," he commented.

"Who are you to say what I shouldn't do?"

"Nobody, just a chap you met in a bar and brought back to a motel room."

"Who *I* brought to a motel room?" She was suddenly standing with one hand on her hip, her legs set firmly apart.

He didn't answer; instead, he smiled with a cigarette between his teeth.

"So, why did you bring me here anyway?" she asked.

"Why do you think guys bring girls to motel rooms? To talk?"

"Maybe."

"Well, a girl who wears as much makeup as you isn't interested in talking, isn't that right?" He stood up from the bed.

"You still haven't told me your name."

"I don't have one."

"What do you mean?"

"I have my father's name. I'd rather not use it."

"Should I call you junior?"

"Don't call me anything."

"Okay, I'll just have to call you mister."

"Call me sir."

"Sir?"

"Yes, sir. Say 'yes, sir.'" He tugged on her hair firmly, but not so hard that it would hurt her. Then he moved his hand over her breast and kissed her.

"Yes, sir," she breathed into him. He began to undress her.

"Do you like me?"

"Yes."

"Say it. Say it like I told you to say it." He was getting rougher and she let out a little cry. "Say it, you whore, you makeup whore."

"I like you," she said. He pulled her hair harder. "I like you, sir!" She was trembling.

"Good girl," he whispered in threatening tones. There was something sinister and animalistic in the jerky rhythm of his voice and movements. His hand moved to her neck and he caressed her throat. She was wearing a pale-coloured scarf, double knotted. It was her noose, he mused.

Suddenly, he hated her. She was the same as every other woman. She had breasts and hips that lured him, just like every other woman that his father had lured into motel rooms. She was a trap, and he hated her because he wanted her. He decided to punish her for all of her female crimes—her conniving ways, her casual words, her pouting lips—for all of her wiles. He took off her scarf and pushed her onto the single bed. He pulled her arms behind her back.

"What are you doing?"

"Just a trick I know." His voice was unaffected, steady, and calm. He held both of her slim wrists in one of his hands and slid the scarf around her pale skin. Her fingers folded slightly, but she didn't struggle. It was the alcohol she had drunk an hour before, perhaps. She was like a weak animal who knew something was happening but couldn't turn her head to see her enemy, and who was too confused or naïve to know the danger. He pulled the scarf tight and doubled the knot. She was caught.

"That's very funny." She turned her head to see him lying on the bed next to her, admiring her. "Now let me loose."

"I want to watch you get out of it."

"What?"

"You heard me. Try to get yourself free."

"You're a sick bastard." Her hair was in her eyes and she was still wearing her short skirt. There was a strong definition in the line of her back and he could see the curve of her breasts pressing against the mattress. She began to wrestle for a few moments, her hands writhing to reach the knot. Then she lay still, breathing. She lay defeated with her hair strewn over the pillow. He thought she was pathetic and beautiful as he rolled her onto her back, roughly. He moved the hair out of her eyes and she gave him a swift kick in the leg.

"Let me loose!" Her eyes were brimming. It was the alcohol, he presumed. He tried to hush her, but still he felt no sympathy for her. This was how he liked her. He wanted the women in his life to feel helpless. He began to remove his trousers.

"No," she said softly, afraid.

"You want me to. I know you do." His voice was soft and hoarse. He pushed up her skirt, put a hand over her mouth and mounted her. Her cries were muffled in his meaty palm. He withdrew after a while, not yet finished, and flung her onto her stomach. Her wrists were still tied, but the knot was beginning to loosen. He caressed her buttocks, trying to forget about the human being beneath him. He only thought of his desires, and he then realized he didn't even really desire her. She was symbolic of everything in his life he could not control and everything that had tried to control him. He was relieved not to see her face and the little girl in her eyes. He had seen those same eyes somewhere before.

He moved the hair away from the back of her white, bird-like neck. How easy it would be to snap, he thought as he saw his hand move towards the nape of her neck. He watched his hand, as though it belonged to someone else, as it trembled with the touch of bone on bone. Perhaps it was simply her trembling, but he felt the rush in his palms and the tremor in his arms. Adrenalin coursed through him, and he sobered to his positioning and the frail girl lying beneath his bare weight. He heard her small cries muffled in the bed, her cursing anguish. He saw, for the first time, the movement of her back muscles contracted with fear and disgust for herself and him. He thought of his father and wondered if he had ever sunk so low as to hold a woman hostage in his own prison.

"Damn it." He withdrew abruptly, pushing her away from him, as though she were the assailant. He withdrew the scarf, which she had almost managed to free herself from, and sat with his back to her on the edge of the bed. For a while she didn't move. Then she slowly hoisted herself into a sitting position at the far end of the bed. *She has every right to be afraid of me*, he thought. He didn't turn around, but he could see her reflection in the oval mirror on the opposite wall. Her hair hung in her eyes and her body was rigid. She pulled down her nylon skirt from around her waist and twisted her hair in her hand.

"Go home, Jodie," he said.

<hr />

After she had left in her spiked heels, cursing him just before she closed the motel door hard behind her, Willis got dressed and went to the front desk to check out. It was 3:00 a.m. and the motel was closed, so he proceeded to bang on the entrance door. A few minutes later, a light switched on from somewhere in the back hallway, and the old man who had given him the room key appeared in the doorway wearing a thick robe. He stared at Willis with puzzled eyes that had not yet adjusted.

"Do you know what time it is?"

"Not really. I just want to check out now."

"Check out time is 8:00 a.m."

"Well, what time is it now?"

"Three in the morning."

"That is early. I don't want to have to wait around, though. Would it be alright if I checked out now?"

"You don't want to wait around? Why don't you get some sleep? Aren't you the man who said you didn't want to disturb your friends?"

"Good memory. Uh, yes, I did say that, didn't I?"

"Well, it looks like you don't have any trouble disturbing people."

"I am sorry."

"Sure," the old man said, sourly dismissing his apology. "So, what will you do at this hour instead?"

"I'll wander for a while. I'm an early riser. There must be some-place I can go."

"The bakery, maybe."

"Surely there must be a night club around here? A tavern?"

"You want to drink at this hour?" The old man eyed him disapprovingly.

"Well, it isn't unheard of."

The old man gave a small harrumph under his breath, which didn't go unnoticed.

"They'll all be closed by now."

"I'll find something then." Willis grimaced.

"Suit yourself." The old man shrugged as he took the key from this strange man who liked to wander in the middle of the night.

Willis wandered deeper into the dark streets, not paying attention to the names on signs or the direction he was heading. He wanted to become physically lost, as lost as he felt he was already. He wanted to lose himself. It wasn't easy, because with every step and every turn, he was still there. He could not escape the bondage of his own incriminating thoughts, the memory of his deed, and his disbelief at the man he saw himself to be. Was he really this monster? Was he becoming everything that he had despised in his father? Was all of it unavoidable?

He shoved his hands into his pockets, keeping them impris-oned. They were weapons, his clenched fists trying to burst through the inner lining. His hands had a mind of their own; he couldn't trust them now, whether they were reaching for a glass of alcohol or reaching out to strangle a young girl. He wanted to chop them off and make himself an invalid. Already, he was not much more than a shell, confused and lost. Most of all, he was irate with his own cowardice and impotence.

He felt a mist on his face and shoulders, which turned into a downpour. He was a raging fire setting off sprinklers. He was thankful for the rain, the feel of something beating on him and adding to his damp thoughts. The rain seemed to seep into his skin, drenching his organs. His heart became a sponge. It was as though the heavens responded to his sordid ways by casting a bucket of piss on him. The thought sadly amused him. He was a rogue. He was a failure. He was his father without the bank notes.

Chapter 19

MARTIN

The train to Calais began to pull out of Paris, and Martin and Evelyn watched the platform roll away. As soon as they could see the countryside, Evelyn relaxed back in her seat and leaned her sleepy head on Martin's shoulder.

"Don't you want to see the scenery?" he teased her.

"I can feel we are moving, and that's all I need to know. I don't need to know where I'm going anymore." She smiled with her eyes closed.

"I guess it all looks the same after a while, doesn't it?"

"Hmmm … I've seen it all before," she replied sleepily, "too many times."

"Well, this time, I'm carrying you away to somewhere where you don't have to be afraid anymore. I'm taking you to shore, Ev," he mused, but soon realized he was talking to himself, because she had dozed off. He kissed her smooth forehead. She was having good dreams.

After an hour of watching the trees move backwards, he gently lifted her from his lap and stretched his legs. He moved towards the front of the train, steadying his rocky movements on the backs of headrests. Most of the passengers were asleep, and a few arms dangled in the aisles. Somewhere in his mind, he compared this to strolling down an overgrown path in the woods, but he could hardly pull back these human branches. Then he heard the low voices of two men coming from a row up ahead.

"Goddamn it. I can't believe she got away. We have to find her. You know that, right? Frank will have a bullet for each of us if we don't. And there's no way I'm going to die for some whore!"

"I can't believe she was so stupid to try and run away," said the other one. "Selfish bitch, I can't believe she'd do this to us. We were her family, right?"

"Who the hell else is going to give a shit about what happens to her? And now she runs off and leaves our nuts in the cracker."

"Listen, she was a sweet girl ... but that Yvonne hasn't got a brain in her head. None of them do. You listen to me."

"... I don't know, Maury. Part of me wants her to get as far away as possible. I don't want to be the one to bring her in to Frank."

"Listen." Maury grabbed the other guy by the collar. "I don't like this shit anymore than you do, but you can never leak that you feel that way! Frank's word is law. Remember that. We don't have any say in this, got it? Unless you want a bullet through your head."

"I got it, I got it. Ease up, Maury. Christ, I'm just speaking my mind."

"Then you don't have a brain in your head, either. Just shut up and eat your potato crisps."

Martin moved backwards slowly and stepped on the person behind him.

"Hey, watch it. We're trying to get through to the loo," said a man with an English accent, and his face pruned up indignantly.

"Sorry," Martin yammered as he moved past the gentleman and his entourage. The two men working for the infamous Frank craned their heads in their seats to see the commotion. Then they turned back, uninterested in the back of Martin's head.

"That guy looks a bit confused," said the softhearted one.

"Who the fuck cares," replied Maury. His companion proceeded to munch his potato crisps in silence.

Evelyn was still asleep when Martin returned to their seats. He wasn't sure what to do. He didn't want to frighten her, but he had to find a way to get them off the train before they reached Calais.

She began to wake up. "I'm sick of all this movement," she said groggily. "We should have flown."

"Yes, babe. We should have flown away."

She gave him a one-eyed look and then smiled. "Silly." She leaned against his shoulder again, and he put his arm around her and stroked her hair, partly trying to conceal her face. Then he saw the two men up ahead get out of their seats and begin walking towards them. One of them, not Maury, looked down as he passed by and a strange look crossed over his face. At first he didn't look certain of what he saw, and then his expression leapt and his mouth began to open.

"Maury! Maury, look!" Martin jumped up and punched Maury in the nose and kicked him in the shins. Maury fell in the aisle and hit his head on the arm of a chair. He lay unconscious. Evelyn gave out a small scream and the crowd around them gasped and murmured.

"Get security!" yelled one nervous passenger.

"Listen, buddy," Martin pleaded to Maury's accomplice. "I heard what you said about Yvonne. This is her only chance. Just let her go, okay? No one will know. Trust me." The man stood frozen. He was nothing without Maury. He was a lackey. A drone. Then he came out of his stupor.

"You aren't going to screw with my head, pal. You're not getting off this train!" He ran down the aisle yelling, "Frank! Frank!"

Martin turned to Evelyn. He told her to go to the lavatory, lock the door, and stay there. He would keep a lookout for Frank and his cronies, and when the coast was clear and they were at the next station, he would come and collect her. She started to speak, to apologize for the danger she caused them.

"Hush," he said. "None of this is your fault." *She is a bottomless lake covered by thick ice, and the ice is cracking*, he thought. He knew what it was like to be trapped beneath the ice for too long.

Evelyn took her purse and obediently left her seat. Martin was scared for her. A few minutes after she had gone, Frank came barrelling down the aisle with his lackey in tow.

"Where is she?" he pointedly asked Martin, barely suppressing his rage.

"Who?"

"Don't play stupid. That whore, where is she?"

"I'm sorry, I don't know what you're talking about." Frank whipped his head around at his crony, who stood there speechless.

"Jesus, Frank, she was sitting right there!"

"You mean that slut I paid six thousand francs for in Paris?" Martin asked without looking at them.

"Yeah."

"Yeah, she's on the train. She's not worth what you charge for her, you know."

"That right?" Frank seemed amused.

"Yeah, that's right. And yeah, I saw her. She even came over and tried to pick me up again."

"Okay, now we're getting somewhere."

"I don't know where she went, though."

"There are only two directions she could have gone."

Martin looked up at Frank then, square in the eye, like he was an idiot, "Listen, asshole, I don't pay that much attention to whores."

"Right." Then Frank turned to his lackey, who looked pretty rattled. "Wake him up, and clean up this fucking mess." Frank nudged Maury with his shiny, wing-tip shoe. Then he turned on Martin and poked a finger in his face, "I'm not through with you yet." As he walked away, he checked every seat and opening. As soon as Frank and his men were out of sight, Martin sprinted to the lavatory down the aisle and banged on the door. Fortunately, the train was approaching the station.

"That guy's been in there forever," one man commented from a nearby seat. Martin ignored him.

"It's me, Marty," he said in an urgent voice. She came out, with a bewildered look in her eyes. She was like a doe caught in sudden danger, but there was a faint fierceness in her eyes, too.

"Let's go," she said.

The train was slowing down, and the relentless, hypnotic message in the click-clacking of the wheels could almost be deciphered. Once the train was in the station, Martin and Evelyn stumbled through the passenger door like newborns coming into a strange world. They stepped foot on the dirty platform, disoriented, and running. As they came into the terminal, their mad dash dissipated into a jog so as not to bring unnecessary attention to themselves. Although their appearances brought unwanted notice, they were perceived as a young couple running to catch a taxicab rather than fugitive-types fleeing from a pursuit on their lives. Finally, they spotted a man in official attire and ran over to him.

"*Excuse-moi*." Martin was short of breath. "Um ... *où est le* bus stop?" The man sized up Martin and Evelyn, and then smiled a smile that conveyed hidden thoughts. Martin was momentarily confused, and he looked at Evelyn wondering what this idiot was staring at?

"There is a bus waiting right out there ... through the main entrance doors," he said after his short pause, and then he explained the joke. "*Monsieur*, your French is not so good, it would be best if you kept to English."

"Hey, buster, ..." Evelyn blurted out, but Martin pulled her arm and began heading towards the doors.

"*Merci*, um ... thank you." Martin was in too much of a hurry to quibble with the man. Besides, he could hear the faint rumble of angry voices coming into the terminal. Evelyn seemed to hear them too, because she looked at him with wide and intense little-girl eyes. But she didn't look over her shoulder. She knew the noise too well. Her eyes asked questions and gave orders all at the same time. They said to him, "Where can we go? Why are you taking me with you?" and, "Run, dammit!" The bus was parked outside, and without hesitating or inquiring about where it would take them, they hopped on. The backbench was empty and they swung frantically from pole to pole to reach it. It felt good to press against the back of something moving forward, like the sensation of being caught by gravity.

One elderly woman quickly glanced back, her gaze preceding her head so that she wouldn't be thought of as staring. Only then did Evelyn look out the back window, and Martin wasn't sure if it was to avoid the woman's glance or to retrace her steps.

They were slowly pulling out of the parking space and she could see herself moving away from Frank and his men jumping up and down on the concrete. They looked like bumbling fools in a silent motion picture ... and everything seemed to be moving in slow motion. She could feel the weight and thickness of the glass between them, and she felt so removed from her pursuers that she flashed her teeth at them. To her, the window seemed bulletproof. Frank threw his hat on the ground, and she laughed. She could see him running towards the bus, but she was already gone, and she could see that he knew it. Then he made a threatening sign to her, and her smile faded. She jerked her head around and stared at the backs of every other head on the bus. She envied the simpler lives she imagined they all had.

Martin was still catching his breath and he noticed Evelyn's hands were shaking a little. They had stopped holding hands as soon as they boarded the bus. There wasn't a need to anymore, because now they were both being led down the streets of Calais. After they had calmed down, he noticed her glancing out the side window at the people and shops. She was smiling again—taking it all in—and he could see an unspoken freedom on her lips. She was breathing normal and her shoulders seemed more relaxed, and he was glad to see it. She had not even reached for a cigarette.

Martin silently compared themselves to the harried couple in the romantic last scene of *The Graduate*. They had escaped imminent danger and were now sitting side by side. They hadn't spoken to each other or touched since boarding the bus.

Then she said something that rocked him. "They will come looking for me." Her face had grown into stone. Her eyes were fixed and chiselled, and she looked at nothing when she spoke. Then she started to cry, in spite of herself. "I'll never escape my life."

The romance was gone. Martin wanted to keep the mood light and to reassure her of everything. He wanted to tell her she was being silly. And, deep down, he wanted the movie to end and the lights to come on so they could go home. Then her eyes came alive and she turned to him, "What if he finds us?" He was growing tired of that question. He wasn't annoyed with her; instead, he was frustrated that Frank had such a hold on her. She was brave enough to try to escape him and leave behind her old life. He wasn't letting her do that easily. Obviously, Frank had high stakes riding on Yvonne. But Yvonne was dead, and Evelyn could not outrun her ghost. And then it struck him. He was involved, as well. The word "us" had never completely occurred to him before. It was too powerful. Somehow, he had been telling himself that this was still her problem, and he would remain an innocent supporter. He had not imagined there would be any targets on him. He had seen a young girl in trouble, and foolishly, he tried to help her. And now he was stuck, derailed, and more confused than ever. And the truth was, they were joined by this annoying, self-manifesting "us" as the result of their actions. He had jumped overboard to save her, and he braved the sharks. How did this happen? Martin attempted to soothe his own worries, as well as hers.

"We can head back to Paris, you know. Paris is a big place. They didn't find us until we left Paris," he said unconvincingly, as though Paris was suddenly their home base. But it seemed she needed to hear something and his feeble words sufficed for the moment. She nodded dumbly and glanced out the window again. She felt comforted by the way the bus wound its way down stray, narrow streets, taking them farther into the centre of the city, and leaving no traces from the outer world.

"Still," she said, "I don't feel safe in France anymore. We shouldn't stay long." Martin nodded silently. She wasn't looking at him.

Chapter 20

WILLIS

Willis roamed the streets most of the night, and each thought smouldered like half-exhaled cigarettes. He couldn't keep one lit. He thought about the poor girl he had lured into the motel room. Wasn't that what she had wanted? Didn't she want someone to make a decision for her? No, of course not, and he berated himself for trying to justify his actions. Was that the sort of place his father took women? No, he would have gone somewhere classy and planned his moves better. He would have seduced them. He was calculative, and the women were sophisticated. If anything, they probably took control of *him*. It was what his father really wanted, not Tuesday pork chops. His mother certainly didn't wear the pants in the family; she was cut from the same cloth as June Cleaver. His father wanted women who were married to their work and never wanted kids, women who spoke crisply and kept their business as quiet as carefully sealed envelopes. *"Confidential,"* they whispered—a single breath in his ear. Willis wasn't as smoothly cut. He was a fragment torn from his father's three-piece suit, living off the prestige of his title, with no significant achievements of his own. His father had money and intellect, but he didn't have a heart. Willis imagined his mother wore a padded vest to protect her heart from all the stray bullets. Willis wore the sleeves of his father's jacket like two casts, helplessly swinging his impotent arms at his sides as he walked in his father's shoes down the dimly-lit street. His laces were unraveling.

His simmering aggression was beginning to break surface, and it frightened him. He had always been considered a playboy, and perhaps he had one too many social drinks on any given occasion, but he never thought about the reasons for his excessive behavior. Whatever it was that he was attempting to drown wasn't staying submerged. Instead, it was growing larger from his constant feeding. He thought of the look on the girl's face before he had flipped her over and pressed her into the pillow. The pillow cover had daisies on it, and if his hand had not been there, she might have been a young girl muffling her scared and confused tears into the daisies on her own pillow and in her own room because of a relationship breakup or some other trouble—but she wasn't. She was trapped in that sleazy motel room and crying because of him. Worst of all, he knew on some level that she was being forced to absorb all of the horrible things he felt, just the way he wanted her to. What else could she do? She didn't know what was happening, but she knew she was being used for something. The poor girl was relenting to him out of her own dignity and strength and a fear that the situation could turn worse if she dared to struggle.

He realized now why he had flipped her over. He didn't really know at the time, but it was because he couldn't bear to see her face. He wanted her to be faceless. She was his mother, she was every woman his father had cheated with, she was every loose girl he himself had slept with, she was a prostitute, she was every woman that had said "no," and she was the dead Mrs. Harris. In that motel room, she was nobody's daughter. Suddenly, now she was. She belonged to someone, anyone, and everyone.

Willis looked at his hands. They were unscathed, almost too pretty. They had never held a hammer or dug rocks out of the earth. They were manicured and smooth as a man's hands could be. They were hideous. He wanted to take a pocket knife to them and show what they really looked like. Instead, he hid them away in his pockets and headed straight towards the Accident and Emergency Department at the Royal London Hospital.

In the waiting room, there sat a short row of tattered patients. He saw everything from a nose bleed and a broken wrist to a bronchial cough and a child's ear ache. He turned to the woman calmly seated behind the half-plated plastic window.

"Hello, sir." She looked bright, but her voice betrayed tiredness.

"Now, what seems to be the trouble?" She scanned him momentarily for cuts and bruises or signs of a bad cold. There were no exterior signs of illness, which made her frown a little.

"I need to talk to someone," Willis answered in a soft voice. He could sense the other patients leaning in to hear the conversation.

"Talk to someone? Well, the doctor is very busy. What is it you need to talk about?" Her voice was less than discreet, and Willis tried to motion her to speak in lower tones.

"It's a sensitive matter," he started. "I don't feel well. I mean, I don't feel quite right. I think I might have a problem. Please, can you help me?" The nurse frowned again, but her face seemed softer.

"We have a Doctor Horowitz on staff," she said. "He's a psychiatrist."

"Thank you," Willis murmured appreciatively. Then the nurse took his information. She had kept her voice low enough that the other patients briefly knitted their eyebrows, having no real clue as to why he was there, and he took a seat at the end. As long as he wasn't being pushed ahead of them, they didn't care and went back to nursing their own illnesses. Two hours crept by as, one by one, the patrons ahead of him left their seats empty and went through the little door. They eventually reemerged with slips of paper and, perhaps, looks of relief. He was alone in the waiting room when the little door opened again and the same nurse emerged wearing her white, knee-length skirt and running shoes.

"The good doctor will see you now," she announced to him in warmer tones. The good doctor? Were all the rest of them bad? It seemed to him a strange adjective to use, especially to someone who was already feeling poorly. Nevertheless, Willis left his seat empty and followed her through the little door. She led him into an empty room down the hall, second door on the left.

"Please take a seat in here. The doctor will be with you in a few moments," she said. Then she swung a chart on the inside of the door and was gone. Why was it that the doctor was never in the room waiting for you to arrive? Would that be too much of an imposition? Was this a way of allowing the patient a grace period to collect themselves and be greeted by the doctor at his own leisure? At any rate, it wasn't long before Doctor Horowitz rapped briefly on the door and breezed in without waiting for a response before he entered.

"Hello there, young chap. I'm Doctor Horowitz. And you are?" He jerked at the pages on his chart. "Ah, Willis Hancocks."

"Willis Hancocks Jr.," he corrected out of habit.

"Ah, yes," the good doctor mused. "Well, Willis, my nurse says you would like to have a chat."

"Well, more than a chat, I guess." Willis wasn't sure where to begin. "I don't trust myself." The doctor let go of his pen and let it hang on his clipboard.

"You don't trust yourself? With whom or with what?"

Where to begin? Willis thought. *Women. Alcohol. Being alone. The rage he felt towards his own mother.*

"With myself, I suppose," he muttered. He looked and felt subdued with his hands lying defeated in his lap. He felt nauseous and his head pounded. "With myself"—those two small words were self-damning.

"I see … are you afraid you might hurt yourself, then?"

Willis looked at the doctor as though startled from a dream. This thought had not even occurred to him.

"No." He answered as though it was obvious, and the good doctor, in turn, looked more troubled. Perhaps it would be the answer to the rest of his issues, Willis thought morbidly. Unfortunately, he knew with a sicker feeling that he was too cowardly and vain to inflict any injury on himself.

"I see," said the doctor again. Willis wondered how he could see. How could he see the confusion and uncertainty he was feeling? How could he see the way his boyhood years were never encouraging and his lean frame was never held by his mother, who locked her bedroom door and cried herself to sleep night after night? Willis had been bitter since an early age. He spent his words and emotions frugally. There was no point in allowing anyone to venture too close. He had freely given himself up to the whirlpool current, and anyone who came too close to save him would be capsized and pulled under. He had been swimming farther out of reach, ever since the news of his father's death. He looked around him and could see no land, no solid ground, except the good doctor floating there beside him. The odds of being rescued were laughable, Willis thought. Perhaps he was merely seeking a professional ear to help console his mind before he was flushed down into madness.

"I have a tendency for depression and, I believe, some anger management issues." Willis brought his attention back to the doctor and tried to list his symptoms as specifically as possible. The doctor softened his eye on him. The corners of his mouth were turned down slightly in satisfaction.

"Well, you seem to know yourself quite well. Most patients I have diagnosed with depression or aggressive behavior have been the last ones to admit to their condition."

"I am educated," Willis replied. He could hear the pompous tone in his words, but that wasn't going to change.

"Do you feel angry now?" the doctor continued, seemingly

unimpressed by his self-accolades or his tone. Willis took a moment to answer.

"Well, no," he said calmly.

"Have there been any recent dramatic events?"

"My father passed away this year."

"I see. I'm sorry. It's not uncommon for adults to seek counseling after losing a parent. It's never an easy thing, death. However, counseling sessions of that nature are more often set up for young children and teenagers. They are especially useful for older siblings who feel an obligation to step into the role of one or both parents. You see, they are the ones who must be able to reconcile such a death in order to maintain balance in the rest of the household."

"Yes, of course." Willis muttered..

"Ah, but I am wondering if your inability to cope with this death may be a factor in the other, um, problems you are having," the doctor continued, leaning in slightly, taking off his glasses and chewing thoughtfully on the ear piece. His voice carried tones of interest, as though he were slowly making a new discovery. "Tell me, do you know what makes you angry? What sets you off?" Willis thought a moment longer.

"I don't know. I suppose it is a sense that I'm going to lose control of something. I often have a feeling that what I want won't stay in one place. I have to tie it down, and then I become angry with it because I know that I am holding it against its will. It doesn't really want me. You see, I need to have this control, but hate being aware that I have to be in control in order to have what I want. It seems that the things that are free are floating away from me like soap bubbles you blow through a wand. Whether you try to capture them or let them float away, either way, they will eventually disappear. I have to keep the cap on the bottle shut. ..." Willis stopped talking and acknowledged the doctor again, as though he had come out of a trance. He felt helpless, like an animal being surveyed with no bush to scurry under. The doctor sat very still, eyeing him, not with scorn or surprise in his gaze, but with interest. He removed the ear piece on his glasses from his slightly parted lips.

"I think I can help you," he said at last. He replaced his glasses, completed his scribbling on the hand-held chart, and then stood up with hands on his knees. "We'll help you find your way, son," he continued, with a hand patting Willis' shoulder blade, partly as a consolation and partly as a gentle nudging towards the door.

Chapter 21

EVELYN

A lone cabin stood in a large patch of land in the American heartlands. The cabin was dark and the floorboards were starting to bend upwards, so a person never felt stable walking across the room. A little girl stood by the kitchen table, playing.

"Evelyn!" her father's voice slurred. Startled, the little girl dropped a handful of marbles on the table. They rolled towards the rounded corners, fell over the edge, and crashed to the floor, unbreakable; red, yellow, blue, green, see-through, sparkling.

"Oh, daddy!" she cried and ran to gather her gems, grasping them in her chubby little hands. Her palms were soft and meaty, but her fingers were long and slender.

"Come over here," her father said. Another man stood with him, a man she had only seen once or twice before.

"Come over here and say hello to your uncle."

She was afraid. She was only five and she could feel strangeness in the room, as though something was going to happen, and she didn't know whether to disobey him or embrace this new person. She decided to obey and crossed the room, clutching a sparkly marble in her right fist.

"That's a good girl. You're daddy's girl, aren't you?"

Evelyn squirmed in her shoes. "Yes, daddy."

"This is your Uncle Ted. Can you say hello?"

"Hello, Uncle Ted."

"Now give him a kiss like a good little girl." The strange man bent down, waiting.

"She sure is a pretty little thing, isn't she?" he smirked at her father. Her father stood tall and said nothing as he took a swig from his beer can. The man offered her his cheek, and just as she was about to kiss it, he turned his head and kissed her on the mouth.

"Ha, ha, gotcha!" he chortled.

Instinctively, Evelyn wiped her mouth and gave the man a sour look. Her father saw this.

"What did you just do?"

She didn't answer.

"You smart little tart!" her father said.

She began to feel her lips quiver. "I'm sorry, daddy. It was so wet. I'm sorry ... I didn't mean to."

He grabbed her arm and the marble fell to the floor. "Hiding things, are you now?"

"No, daddy. I wanted to show Uncle Ted my marble." She was crying now because he was twisting her arm. He dragged her over the bumpy floor.

"Get in there." He threw her in the hall closet. "You're going to stay there and think about what you did until I come back." She could hear the latch come down as she hugged herself in the dark.

This wasn't the first time she had been there. First, the darkness came alive and then the closet walls would disappear. She waited to give into the blinding solitude. Evelyn closed her eyes tight enough to see vibrant colours appear; first, the shape of her own eyes behind the lids and then dream-like friends. She carried a cosmic imagination behind curtained eyes; the colours were real enough. She would invite soldiers, sorcerers, horses, and heroes into her boundless world. Once her eyes adjusted to the dark, wonderful friends would also appear through her hands, shaping mouths. Her fingers spoke volumes, turning into butterflies, dogs, and dinosaurs. When the secret conversations ran out of words, she would lie down and clench herself into a ball, trying to disappear somewhere. To follow the friends that had left her. There must have been some secret portal in the floor from where they sprung from each time. They waited until she needed them to take her away. They always knew when to come.

But now she was alone again. She closed her eyes, creating more bright colours. Smiling to herself, she brought forth new mommies and daddies. She reunited with her real mommy and daddy, as though she had never left them. She could never see their faces, but it didn't matter. She could almost feel gentle hands brushing her hair, calming her, cooing to her. The hands were so soft, and she always felt loved and safe. And then a man's arms would come rushing towards her, but she was never afraid. She would be swept up, giggling. And he would dance with her to music she could touch, laughing. He would hold her in the way daddies were supposed to. Somehow, she knew there was a difference. There had to be, because in this fantasy, she never felt confused or afraid.

Somewhere deep she sensed that her dream continued living. Somewhere. She believed in her childish mind that these people she fantasized about had been ripped from her, or she from them. How could real mommies and daddies be so awful? The images faded away from her with reaching arms. And she squirmed in her sleep, trying to hang on to them. Someone said, "We're sorry, Evie. We're sorry ... so sorry ..." She opened her eyes to see light coming into the closet, and her mother's tear-streaked face; the mother she knew.

Uncle Ted visited often throughout the years. Evelyn was now twelve years old and almost broken by her father's abuse and her mother's drinking. She was too big to be thrown in the closet, so she went there on her own to seek moments of oblivion from her violent world. She never cried. She had grown bored with her tears years before. They never changed anything and they only made her weaker. Instead, she hid from her parents, and herself. Her mind was the only place she could escape from everything else.

"Evelyn! Where, the devil, are you?" she heard her father's booming voice. For a moment she thought about rebelling and choosing to stay in her imaginative place. She wasn't ready to leave the darkness. She couldn't tell if he had been drinking, but she assumed he had. She opened the closet door just a sliver, undetected, to witness his tall, bulky frame across the room. Then he turned his head towards the door and caught her flickering eye.

"Get out of there." His voice was gruff, but nonthreatening. "You're not a baby anymore, for Chrissake."

She could never tell how he was going to be. She crawled out of the closet. Her father was standing with Uncle Ted.

"Hello, Uncle Ted," she muttered and gave a half-hearted curtsey. This was how her father had trained her to greet him. Her father eyed her closely, but he decided to take another swig of his beer rather than reprimand her.

"See that, Ted," he muttered, "she's turning into a little mope. Thinks she knows it all, too." Evelyn fussed with the pleats in her dress. Uncle Ted just stood there and stared at her with eager eyes. She didn't look at them, but she felt them.

"She is a young lady now, Gus," Ted drooled. "You oughta treat her like one."

"She ain't no lady."

"No, maybe she isn't. But she's close enough."

Evelyn kept her eyes on her bare feet. Her legs were thin and long with small knobby knees.

"Now then, Ev, where's my kiss 'hello'?" Uncle Ted pretended to pout. Evelyn sucked in her breath. Her latest bruise had only just healed; punishment for what her father called stubbornness. Uncle Ted didn't have to lean down very far anymore, and his kiss was always the same. A trick. She felt his lips on hers. And then she backed up quickly, shyly. Her father smirked.

"I think she's ready, Gus." Uncle Ted's eyes flashed. Her mother stood up quietly from her chair in the corner, agitated, and left the room. Evelyn looked up at her father with confused, terrified eyes. She didn't know what this meant, but she had begun to notice the first tender budding of her breasts and the changes happening within her. The men had saliva grins and it scared her down to her spine. She could already sense their blundering tainted hands on her newfound skin.

Chapter 22

EVELYN

The little girl stood frozen in a circle of eyes. Then her father's lips parted, "I believe you're right, Ted. Come by tomorrow. I'll have her ready." Then he put his beer can to those same lips and turned away.

Her mother entered the room again, like a servant, twittering about a fresh pot of tea being made and would anyone like some? Evelyn's head was spinning. She felt naked and bewildered. To her, it was like watching two devious, lusting men speaking a foreign language as they closed in on her little world.

"No thanks, Ma," Gus murmured. Uncle Ted tipped his hat to her mother and then tipped it a little lower for Evelyn. He left with a grin. Her mother stood rooted to the floor, comically, holding a scalding pot of tea. Gus tugged on his pants and sauntered over to her mother and whispered audibly, "About time you had your female talk with the girl," as he passed her. He struck up an old whistling tune, disappearing into another room in the house.

Her mother gave her a flustered, plastered smile and continued to twitter, "Now, come on, girlie, have some tea. Heavens, you're such a waif! We need to put some colour in those cheeks." Evelyn already knew her mother had slipped a healthy dose of brandy in her own delicate cup. *Good for the cold*, she said. *Good for the cold.*

Later that night, as Evelyn was brushing the knots out of her hair, her mother slipped into her room. She had not come into her room at bedtime for years. Her mother fluttered about most of the time and lived in a stupor of brandy and battering insults. Evelyn always thought her mother was just as afraid of her as *she* was of Gus.

Her mother lurked near the door, like a first-time lover, afraid to come too near, yet desperate to be close.

"What is it, Mama?" Evelyn softly put down her brush and sat, quiet and anxious. Her mother hesitated and then came towards her in determined steps. She picked up the brush and gently took a thick strand of Evelyn's hair. She began to brush, smiling at her in the mirror. She had never brushed her hair before. At least, Evelyn could not remember the last time she felt her mother's nurturing strokes.

"My heavens, girlie, wherever did you get such thick hair?"

Evelyn didn't answer. "Mama?"

Her mother didn't answer for a long time, either. Then she said, "You're not a little girl anymore."

"No, Mama."

"You're becoming a woman now. And being a woman means doing certain things."

"Like what, Mama?" There was another long pause. Evelyn's hair was beginning to separate and become static, but her mother wouldn't stop brushing. She seemed determined to get out all the knots, to make everything smooth.

"Do you like Uncle Ted?"

"He's my uncle."

"Yes, I know."

"Of course I like Uncle Ted."

"Well, good. Good."

"Why do you say that, Mama?"

"I'm— I'm just glad you like him. It helps if you like him."

"I don't like him, Mama, but he's my uncle. I have to like him, don't I?"

Her mother stopped brushing her hair.

"What's wrong, Mama?"

"Well, you do have to like him. There's nothing else for you to do. You have to become a woman tomorrow. You want to become a woman, don't you?"

"I don't know. I'm afraid. I'm afraid of Uncle Ted."

"He's not going to hurt you. Just shut your eyes and let him do what he has to do ... to make you a woman."

"What will he do to me, Mama?"

"He'll only do what's natural. What's right."

"It doesn't seem right. I don't believe in it." Then she was thoughtful for a moment. "This is what they did to you, isn't it, Mama!"

Her mother's face looked wretched. "That's nothing for a daughter to know about her ... her mother."

"You're going to do the same thing to me that was done to you. Oh, Mama, who was it? Who made you do this when you were my age? Was it your Mama? Oh, Mama, how can you let them do the same thing to me?"

"Because it's time for you and this is how things are done, according to your father. We must listen to your father."

"He's not my father."

Her mother's hands were shaking. She didn't know what to do with them, so she tried brushing Evelyn's hair again. Evelyn wouldn't let her; she took the brush and slammed it down hard on the vanity table.

"He is so your father! He's the only father you've got! The only father you've ever known! You miserable, stupid child, ... you have to learn to obey your father so that he … so that he won't beat on you." Then her voice softened, exasperated. "You've been so good, Evie. You don't want to ruin that, do you? It will all be fine. You'll see. It won't last long."

Evelyn was so frustrated and scared she could barely see. Her face was soaked in tears and her eyes were raging. There were so many violent voices in her that she wanted to thrash out against the crippling walls around her. *Beat on me?* she wanted to scream. *What about you? What the hell about you, Mother? How can you be my mother when you won't protect me? How can he be my father and casually toss me off to some horrible man who will rob me of I don't know what? How can you be my parents when you both hate me so much?* The incessant voices volleyed in her brain while her mother picked up the brush again with increasingly shaky hands and clumsily smoothed the young girl's hair. Her voice was soft and psychotic.

"Now, never mind all that. We'll forget. Make sure you rest and remember to wear a pretty dress for tomorrow. How about the lavender one? Shades of purple always look so nice on you."

"Yes, Mama."

The next morning, after a night of sleepless transition, Evelyn descended the stairs from her bedroom. She emerged in front of a parental firing squad at the breakfast table to surrender herself to a womanhood she wasn't ready for. She had not finished her childhood. She couldn't conceive of this dimensional day and, instead, clung to breaking strands of innocence. No one made eye contact with her. They knew her impression was fading like the morning light on dusty windowpanes. Soon she would no longer recognize the world outside or her own home. She would not be able to find her reflection.

Evelyn ate her cereal without incident, and only the faint crunching existed in her ear. Before she had finished her last spoonful, the front door opened, and Uncle Ted stood there shifting in the doorway. He took off his hat like a schoolboy and Evelyn wondered why. There was nothing to respect in that house. Her mother chirped, "Cup of tea, Ted?" Tea. Even tea didn't seem normal.

"Go on, girlie," her father mumbled between bites of toast. "He's waiting for you." He didn't say "uncle." He didn't say "Uncle Ted is waiting for you." Somehow, that would make it incestuous. If they just made him a man, a stranger, stripped him of any personal connections and erased him of blood ties, then this was okay. Evelyn tried to finish her last spoonful, but Gus pushed her bowl away, spilling milk.

"Go on," he growled without raising his eyes. Part of him sounded sad or confused, but Evelyn was sure he felt neither. She knew all he meant was disgust and annoyance. He pushed himself away from the table and stalked into the kitchen so he wouldn't have to be a witness of his own evil. Evelyn put her spoon down gently and stayed in her seat. Her feet planted themselves onto the floor like the roots of trees searching for water. Uncle Ted didn't speak as she balanced herself, feeling her feet breaking away from the floor, and then eventually trudged past him like a prisoner on death row, through the door he held open for her. He was a real gentleman.

The morning was fresh and she felt she could run into the flowers, the garden, the trees, over the grassy knoll, until she disappeared. But she knew she couldn't. She was shackled, walking in front of her uncle, her warden and perpetrator, out to the shed. She knew she couldn't run from him, not fast enough. She also knew *this* had to happen somewhere inside, hidden: the shed. She walked as though he was poking a bayonet into the small of her back, and she envisioned him piercing her. She wished for it. Her soul was torn and she wanted the air to be sucked out of her. She wanted to deflate beyond use and escape from her skin. Then maybe she wouldn't remember. She stopped at the shed, not wanting to enter on her own accord, admitting herself into captivity by crossing the threshold.

"Get in there now," he breathed. His voice wasn't threatening. Again she heard sad tones, almost as if they had both been bullied into violating each other. Perhaps Gus had an equal power over his brother, although she couldn't see how. Hadn't Ted been the instigator? She remembered his leering eyes. She wanted to turn and look into his eyes now, but she was afraid she might see something horrible, like sympathy. Somehow, it would be easier if he were filled with lustful wrath or if he didn't care.

The shed was empty, save a few tools hanging on the wall. But the tools didn't scare her. The lack of windows and the mouldy smell did. She felt she was trapped in a larger closet. Imaginations died in there. Evelyn cowered near the rear of the shed and glared at the man in front of her. A man. She was too afraid to look away. As much as she dreaded this moment, she wanted to see it coming. To know that it had happened and know the first man that happened to her. It was a morbid thought, and she couldn't explain it, except to know that she wanted to hang on to whatever piece of her was being stolen, even if it meant hanging on to a disquieting rage. But nothing was happening. He stood there, lost in his own fear, desire, and shame.

Then his face hardened and he came at her with impatience and new aggression. He grabbed her with his farmer's arm and forced his chapped, sweaty lips on her mouth. He pulled at her violet dress and tore the sleeve, and then busted her front buttons with his free hand. She stood there as he peeled her open and tore into her like a mandarin orange, seasonal and sweet. Then he backed away from her. He stood there, looking bewildered. Like a child after a tantrum, forgetting his real desire and only remembering his violent outburst. He looked at her in a way that said he was hearing her stifled fear for the first time and seeing her tears that wouldn't dry fast enough. She was suffocating herself and trying to be a good girl, standing there, holding up her dress and shaking in her bravery.

"Get out of here, Ev," he whispered in a broken voice. He was trembling. She was even more afraid of the sudden freedom, of the urgency in his words.

"You're not my uncle, are you, Uncle Ted?" she cried. He shook his head and covered his face.

"There is a highway on the other side of the woods. It's not far.

Now go on." He wanted to scream at her, but he didn't want Gus to hear him from the house. "Go."

She started and then ran past him through the shed door left ajar. She was afraid to say anything, to question him, to touch him. He was the warden under a brief influence of mercy, and all she could see was her chance to disappear. But Evelyn did not run into the woods. Instead, she ran back towards the house. Her little girl spirit was raging as she burst through the door.

"Liars!" she hollered in her quavering voice. "You liars!" Her father looked at her, stunned and outraged. He was about to rise from his seat, but something in her fiery eyes made him check himself.

"How could you ..." she began and then faltered. "I'm leaving." She found strength in her words, knowing they were as powerful as actions as she was standing there in her torn dress, feeling raped. Not by the man in the shed, but by these people who had incarcerated her without care. These people were the ones guilty of her torn dress and absent childhood. These people.

"I know the truth. I know you are not my parents. And now I'm leaving."

"You can't ..." the frail woman in the corner blurted out. Evelyn thought the woman was on the brink of fainting or going into hysterics. Either one would have been a refreshing change; she would realize the weight of her own body or her voice and the power unleashed in being able to express anger and sorrow. She stepped out of the shadows, but still lingered, uncertain, behind her husband's presence. "You can't," she said again, wringing her hands. "You belong to us." Her husband held the woman back with an outstretched arm, like an iron bar. But there was nothing really there to hold back, and his eyes flashed with anger and defeat. His lips remained firm.

"I belong to no one," young Evelyn said simply. She was a grown woman inside. "I never did." She turned and left, the dull echo of her soles on the rough wooden floor, and let the latch on the door fall behind her.

Chapter 23

EVELYN

Evelyn walked away from the shack like someone walking away from an exploded building. She was fighting back tears. Not tears for leaving her bereft, imbecilic mother or her tyrant father, but tears for being twelve years old and lost with no direction as to where to go next. She walked forward in a straight line into the woods that surrounded the property. These were trees she had never dared or even thought to enter before; her father always had such a close watch on her. The trees cast long, black bars on the ground, shadows from the sun, which she could walk between. She stepped on the sodden ground in her broken sandals, her feet sinking. She silently wondered if this was how it felt to walk on the moon. She was a bit nervous about the possibility of having company in the forest, and her eyes darted around at the sound of fluttering birds and singing brooks.

After thirty minutes or so of walking, she spotted an opening in the distance that seemed to lead out of the woods. The makeshift path shone open like a burst of sunlight. As she exited, she realized she was on the side of a two-lane highway, with no car in sight. The land was flat and she could follow the road easily and, seemingly, without danger. Evelyn felt an odd mixture of melancholy and exhilaration. She'd always felt alone, but she had never actually been completely alone before. With one foot in front of the other, she was stretching her limbs for the first time.

The late morning sun left a slow burn on the top of her head and shoulders. She began to feel weary and had no idea how long she had been walking on the highway. She looked ahead to see a ribbon of asphalt stretched out in front of her, and she imagined this highway must travel clear across the country, dividing north and south, in whichever direction she decided to head. It was eerie and barren, as though forgotten. This was the right highway for her to be following, even if it meant she might be walking alongside it for the rest of her life.

A grey Plymouth had slowed down behind her as she was caught up in these bleak thoughts, and she hadn't even heard the subtle rubbing between the tires and gravel. She jumped a little when she caught sight of the rusty hood sliding up beside her like a snake. Then the car slid up a little farther so that she was parallel with the driver as she warily bent down to look inside.

"Well, hello there, darling. It's a hot day to be walking. Can I give you a lift into town?" The voice came from a young woman. She wore a flimsy, short-sleeved blouse; large, gaudy earrings; and oversized sunglasses. She took the sunglasses off to reveal her small, twinkling, blue eyes and long mascara lashes.

"Well, hop in before you burn the tops of your ears. Wait a second." She grabbed a t-shirt from the back seat and placed it hastily on the passenger seat. "The car seats are really hot. You don't need to be burning anything else." The woman winked. Evelyn opened the latch on the door as though handling a hot potato and slid into the car.

"So, where are you coming from?" the woman started. Evelyn

looked out the window and watched the blur of trees passing by, thinking of how strange life was and the circumstances that had propelled her into this uncertain future. Just that morning she had been cowering at the breakfast table, trying to eat her cereal under her father's supervision, and afraid of losing herself completely. She just looked at the woman and gave a little shrug.

"Nowhere special," she muttered and cast her eyes downwards. The woman glanced at her for a second, curiously, and then set her eyes back on the road.

"That's alright," she said. "It doesn't really matter where people come from anyhow; all that matters is where you think you're headed." Evelyn didn't respond. Then the woman said something a bit strange, like she had forgotten that Evelyn was still in the car. "I wish I'd paid more attention to where I was heading." Evelyn looked over and saw a purplish bruise peeking out from under the sleeve of her blouse.

"I'm Bonnie," the woman said. Again, Evelyn didn't respond. When Evelyn looked up, she could see a small gas station on the side of the road.

"We're almost in town," Bonnie remarked as she passed the gas station and nodded at the man standing in front of the gas meters, looking for customers. He gave a short wave. He looked a little abandoned. Evelyn wondered if she was merely trying to find reflections of herself in everything else so that she wouldn't feel so alone in her newfound skin.

◆◆◆◆◆◆

A few miles down the road, more buildings began to emerge out of the flat horizon. The woman pulled over in front of a small strip mall and turned off the ignition.

"Are you going to be alright?" She took off her glasses and examined the young girl. Evelyn nodded dumbly. The woman fished a safety pin out of her purse and quietly handed it to Evelyn; the younger girl pinned together the front of her dress.

"Thanks for the ride," Evelyn stammered as she reached for the latch on the door.

"Hold on." The woman reached into her purse and took out a small wad of money. "This should cover you for a bit. There's a hostel just down the block." Then she grimaced. "Are you sure you're going to be alright?"

"I'll be okay. Really." Evelyn didn't want to be a burden. And she felt a little uncomfortable with the way this woman looked at her. She wasn't used to people being concerned about her.

The woman turned her eyes back on the road, turned on the ignition, and left her standing on the curb in the disappearing sunlight. Evelyn looked around her before deciding which direction to move in. She headed down the block in search of the hostel. She knew she had found it when she came across a front step that had a few young people hanging around. She picked up on an accent or two and shimmied past them and through the front door. A middle-aged man was seated behind the front counter. He was talking on the phone, giving someone directions to the hostel. He hung up the phone and looked up to see this strange, tattered slip of a girl fidgeting in front of him.

"Hello, there, little girl," he said pleasantly. "Can I help you?"

"Yes, I'd like to stay here." She felt an odd pang from being called a little girl. She may have looked very young, but inside her, there was no little girl left. The older man looked a little disturbed.

"Well, now," he began, "first of all, how old are you?"

"Fifteen," she lied, but her eyes met his with new confidence. She could see he was weighing this bold statement, but she didn't falter.

"Fifteen, huh," he inquired with suspicion.

"Please, if you don't give me shelter, I'm not sure where else to turn." Her defiant voice dropped and she revealed her true age in her mannerisms. She was apprehensive, and he could clearly see it.

"Alright," he said and brought out his ledger. "That will be $12 a night. How many nights would you like to stay?" Evelyn's eyes glazed over.

"I don't really know. Do I have to let you know right now?"

It was becoming more and more clear to him that he had a very frightened, lost girl on his hands. Possibly a runaway.

"Don't worry. ... I tell you what ... can you work?"

"Oh, yes."

"Well ... I run a diner in the hostel. Would you be willing to help out waitressing to earn your room and board?"

"Oh, yes. Thank you, sir."

"Okay, it's a deal. Here is your room key. Where's your luggage?"

"I didn't come with any," she answered in a quiet voice.

"I have a daughter who is your age ... I mean, well, she's about the same size as you. I'll lend you some of her clothes. She won't be back for a while. Visiting her mother, you know. Anyhow, I'm sure her clothes will fit you." Evelyn beamed as she took the room key and walked quickly up the stairs to her new room.

The next morning she awoke in her bunk to find three other girls sound asleep in the room with her. And at the foot of her bed were a couple of dresses, folded neatly. She smiled, not perturbed at all that the man had come into her room to supply her with fresh clothes for the morning. She also noticed that the dress she had been wearing the day before was gone. She lay in her bed for a minute, adjusting to the new day and smiling to herself. She slipped into the blue dress folded on top, while sitting in her bed, found a used pair of shoes that were in good shape beside her bed, tugged them on her narrow feet, and deftly left the room. She arrived in the lobby with her hair thrown into a ponytail and a hopeful smile swept across her face.

"Well, good morning," the man greeted her, amused. "Did you sleep well?"

"Yes, thank you. And thank you for the beautiful dresses."

"Well, I don't know how fancy they are, but that blue looks nice on you."

She beamed.

"Are you ready to get to work?" he asked.

She pretended to roll up her sleeves, "I sure am."

"Good. Follow me," he said as he moved through a curtain into another part of the building. She followed him into the diner, and they wandered behind the counter into the kitchen area. A tall, young man was already placing bacon strips in a frying pan and preparing the batter for pancakes.

"We'll be opening in a few minutes. We always open at 8:00 a.m. and stay open until 2:00 p.m.," the man explained. "This is Tim, our chef." The young man smiled in her direction.

"I'm sorry, I didn't even catch your name?"

"My name is Evelyn," she replied brightly.

"Nice to meet you, Evelyn," he said, then he moved on with his orientation, and he began training her about how to signal Tim for orders, the breakfast and lunch specials, and how many tables she was expected to take care of. He wrote *Evelyn* on a label and told her to put it on the front of her dress. He was amazed at how well Evelyn was taking it all in, or so he thought. She was fine until the customers began filling the chairs.

The first wave of customers to arrive were the truckers, who brought their giant trailers to a 20-foot halt, and lumbered in with their unkempt beards, insulated vests, and weathered baseball caps that read John Deere across the fronts. They barged through the door good-naturedly and called to the man in charge, "Morning, Jack!"

"Morning, boys. What can I do you for?"

"Ah, we'll have the regular." One of the men trailing in behind waved his hand vaguely and followed his crew into a booth by the window. Jack saw the nervous expression on Evelyn's face and whispered to her with humour, "A round of black coffee and flap-jacks with syrup."

"Okay," she replied and smiled, trying to conceal her nerves. She moved into the back of the kitchen to give the order to Tim as she heard Jack exclaim to the waiting table, already loud with banter, "Coming right up, fellas!"

As she approached the table, looking like a circus act as she balanced the mile-high plate of flapjacks and six cups of black coffee on a small, orange plastic tray. She felt like a rabbit approaching a pack of wolves. They seemed to eye her inappropriately as she came towards the table. Obviously, she did not look like a twelve-year-old girl to them.

"Well, hey there, sweet stuff. You must be new here," the man who had given the order to Jack piped up.

"Yeah, I'm the new waitress. So just call me if you need anything."

"Oh, I'll be sure to do that," he replied in a slithery tone. The rest of the table tried to muffle their smirks and sniggering, and as she turned to go back to the kitchen, she felt a hand press on her behind. Another group of customers were emerging through the door, including two men in clean suits, as she whirled around and glared at the trucker. Before she could think, she grabbed one of the cups of steaming black coffee and poured it in his lap, and then she grabbed the syrup and squirted it all over his baseball cap until it oozed off the rim. Amazingly, the other men just cheered and laughed at their buddy.

"Didn't anyone ever teach you any manners about how to treat a young lady?" she seethed through her teeth, "you old, fat blob of diesel grease!" Still fuming, she turned on her heel, leaving a trail of jeering remarks, and then she saw Jack emerge from the kitchen.

"Jack, this is the worst service I've ever had in this place! You should screen your employees better. This little tart just went bonkers on me; look at me! Look what she's done!" the trucker hollered indignantly.

"Jack, he ... he ..." but she was too embarrassed to tell him what had happened.

"What the hell do you think you're doing, little girl? Is this how you repay me for giving you work? I'm sorry, I can't put up with this sort of behaviour. Now those are good boys over there.

I can't believe they'd start anything to deserve that." He looked at her with the disappointed eyes of a father of some kind. That's how she maybe saw him.

"Please just give me another chance. I told you, I've got nowhere else to go," she could hear herself begging, and she hated the pitiful sound of her voice, but she was desperate for a place to stay. Jack drew in his breath slowly.

"Alright, I'll give you one more chance." He glanced at her sourly as he moved towards the table to tell the men breakfast was on him.

Chapter 24

EVELYN

The next morning the same truckers came in, but they didn't harass her. They eyed her cautiously and treated her like the servant her apron signified she was. She felt relieved, and at the same time, a little sad and disturbed. The other girl who worked there before her must have been accustomed to their behaviour and took it in stride. It must have been something they were all used to, an unspoken understanding and a means for her to get better tips. But she was not that other woman. She wasn't a woman at all. People forgot that since she had a tall, blossoming body and the eyes of someone much older.

She also noticed the other men in suits who had entered the café the day before. She recognized the Plymouth they were driving and frowned a little. Then she straightened her spine and approached the suits' table, trying not to appear intimidated or impressed by their attire, neatly combed hair, and close-shaven faces.

"Good morning, gentlemen. What can I bring you?" She smiled

brightly. They turned from their conversation and gave her an amused look.

"How old are you?" one of the men asked. He had a crisp British accent and a suspicious twinkle in his eye. He unnerved her a little.

"Excuse me?"

"I saw you yesterday morning with those rowdies over there."

"Oh, look, I didn't mean ..."

"I thought you handled that very well."

"Oh."

He eyed her carefully, and then he did something she didn't expect him to do.

"I'll have this," he said, pointing to an item on the menu. Then he looked at her expectantly.

"Oh, I can't quite see it from here, sir. Could you please tell me?"

"I'm sorry, here, I'll make it easier for you." He brought the menu closer to her face as she stood there silently shaking, with her pen and pad in hand. "This."

"Okay, thank you, sir." She nervously made an indiscernible scribble on her pad.

"You have no idea what I want, do you?" he said with a gentle, mocking voice. She felt her face grow hot. She wanted to turn to the other man and ask him what he had decided on, but she was afraid the man with the British accent would complain to Jack that she was being inattentive and rude. Instead, she stood there with her eyes downcast, frozen, feeling trapped. She had tried to keep her debilitating secret. She had a wonderful memory. How would she survive when the truth came out? *She couldn't read.* She glanced up at this man, this man who was a complete stranger and who was now in complete control of what happened next. There were volcanoes in her eyes.

"Just as I thought," he mused. How did he know? Did she reek of low breeding? Did she sound like she had never gone to school? Did she have a sign on her forehead? Maybe he had just toyed with her for fun and then surprised himself by finding out the truth accidentally.

Maybe he was so arrogant that he tested the IQ of anyone in an apron. Maybe he was just an asshole.

"Are you going to get me fired?" she said in the most composed voice she could manage.

"Yes and no." He glanced briefly at the other man. He liked having this control.

"I'm going to employ you in a more suitable occupation. My name is Frank." Then he walked over to Jack and complained that his waitress was so incompetent she couldn't even read the menu. Jack fired her, and then she had nowhere else to go, except home with Frank.

Once they were in his car, the same grey Plymouth that Bonnie drove the other day, Frank read the nametag that was stuck to her dress.

"First of all," he said, "lose the nametag. That name doesn't represent you anymore." Evelyn recognized the ominous tones in his voice, and she didn't want to be kicked out of his car in the middle of nowhere, so she silently obeyed and peeled the nametag from her dress. The other man sat quietly in the backseat.

"Good girl," he said from behind the steering wheel, not looking at her. "Now, why don't we decide on a new name? How about Eve?" Suddenly, he was talking down to her like she was a child, like they were playing a game. She was more than a little afraid of him, so she played along. But she didn't like Eve, and she said so.

"Yes, you're right. Too pure, Eve." Then he became excited. "I've got it!" Evelyn, who was soon to no longer be Evelyn, gazed at him. She felt herself slipping away again. She was confronted by all of these men who had so much power over her. Where was her power? Her words seemed to belong to someone else.

"What is it?" she heard herself say. "What is my new name?"

"Yvonne." He stretched the name out evocatively, letting the vowels roll around in his mouth. It was a woman's name. It was glitzy and sophisticated. There was a part of her that was rebelling against this manipulation, just like when Gus and Ted had taken property of her. She had no relations, and still, she knew she didn't belong to herself anymore, either. And now this man, this Frank, was doing the same thing, only she didn't quite recognize it as being the same thing. There was another part of her that wanted a new name and a new identity. Maybe she would gain more control in her world and drown out the little girl.

"Yvonne ..." she said, quietly tingling.

Chapter 25

MARTIN

Evelyn's eyes fluttered open, and she focused her gaze on Marty.

"You fell asleep," he crooned. He stroked her hair away from her eyes.

"I wasn't sleeping."

"Weren't you?" His mouth creased into a boyish smile, not believing her.

"No. No, I was reliving something."

"You were dreaming."

"I was remembering."

"Memories can chase you. But don't worry, they won't catch you here."

She looked around the room in response to his last words, "Where is here?" She remembered they had gone somewhere after getting off the bus, but she had been too tired and it was too dark when she last closed her eyes.

"A hotel room ... I've decided that tomorrow we will leave for Germany. We can go anywhere, Evelyn."

"Another hotel room," she said, drearily surmising her surroundings.

"We won't stay long. You were too tired to travel last night. I wanted you to have some rest."

She smiled up at him. "Why are you carrying me?"

"You don't need carrying."

She began to rise and the blankets and sheets fell away from her. He smoothed her back with his hand, feeling her spine. She was sturdy and fragile all at once. Her long mane of hair fell in torrents. He wondered silently what secrets she kept, this wild girl. She was still a girl, somewhere deep inside.

"I'd like to keep going east; I want to get lost in some mystic land where no one, not even Frank can find me."

"There is a risk in going farther east, remember. We may have more difficulty travelling across borders with the Russian security."

"Maybe you're right." She broke out of her sleepy state and flashed her eyes at him. "I don't want to feel trapped anywhere." She had transient blood, and she wouldn't allow herself to feel caged in a room, an emotion, or a country. It made her nervous, as though if she stayed in one place for too long, the world would close in on her again.

She was still running, and Martin kept trying to be her cushion to crash into, to hold her until she decided to go upwards instead of forward at lightning speed. Whenever he could see her trying to hide behind those translucent eyes, he tried to banish the ghosts and monsters that chased her. Every time she turned her head away so that he wouldn't see her fear, he knew not to touch her. Like touching the electricity coursing through a broken circuit, it would feed on him. He was the conductor, and he knew only too well how it would suck them both dry.

He wanted to pull her out of the ditch and then watch her run away from him, thankful; like a wounded bird, he wanted to take the rough splint off her leg and watch her fly out the window. He wanted to be a saviour, not a guardian. He didn't want this—he didn't want to love her. Love was a responsibility. He hadn't learned how yet. He didn't know if he could learn by staying with her—something told him there was more he needed to do first, without her. She was not the last puzzle piece. She was a means to the completion of the frame he had to fill in. She had pulled him out and woke him up. He was a wounded bird, too. Once he flew, he might never come back; it scared him. She was becoming a security blanket that he didn't want, and he felt they were tugging on the same blanket, fighting for a corner to keep them safe and warm.

Neither of them wanted to think about the "real world" yet. He had been alone before, but this was different. He was kidding them both with the belief that he could uphold them and bring them to shore. Together, they would only tread water. It was easier to be alone and to watch the world move by you and around you, like pockets of wind whirling around scraps of garbage, and think to yourself, *I'll never be there. I'll never have a cup of morning coffee in one hand, and a briefcase in the other*, and curse all of those who sweep by you with their wrist-watches, eyes down or unfocused, not wanting to see you moving in your helpless circles.

He only half-envied those people. Sure, they had the fat pay cheques and large houses—but they also had the mortgages, moody bosses, and tight lunch breaks. They had the work that had to be completed by 5:00 p.m., which everyone's lives depended on. They had everything hanging in the balance, and all of it was small and intangible on the larger scale of human happiness. Those people drank at the end of the day, dragged their bodies around like luggage, sighed heavily, and had trouble sleeping. They worried about conversations, deadlines, numbers, and protocol—all of it air. They were forgetting to live and, instead, heading towards early graves. Who signed up for that?

Martin still didn't want to be a part of it, but he knew he had an opportunity, and a responsibility, to be part of something that involved more than him. He also knew that Evelyn couldn't come with him. The thought struck him in the chest as he watched her. It wouldn't be fair to drag her through, and possibly down, his unmapped journey. He would continue farther into the continent, alone. He knew she was a strong swimmer and would find a shore; she had to discover that, too.

When she closed her eyes again, he kissed her softly between the eyes. Those beautiful eyes he had watched turn to stone and soften again, like sea-washed sand. He sat on the corner of the bed, watching her for the length of the sunrise, as it crept across her face in sharp slashes from the blades of the window blinds. Then he whispered, "Sweet dreams," to her, and as he crept out the door, he mouthed the unspeakable word. "Goodbye."

⟶•◖◗•⟵

Martin checked out at the front desk, and the clerk put on a cheerful air, but still eyed him with curiosity. He wanted to ask about the young woman who had accompanied him to the room, but he didn't want to pry. Martin answered his unspoken thoughts by saying, "She's still asleep in the room."

He was Martin again, Martin from the Hyde Park tunnel, Martin who only spoke to Joe. He could feel himself shrinking back into his solitude, but this was different. She had started to depend too much on him. What did he need to feel guilty about? She had been able to get herself around quite nicely. Or was that Frank who told her where to go and when to go there and who to go with?

Shut up. Quiet. She wasn't his responsibility. He had brought her out of harm's way and he didn't have the strength to drag her around with him. She was fine now. Wasn't she? She understood now. She could see her past and her future and how they weren't the same anymore. He had his own future to pursue, hurdles to conquer, and questions to answer. She was like a stray animal that you bring in for a saucer of milk, but eventually you have to let it go out again, into the world. Let go. She said so herself, she didn't want to feel owned or trapped. Stray animals are wild animals, and he didn't need her to give him any scratches or scars after the milk ran out. They were both free spirits, wandering and not accustomed to being cared about. They had learned something from each other ... the touch of another human being. But this touch was beginning to turn into a rash for Martin. He knew, with some trepidation, that this was his stop. This was where he needed to get off and catch another train.

Martin's stride quickened as he realized he was already many blocks away from the hotel. He had asked the front desk man for directions to the train station, and he had managed to find his way, blindly, down the careening streets with another world unravelling in his head; the world of Yvonne or Evelyn or whoever she had decided to be. No, that wasn't fair. He had decided what to call her without really asking her. He was the one who had smashed her trick mirrors and made her look at her true and naked self. He was the one. She was better off without him. Why not live in a fantasy world? It almost seemed safer at times, to forget who you really are. To become what others see you as being. Being. They were all just humans being, moving in zigzags. Moving like ants. One could die from thinking too much.

He looked up and realized he had arrived at the train station. He was back in the chaos of people and suitcases and hellos and goodbyes, and arms opening to engulf those arriving or leaving. There were people clinging to each other, pulling on hands, giving adhesive kisses, and touching faces as if they feared death would keep them apart once they boarded that platform. Crossed borders were real: the transient places where there were no guarantees for return, even if the travellers were clutching return tickets. Who knew where those steel wheels would really take you? It was a final point. The red line in the waiting area said so as Martin crossed over it with his torn ticket and moved through the turnstiles.

Chapter 26

EVELYN

The room was filled with light when Evelyn awoke. She thought she had just rested her eyes for a few minutes and remembered the weight of her eyelids forcing her back into dreams that seemed to entangle her. She awoke with a start to find no other presence in the room, no shadow leaking from the adjoining bathroom door, left ajar, no sound of his shoes or running water. The blinds flapped nervously as the summer air drifted into the room, like a lone bird's wing that couldn't take flight. She felt a mild panic.

"Marty?" she whispered in a barely audible voice. She was afraid to crack this silence, and to only have the silence returned. She gathered the sheets around her, slowly moved from the bed, and peered cautiously out of the blinds to see what the day's clouds might bring. She already knew it was a turning day. She vaguely hoped to see him standing on the sidewalk waiting for her, to see him look up and acknowledge her face peering down and wave frantically at her to join him, but she only saw an old woman pushing an overloaded shopping cart down the street. The shopping cart seemed to be filled with all her worldly possessions. Evelyn saw herself in this woman. Only, she wasn't sure what items would fill her own shopping cart. These solitary people who wandered the earth seemed to carry with them the material remnants of a previous life, tangible memories of who they used to be. Evelyn carried her memories too, but she couldn't put them in a shopping cart, except, perhaps, a few torn dresses. She would have to put herself in a shopping cart. And then there was the little girl she tried so desperately to escape from—there would have to be room for her.

The old woman suddenly stopped her cart and peered upwards at the hotel windows. She put her hand over her forehead as a visor to block out the sun. Evelyn wanted to move back from the window, but something made her continue looking down at the woman. She wondered if the woman saw her from this height. Could she have detected her own misery through the cheap window glass and distance that separated them? Perhaps this was her daily routine, to wander the streets with her life in a basket and peer up at the apartments and hotels, dreaming about entering such a building and having her own four walls, a bed, and a mirror, even though she may never look at her own reflection, and having a set of blinds to block out the rest of the world. Evelyn's finger slipped and she let the blind snap shut.

Soon, Evelyn was standing on the same sidewalk, after ten uninterrupted minutes of staring at her own image in the mirror, wondering why she had been abandoned and if it were really a bad thing. She had stood naked in the mirror, covering her breasts with her arms, hugging herself for comfort and self-realization. She wanted to smash the mirror, but she restrained herself because she did not want to break anything else. Maybe she had anticipated this. To wake up with only herself ... She had not done so in years. She quietly collected the small bundle of money Marty had left for her on the corner of the bed, put it in her bag, and deftly left the room.

The day was cool and the air was foreign on her skin, a teasing breeze that made her small, protective hairs stand up. She held her elbows while standing on the sidewalk. The man at the front desk had given her a kind, fatherly look when she checked out.

"You don't need him, *mademoiselle*," he said. Then he nodded reassuringly, as if saying that was all that needed to be said. She didn't answer. She didn't believe him yet. She lifted one corner of her mouth and went out. She didn't call a taxicab; instead, she began walking in the sunshine, with her heels dipping in the shallow cracks in the cement. She felt as though she was learning to walk; her legs were thin and unsteady, and she held her chest in. She was afraid everything might fall out, loose, onto the pavement, a cartoon vision of her ribs breaking and her vital organs, even her eyes, falling out, and her kneeling on the ground, mortified, and people walking by and watching. The thought made her hold her elbows and close her eyes tighter to keep everything in. She had asked the man in the hotel where she was. A small French village outside Paris called *Carrières-sur-Seine*. She blinked. They had travelled nearly all the way back to their starting point. She thought she could hide there for a while, but she didn't know how she could manage. Marty had left her money, but it felt greasy in her hand. She had not begun to forgive him, and the money was linked to a part of him she didn't know or trust. She didn't care about the money; she had never had money before. She had also never been entirely alone before. She was trapped again. *Screw him*, she thought, not sure which *him* she meant. Every man that thought they had her or decided for her who she was or what was best. They didn't have her now.

As she walked through the quaint, sunny village, trying to calm her thoughts and decide what to do, she noticed the old woman with the shopping cart coming towards her. She must have looped around again. This was her village, her home. Everyone needed a landmark, a center. As the woman came closer, Evelyn noticed she was not old. She looked haggard, but no older than her mid-forties. Her hair boasted long grey streaks, partly tied back off her tired, weathered face. Her eyes were large and had seen too much. She didn't see Evelyn and was about to jostle past her with her life in her cart, but Evelyn spoke, "*Excuse-moi.*"

The woman stopped as though a stone wall had suddenly been thrown up in front of her cart wheels, and she slowly looked up at the jittery, younger woman standing in the street. Evelyn reached into her bag and took out the money. She pulled a few large franc notes out of the wad in her hand and gave the rest to the woman. "Find shelter," she said. She knew the woman could find a new life, if she wished for it. It would take more than money, but it could be done. The woman grabbed the money in both hands, clearly not sure what to do next. She nodded at Evelyn, her face pale, her eyes moist, and her lips twitching. "*Pourquoi?*" she finally said, in a voice that seemed to have not been used for years. Evelyn shrugged and smiled, "Please find shelter," she repeated and then, with her heart pumping, began to walk away from the older woman, feeling less helpless. The village was another respite; prettier and not so remote. She hadn't kept much of Marty's money, but she had enough to make a decision. She headed towards the train station. She was going back to Paris. She wasn't going to be afraid anymore.

Chapter 27

EVELYN

When the train pulled into Paris, Evelyn felt a sinking sensation. She wondered if she had been wise to come back. She was angry with Marty, and as much as she knew she had to move on, she wasn't ready to make any hasty steps. The unknown was too much to wrestle with right then. She was walking inside a dream she couldn't control, and that scared her more than Frank. Frank, who could be around any corner she turned. He still lived in her head, and she needed to exorcise him. Still, she wasn't ready to make any life-altering changes. Not yet. She knew who she was, but she also still believed in what she was—what she had been made to believe—an uneducated girl who only knew the street life. Except for the few marked days she spent with Marty, she had only known the control and pain others inflicted on her. Her customers weren't harmless; they were lonely and vengeful animals. Frank was greedy and afraid. Evelyn didn't have to be a part of that cycle anymore; instead, she chose to be independent. She could carry on, choose her own customers, and work without Frank. She could be the one in control for a change.

The train ground to a halt and the people around her began to stand up and move towards the opening, and she followed them out into the daylight. She stood on the platform with her small shoulder bag swaying; she was wearing her short skirt and thin blouse; her feet ached in her high heels. She opened her compact mirror and peered at herself with scrutiny. Raccoon eyes and a smudge of lipstick drawn outside the lines; she licked her pinkie finger and gently rubbed out the offending colour. She put her compact away and walked down the platform to the exiting doors, out onto the sidewalk. The streets were filled with life, and her eyes darted around. Perhaps Frank had moved on, too. Surely, he wouldn't continue looking for her or waiting for her. The big city must be a place for her to hide—how could she stand out when she felt so small? This was Paris, and she blended in well. Her attire was bold, waiting for night. She was tall and striking. The men turned their heads slightly, and were jerked back into place by the fuming women on their arms. She exaggerated the movement in her hips as she languished down the boulevard past the yapping dogs and raised eyebrows. She didn't need Marty or Frank defining her; she was a woman who survived them both. She went into a pub and ordered a drink. "A martini," she breathed to the bartender. He didn't bat an eye as he poured a short martini glass, gin and vermouth with one olive, and slid it across the counter.

"*Merci,*" she said. The bartender nodded and moved on to the next customer, with his towel in hand. She sat on the barstool and nursed her drink. The men in the pub didn't seem to notice her; they were too tied up in their memories and regrets. She felt happily invisible in the dim light. She picked up on the little bits of French floating around her like pieces of familiar music as she finally tipped back her last drop. She was ready to pay the bartender and leave, already opening her shoulder bag, when a voice behind her told the bartender to pour her one more. She froze; she knew the voice. She half-spun around on the stool.

"Maury," she said. The man looked uncomfortable as he sat down next to her.

"A beer," he said to the bartender. He didn't say anything to her at first; he only glanced over at her.

"*Bonjour*, Yvonne," he said, finally. "Where have you been?"

"Jesus, call me Evelyn, Maury," she bristled.

"Is that what you're calling yourself now?"

"Evelyn is my name."

"I see."

"Is he looking for me?"

"No. He gave up on you."

She let out a quiet sigh. "Were you looking for me?"

"I was worried."

"I'm fine, Maury."

"Are you? Then what are you doing back here?"

"I can't come back to Paris?"

"What do you plan to do?"

"Play by my own rules."

"Ah, I see. That other guy dropped you." She sat rigid, concentrating on her drink. "No, no. You don't have to say anything. ... Frank protected you, though," he said into his beer glass, before taking a long swig.

She watched him and then laughed. "Were you there?" she retorted. "Who protected me from Frank?"

Maury was silent. He gave a head nod, as if to say "touché."

"Are you going to continue hooking?"

"Keep your voice down."

Then he laughed, "You don't exactly look like you're going to the opera."

"How did you find me?" she asked.

"I thought you might come back; I've been hanging around the train station for a few days. I didn't think you'd last out there."

The bartender gave them a look of intrigue from the other end of the counter.

"I'm on my own, Maury."

"What if he sees you?"

"He can't do anything to me now. He knows I'm not his anymore."

"I guess you're right. He still has Bonnie, and another young girl he found," Maury reasoned. "You're not so young anymore. It's just as well, I guess."

"You make me sound like a retired ballerina," Evelyn said. She tried to ignore the casual way he talked about the new girl. Who was she? How old was she? Where were her parents? What had happened to her? There were so many young girls falling through the grates. Was anyone counting?

"I wouldn't go that far—ballerinas go out with style," he answered. "You are deserting Bonnie, though. You know that, right?"

"Bonnie is a big girl. She survived before I came along. She can take care of herself." Evelyn looked at him and ran a tired hand through her hair. She knew she could become more than this, but there was still the fear of crossing into the unknown. Maury put some money on the table and dismounted his stool.

"We did what we could for you, *Evelyn*." He sounded disappointed. She wondered if it was a cover for his concern. She almost wished she could save him, too. Frank was nowhere around, and yet he seemed to have an unrelenting grip on everything that walked into his web. Frank was no longer a person; he was a mentality. Evelyn shook her head. It wouldn't matter what she said to Maury.

"Good luck with business," he said and then touched her shoulder. "I won't tell Frank."

Tell him, tell him! she thought. *Tell him that you can't keep living things in jars!* Then she was alone again, with another empty martini glass.

Night came, and like a cat, she answered. She stepped out of the alleys to her old, familiar haunts, the corners she put herself in, with her back against the wall. This was something she knew how to do. This was home. Only, the landscape had changed. In a short time, she had become a stranger. The girls were strange too. They strutted and hissed, telling her to get off their curb and find another goddamn streetlamp. She kept moving, bewildered. If she wasn't with Frank—if she wasn't with anyone—she was nobody. She moved past the bent stars that seemed trapped in the murky and polluted Seine River. Finally, she stopped by a streetlamp and stood shivering. The streets were quiet. She thought about the people who were warming each other in their beds, sleeping. After a long while, a human shadow moved along the street. At first, she couldn't tell in what direction the figure was moving. The shadow moved closer, until Evelyn was in the presence of a man in a thick overcoat and a baseball cap.

"*Bonsoir*," the man said.

"*Bonsoir*." Evelyn leaned towards him, invitingly.

"Do you have a place we can go to?"

Evelyn looked around. There was no convenient place nearby. She gave an embarrassed, school-girl laugh and shrugged with a smirk.

"No matter," he said. "It is summer, no? We have the earth." This wasn't completely foreign to her, but it wasn't her first choice either. She wished she had picked a more central spot to pick up customers and pitch her lines, but it seemed she had been run off the popular spots. She was lucky to find anyone out here, she thought.

"*Oui*," she answered, trying to sound confident.

"Those bushes," he smiled, and grabbed her arm. She didn't like his force.

"Do you want to know how much?" she asked, hoping her price might put him off. She didn't have a good vibe about him, and some signal went off in the back of her mind.

"Oh, I'm not going to pay," he said. "You are just a hooker." He wrenched her arm behind her back and tore her blouse open with his free hand. There was no one around. She tried to scream, but he kissed her to muffle her cries and bit her lip hard. She tried to kick him, but he grabbed her leg and flung her backwards, landing on top of her. The grass was wet. She felt cold and the ground was slippery, but she couldn't slide out from underneath him. He was pressing half his weight down on her shoulder as he fumbled with his pants. He had opened his overcoat while they were talking before—one less thing for him to do now. He was inside of her, grunting. When he was done, which didn't take long, he playfully bit her ear and said, "You are really lousy." She lay still. Maury's words flashed through her mind—*Frank protected you*. Her eyes began to well up from anger and defeat. They all betrayed her, every one of them, every man who walked the earth.

"Don't tell anyone," he said. "Well, you have no one to tell, do you?" She shook her head violently and was thankful he was not going to kill her. Then he was gone.

Chapter 28

EVELYN

Evelyn sat on a bus bench the next morning and, as she reached into her bag for her compact, felt her shaking hand land on something unexpected. She pulled out a small notebook and stared at it. With some trepidation, she opened the front cover to find the words: *Write your way out. Love, Bonnie.* She flipped through pages filled with her friend's handwriting. As she read the words, she felt closer to Bonnie. Here was a part of her friend that she may not have known otherwise. Bonnie's writing was disjointed, but Evelyn could tell that her thoughts came from a different place, some place that didn't include Frank. Evelyn was in that place too. This was a record of Bonnie's life before Frank, another world completely— one that was untainted, or so Evelyn thought until she read farther. She opened the notebook to a random page and, in mid-thought, began to read Bonnie's scrawled writing:

They were killing themselves and I couldn't watch. I knew I couldn't help. I tried. I'm better out here. They don't have to worry about me now, the accidental sperm that careened their lives into recklessness. I tried to help. I tried to hide Mom's bottles and kiss Dad goodnight—every night, for a long time—to talk when no one was listening. I got tired of hearing only myself. There was so much silence and resentment. Out here, well, I'm not sure what to listen for. The group at the other end of the bridge is huddling together, collecting garbage for a fire. Somebody lit a match. Maybe I'll be warmer, at least for tonight ...

The pages continued on to other fragmented entries of memory and lost days. The writing was erratic, only half-thoughts. Bonnie's life was reduced to hasty notes scrawled in the margins. Evelyn flipped through the pages, but she already knew how the story ended. At least, she thought she did. Bonnie hadn't escaped, though. She hadn't written her own way out. What more was there to know?

Evelyn read the first couple of entries and decided to pick up the thread of her friend's attempt to write herself down, and maybe create another ending. That way, maybe she could open another universe, or at least keep a conversation going with someone she missed greatly; two conversations needed to happen there. She wanted to reconnect with her friend, if only in her head. She also wanted to make the conversations with herself more real and valid. It was too lonely out there. She had some wisdom for Bonnie; she'd found a wormhole back into the world. Maybe by committing her emotional map to ink, Bonnie could one day follow. She sat on a bus bench, ignoring the buses pulling in and out. In earnest, and with a childish belief, Evelyn began to write:

DAY ONE

Yesterday when I woke up, I rolled over and faced a wall; I placed my hand on the wall and it was all I could feel. Today when I woke up, I felt the air coming through an open window. In the beginning everything seemed bleak. I began doubting all that I knew, even when I thought I knew everything.

How did I get here? How did I get to be so manipulated by men? Why I am so angry that Marty is gone—I should be glad all of the men are gone. I feel like a newborn deer on my stick legs, trying to balance—to walk forward and keep my head up. I won't lie, though. Being alone out here feels both better and worse. I suppose it's like being in space and suddenly having someone pull your helmet off. It is hard to breathe at first. Bonnie, we get conditioned to things, don't we? You can see the door, but you can't go through it. I know what that's like, only, I did go through. It felt like going through a brick wall. I had been hitting my head against it long enough, and then one brick came loose, and then another and another. I had some help, though. I wish you could find someone to help pull you out too, even if they do eventually leave you. What is that saying? People come into your life for a reason and a season. I don't know where I read that … maybe on a bookmark … Anyhow, they come to teach you something, but not to stay long. Maybe that's what you were to me—or I was to you. It was a long winter …

DAY TWO

It is not easy being out here, Bonnie. I won't sugarcoat anything. I am left to my own devices now, making decisions that are good and bad. I helped an old woman the other day. Well, in truth, she was only old in terms of hardship. It is amazing how young you and I still look … give us a few years, if we continue down these paths we will be reduced to burlap. I hope she left behind her shopping cart and walked out into the horizon, like a cowboy walking into the sun rising, not setting. We aren't over, you know. I gave her a new life, I think. Marty let me do that. At first, I was giving the money away because I didn't want to carry around so much of him. I think I set us both free in that moment. I wish you were out here with me. Imagine us getting away, finding real jobs, setting our alarm clocks for 6:00 a.m. and being normal. I want you to. I know you can, but I also somehow know that you won't. I'll carry you in my pen, in my mind, and in my sight. I'll write my heart to you. I'm tired of the men pushing us down, throwing us on our backs, and thinking we are only skin. I'm going to get out of here; take off my high heels and wear sneakers. I'm going to run. Two nights ago broke the straw. I thought I could be my own boss. I thought I could rein-vent myself by doing the same thing, putting myself out there again, on my terms. I can't. No one respects those terms unless there is a baseball bat or gun aimed at their head. I wasn't armed, and I got ploughed. I got hurt. We've had rough ones before, but there was always back up. A strong arm. Maury would kick open a door, yelling and threatening, and the guys would be throwing themselves out the window to get away from him. I didn't have Maury last night. I don't want Maury. I don't want the rough ones; I don't want any of it. I have to find something better.

DAY THREE

I was wandering today. Wandering and wondering ... Is there anything wonderful left? Is there always going to be somewhere to wander to ...? I'm moving in circles and starting to believe they are straight lines. Paris feels small now, and I know it's only because I've been moving up and down the same old stretch. I am afraid of breaking out, even as I'm being forced out. I've never gone very far—never bothered to look over the fence. I've always been forced in some direction by the hand of someone else. I thought I could confront something by coming back here ... Frank, maybe even myself, but I don't know where the journey, this life, started. Sometimes I think I'm still locked in the closet and dreaming my life, but the nice dreams never come. I never belonged to anyone, you know. If someone told me they owned me, I thought it meant love, or something close to it, or at least a place I could pretend was home. I pretended for too long, and then I started moving away from myself, and I couldn't tell the difference anymore between love, home, manipulation, and protection. I learned from you how to put on the tough act and hide behind the no-sleep eyes. We're made of scales and porcupine quills, aren't we? That is our protection. Marty tried to break through it all; I almost let him. I'm walking in circles trying to find the place where he found me so I can start moving in a different circle or direction. Maybe if I can break the cycle—rub away the part of me he touched—I'll belong to myself again.

As Evelyn stood impatiently on the sidewalk, with her hand in the air and her bare leg stretched out in a power stance, she secretly recoiled from the feeling of familiarity. Those days she used to hail cars and wait for men to take her away and soil her with their bodies and wealth. She never became wealthy in the exchange. She remembered her first night back in Paris and shuddered. Instinctively, she brought her leg in, adjusting her skirt so that it stretched a bit longer on her well-toned thighs. Evelyn held out her hand and hollered at a taxicab pulling up. She stepped into the back seat and said, "The airport, please."

Chapter 29

EVELYN

Evelyn flew the short distance from Paris to London. She was still wary of Frank and his cronies hanging around the train stations and possibly searching for her, no matter what Maury had said. Besides, she felt like flying—leaving the ground for a while. She wanted to feel suspended in space, near the clouds, where no one could snare her. Trains could derail and airplanes could lose their course of direction and plummet from the sky, but she would rather dive from the air than break loose from the tracks. If she couldn't maintain control of her life, she at least wanted to choose her own ending.

She felt the rumble of the wheels beneath her, headed down the long stretch of pavement. The sound was a refreshing change from the familiar click-clacking sound of the steel wheels of a train. She erased the sound from her memory, and the memory of seeing the endless landscape and trees passing by her window. Soon she would only see clouds, and she would feel weightless.

She looked out and saw a blue canvas ready for her imagination, anything she wanted to draw there. So, why could she only draw the past?

After a while, the wheels touched down with a jerky, uneven landing, like two giant feet reaching the earth after a long jump. Once she descended from the plane and followed the other passengers into the waiting area, she felt a strange relief that there was no one to meet her. She felt too tired and disoriented to meet anyone. However, there was one person she wanted to talk to. She headed for the payphones and fished a coin from her pocket. After plunking the thin coin into the telephone and punching the cold, raised steel buttons with a shaky finger, she listened to the familiar European beeping in the phone and finally spoke in a cautious voice, "Bonnie?"

The small voice came through the line like the crackling of a twig just before it snaps, bent and fragile.

"Ev? Ev is that you?"

Bonnie never called her Yvonne, except when Frank was around. She never let Evelyn disappear completely into Frank's creation of a woman-child, that twelve-year-old in spiked high heels that made her too tall to be twelve anymore. She remembered how Evelyn first looked like a newborn doe finding her legs and trying to resist gravity. A Bambi on ice with a painted face; the innocence was gone.

The first few times Evelyn traced the red lipstick around her small, virgin mouth, trying to draw a smile without showing her teeth, she missed the lines of her lips. She had a seductive smirk that drew the men in, but still left them out in the cold, those men who weren't interested in personalities. The girls had tried to make light of it, pretending to be these people that weren't real. They told themselves they were playing dress up, putting on a show, and playing for a one-man audience. But everything was becoming false for Evelyn, and she coped by hiding in her pretend world.

"Yeah, Bonnie ... it's me."

"Holy shit, where the hell are you?"

"I wish I could tell you."

"Okay, I know. Listen, I understand if you can't tell me where you are, but you need to be careful."

"I'm protecting you too. Frank will expect me to call you, he knows how close we are, and he can tell if you're lying. If he asks you where I am, you can tell him that you don't know without trying to lie."

"Jesus, you're right. Hey, are you alright?"

"Yeah, I think so. Yeah … yeah, don't worry about me. I'll be okay."

"You're a tough cookie. You remember that."

"Yeah, I know."

"Don't let anyone take you down the wrong track, okay? Just keep running, baby girl. Hey, did you find my book?"

"I did. I've been writing in it—you know, sort of talking to myself."

"That's good. I thought it might be useful. It didn't help me, but I thought maybe …"

"How did you know?"

"Know what?"

"That I might leave?"

"I didn't—but I hoped you wouldn't stay."

"I don't know how … I mean, I didn't do it alone."

"That doesn't matter. You still did it."

"Thanks, Sis." There was silence on the other end, a movement of lips starting without sound. "There's a whole world out here, you know."

"Yeah …" The voice was determined not to crack, but Evelyn could hear it bending, "I always liked to think of myself as your big sister, you know."

"I know. You're the closest thing I've had."

"Okay, listen, you better keep moving. Don't call unless you have to. I understand. It's too dangerous, otherwise. You just keep moving, and keep writing—you're a long way from out of the woods."

"I will." And before Evelyn could say anything else to her friend, the receiver hummed a monotonous tune in her ear. She placed the phone back in its cradle and walked outside into the bustling city of London, which didn't know her anymore.

There were double-decker buses and old-time taxicabs parked in a welcoming row just a few footsteps from the entrance, but instead, she found her way downstairs to the underground train. The platform was littered with posters and graffiti, which had given a woman in a Gucci advertisement a thin purple moustache. The woman seemed to laugh open-mouthed at herself, showing her white, oval teeth. The train came through the tunnel with bullet speed and braked in front of the waiting passengers, stopping on a dime. The doors sashayed open with an automated, cautionary message to "Mind the gap!" as people simultaneously pushed their way in and out of the train with astonishing ease. Evelyn was soon shoved into the middle of the train, packed in like a piece of live-stock. As she hung on to the pole in front of her, she smiled at the sole feeling of being lost in a sea of strangers.

The underground train pulled into Victoria Station, and Evelyn found herself cast back out onto the pavement. She proceeded to hike along the crowded sidewalks, which were wider than the streets. She reached the first hostel she'd spied, and it was called "The Birdcage." An ironic name for a place with windows she could open while she slept and doors she could exit at her own will. She mused at the name. She liked it immediately.

In the night she listened to her dorm mates softly wheeze and shift on their cots as she looked out at the sky. In London one could see fewer stars because of the buildings and chimney smoke obscuring them. There was a fire escape stairwell outside her window, and after a moment's thought, Evelyn lifted herself down from the high bunk and out of the room, stealth-like, into the night air. She climbed the iron stairs to the roof and lay on her back, scouring the stars and naming them.

She felt the cool breeze and the sweet shiver that moved through her spine and down both legs. She liked the way nothing else touched her. She thought of Marty, and in her mind, she thanked him for this. She understood now. He had walked away because he had sensed her tightening grip. In the beginning, it had stung her, but she could see the pattern of how every time she needed to be close to someone, either she or the other person would let go of hands and they would watch each other fall back into their own skin. She was falling now. She also knew that if she ever found a place to be held, she wouldn't want to leave that place, and she would forget the beauty in being let loose. Marty knew it, too. And so he had let go of her hands.

⟶◦●◦⟵

BONNIE

Bonnie still remembered the day Evelyn had arrived and the look they had exchanged when Frank brought her into the living room. Bonnie had been watching some daytime TV talk show about boyfriends with compulsions to beat up their girlfriends. She was watching it as though she were removed from it, calling the boys losers, and writing the girls off as naïve sluts. She didn't want to compare her own life too closely to what she saw on TV. It might become too real.

"What's that trash you're watching? Turn it off. I've got someone here I want to introduce you to. Bonnie, this is … this is Yvonne. I'm sure you two will become fast friends." Bonnie had turned around from the TV to look into the eyes of the young girl she had dropped off at the side of the road a few days before. Her eyes widened, but she quickly softened them with an indifferent, vacant gaze as she said, "Hey, Yvonne." She talked as though she was chewing gum, but she wasn't. Yvonne gave a half smile and said hello, which relieved Bonnie.

Frank didn't detect any awkwardness in the room. The first meeting had gone smoothly, so he adjusted his tie and left the room. He muttered something about leaving them to get to know each other and then shot a meaningful glance at Bonnie, which Evelyn didn't see. For a few long minutes, the little girl stood rooted to the spot, watching the back of her new friend's teased hair, which was pulled into an uncombed ponytail, and her lazy arm, slumped over the couch, with a rainbow of plastic hoop bracelets cascading on her tiny wrist. The TV was turned off then, but the older girl kept staring at it, examining her own image in the reflection of the grey screen. She looked much younger than she had that day in the car, more vulnerable. Maybe it was because she had been behind a steering wheel, speaking her thoughts aloud like she owned them, and not caring who was listening. Now she was silent and curled up, her legs tucked into her belly, trying to fit into the space of the cushion she was on, and to fit inside the blank TV screen.

Then Bonnie spoke to the TV screen, her eyes in the reflection directed at Evelyn. "You're a pretty good little actress, Yvonne. You didn't even flinch when you saw me."

"Neither did you."

"I don't flinch at much anymore. I am disappointed to see you, though." Bonnie smiled at her, sympathetically. "How did he find you?"

"I was waitressing in that hostel. He got me fired," Evelyn answered briefly.

"That figures," the other girl snorted, but there was no humour in her voice. She sounded tired. Then she turned around to look at the younger girl, and her eyes were sad. She shook her head, her eyes set on her.

Evelyn looked around the room. She had no bag with her; she just stood there feeling dumb in her blue dress with no nametag. There were old-fashioned light fixtures that weren't dusted, thick curtains that were drawn, even though it was a sunny afternoon, and a small mirror hung on the far wall, in which Evelyn could see the reflection of her floating head. The shag carpet was dark green and there was a musty smell in the room.

"Is this an apartment?" Evelyn asked. The other girl let out a short laugh, like exhaust, nearly choking. "Oh, boy ... yeah, sweetie, this is our fucking apartment."

"Did you tell him about me?" Evelyn suddenly asked, feeling a little braver. She wasn't sure how she should act around this girl, or what she meant about the room.

"No." Bonnie pursed her lips, thoughtfully.

"You knew he was coming?"

"I knew he was looking—I didn't know it would be you."

"Looking for what?"

"Pretty faces," Bonnie sighed. "And you've got a pretty face."

Evelyn wanted to say thank you, but wasn't sure what to think. She was uncomfortable. "My name isn't Yvonne, you know."

"I know—but it is now."

"My name is really—"

Bonnie cut her off sharply, "I don't want to know."

"What's your name?"

The other girl jerked around hard on the couch and shot her a daring look, or a warning. "Bonnie, remember?"

Evelyn was afraid to move. "I still think you might have helped him find me."

"I do what he tells me, you're right, but I never volunteer," Bonnie hissed at her, half-insulted. "I wouldn't wish for any girl to be in this place, but he needs more than just me." Then she looked at the younger girl, rooted in the carpet. "You really don't know what I'm talking about, do you?"

"I think I have a good idea."

"You ever done anything like that before?"

"Almost." Evelyn's knee visibly shuddered and her right arm twitched.

"Bad memory?"

Evelyn didn't answer; she just covered her right elbow with her left hand and stared at Bonnie.

"You're going to have to get over that. We'll sort it out."

"What's he like?" She spoke in low tones, not sure if he was standing behind a wall somewhere along the hallway, listening to them.

"Better than some, I guess." She sounded practiced, as if this was an interview she'd given a hundred times before. *"Come on, meet the boss. This life ain't so bad ..."* She was the receptionist, the hard case. "You learn the rules, you'll be okay."

"Where are we?"

"I wouldn't call it home, but try to get comfortable."

"Are we staying long?"

"Just another motel room along the road trip, sugar. We've been here for a week. It's a small town—I've done my work." She rolled her eyes and chewed on an errant, painted fingernail. "We'll be rolling out soon." Bonnie rolled herself off the couch. "I'm going to the can—have a seat, okay?" She chucked a magazine at her. "Here, read the celebrity headlines. You know this one?"

"I'll hold on to it for you," she said, rolling the magazine in her hand like a baton.

"Cool." The other girl looked at her as though she were an alien and then turned to carry herself easily down the corridor to the small, dingy room at the end.

Chapter 30

BONNIE

Bonnie grew up in the Midwest, in the state of Indiana, with her parents. She was an only child and lonely most of the time. She didn't keep many friends, and the few that came over never came back after enduring her mother's loud, half-drunken fawning. She would exclaim in her high-pitched voice, which sounded like peeling tires, "Oh, you brought your little *friend* over! Oh, isn't that niiice!" Bonnie would sink into her shoulders and turn crimson as her friends stood with arms slightly rigid, gaping at her and her mother. *Little friends* were kindergarten age. She was fourteen then. Her mother never asked why her friends didn't return. "You must have done something, sweetie." She would shrug and then toddle down the front walk with her twiggy legs, heading to the grocery store in her red stiletto heels and houndstooth mini-skirt, waving absurdly and hollering greetings at the neighbours.

Bonnie felt sorry for her father. He didn't talk much. He worked hard all day at his blue-collar job, while his wife created more debt buying her frivolous outfits and ridiculous jewellery. After work he would come through the backdoor with his lunch pail, drop it on the counter, cross the kitchen floor into the living room, and park himself in front of the TV for the evening. He shut out whatever was going on in the rest of the house—mostly his wife's nattering voice. She berated him for not cleaning up anything, for not thanking her for dinner, and for not touching her in bed. The latter was something Bonnie didn't need to hear at fourteen years old, or at any age. In response, he would turn up the volume on the television set.

Some evenings, Bonnie would quietly go into the living room and settle into a chair next to him, and he would pass her a beer, forgetting she was only fourteen, and without talking, they would watch the game—baseball, basketball, hockey—or rerun sit-coms. This went on for a few years; the two of them blocking out the noise of the hysterical woman in the back room, when she was there, shrieking about how nobody loved her and how she was going to leave; though, she never did go. Occasionally, her mother would wander into the living room and throw some light object at them ... an empty toilet roll that hadn't been replaced, for instance, or an item of lingerie he had failed to notice.

Later, Bonnie stopped keeping him company and started spending her evenings outside with a few boys at the ball field. She was the only girl who let them do things, and she liked the attention. She didn't think about the harm: she just wanted to feel good. The other girls at school must have known. Girls always knew; she could tell by the way they watched her move down the halls. She rarely brushed her hair and always wore heavy makeup. She liked the tousled, "roll-in-the-hay" look. She was being tough and adventurous, with her red-dyed, naturally blonde hair, stretchy jeans, and small tees. The girls were jealous. *Keep them guessing*, she thought. She imagined chastity belts under their skirts, and their dads who hid the keys. These girls were pure, frustrated little white flowers. They had to fight for the bees to take notice, and maybe they were afraid of the stingers.

There were three boys that she met in the ball field near her house. They didn't like to go anywhere else with her, and there was one boy who always hung back a little. He always seemed fidgety and anxious. He didn't say much. Well, none of them said much. She was seventeen and didn't care. They would kick the dirt for a while and then, one by one, try a few things on her. They didn't hurt her; it was all just touching. She grew up at the ball field, without thinking. The quieter boy kissed her the best and had a light touch. She liked him, though she never reacted differently, or at least tried not to. One night, he looked at her a bit strangely, as though a short zap had struck them both, but then it passed and he put his hands in his pockets and moved away. The next hand that touched her always seemed rougher and without forethought. At night, she dreamed of the one quiet boy, and the other two would fade like ghosts into the grass.

She wanted to isolate this boy and bring him out of his shell, and the pull he seemed to have on her scared her a little. He had a strange uncertainty or a look that made her want to shake him loose and cradle him. She didn't really know what she wanted to do with him. Maybe it was safer to know what was coming at her, upfront, like the boys who talked big and grabbed at her hungrily and awkwardly. She understood that better, somehow. This boy seemed almost apologetic when he kissed her as the other boys urged him on. Then he would turn around and go home, travelling across the ball field and not looking back. He perplexed her, and soon after, she would push the other boys away and say she was bored and wanted to go home to sleep.

"Can we come?" they would ask, elbow-jabbing each other with shallow laughs.

"No."

She would go home and pass by her dad, usually sleeping in the living room, and her mother, lying on her parents' bed, and lie down on her own bed, with the door closed, and lightly hold one breast, her hand over her shirt, full with thought.

The quiet boy didn't go to her school. He was an older kid in the neighbourhood who had dropped out, and he helped his dad fix cars. Sometimes she would walk to his house and stand on the corner of the street, hidden, and watch him move around the cars with his tools. She watched him dive under hoods and twist engine parts into place.

One afternoon he was working on an engine, and he looked over and saw her standing behind the bush on the street corner. He banged his head on the hood. She stepped out from behind the bush in alarm, but was still too timid to move any closer. Instead, he came over, wiping his hands on a towel marked with grease and vaguely rubbing the back of his skull.

"Are you alright?"

"Oh, yeah." He grinned. "It happens sometimes."

"You sometimes get surprised by girls hiding in bushes?" She was fishing.

"Only the pretty ones." He smiled, taking the bait. Then he was quiet again, looking down, not sure what to say next. His bag of wit was empty.

"I see you working on your cars with your dad sometimes," she said softly, wanting to keep him talking. She liked his voice—he wasn't macho and gruff. He was real.

"You watch me, you mean." He didn't look upset by the idea.

"Yeah, I do." She felt herself growing embarrassed, but in a pleasant way. "I wish my dad did stuff like that with me."

He didn't know what to say to that. "Well, it's the only thing we can really do together."

"Why is that?"

"We have a hard time understanding each other ... me dropping out of school and everything. I think he hopes this will give me a skill, maybe to become a mechanic or something."

"Sounds like a plan," she said matter-of-factly.

"Yeah, I think so."

"Why did you drop out?"

"I couldn't keep up with any of it. I guess I'm kind of slow or something."

"You look like you know your way around a car, though. That's something. ... Lots of guys in school wouldn't know stuff like that."

He smiled at her and shook his head. She wondered if he maybe thought she was silly, but she liked his smile so she didn't care. She even told him so, and then she realized how far out she had gone. There was no retreat now.

"I like yours, too." Then he went further, after making a decision in his head that she could see working itself out. "You know, I don't know why you let us fool around at the ball field."

"I don't know." She shrugged. "You don't have to do that stuff, either."

"Yeah, but I'm with my buddies ... and come on, I'm a guy!"

"So?"

"So it's hard when it's right in front of you ... but I don't want to think of you just being that way. I think there's more going on with you."

She wasn't sure how to respond. Suddenly, she didn't want to have this conversation on the curb outside his house.

"There is," she said simply. "I'll tell you about it sometime."

"I look forward to that."

"I'll let you get back to work."

"Okay—I won't see you at the ball field. We'll meet somewhere real, like going for coffee. Okay?"

"Okay," she said softly, making a promise with her eyes, and then she turned to walk away.

Chapter 31

BONNIE

A few days later, Bonnie waited for the quiet boy in the coffee shop. She sipped her coffee, burning her tongue. The boy came in through the far entrance, looked around the room for a moment, and set his eyes on her; a smile spreading over his face. She returned his smile shyly. She didn't want to be the tough, uncaring girl he maybe thought he knew. She wasn't really that girl at all—that girl protected her sometimes. He sat down across from her in the booth, a little anxiously. He seemed as though he might fly out of his seat, but he looked happy.

"What is your name?" she asked suddenly. He looked surprised and then grinned—that grin.

"Yeah, I guess we should start there, shouldn't we?" He seemed embarrassed. "I'm Trevor." She nodded, echoing the name in her mind. It was a safe name, somehow, and soft-sounding. It wasn't Eddie or Tony or Rocco or some other trouble-sounding name. Trevor. This was the boy who kissed her because ... She didn't know the reason … but he never tried anything else. There were times when his friends, if that is what they were, gave him the gears because he didn't try to shove his hand up her shirt.

"Bonnie," she said. How many times had they met in the field behind her school? *This meeting erases those times*, she thought.

"How is your coffee?" he asked, wanting to start in a safe place. She recognized the need for small talk, to start off slow, and appreciated it from him.

"Okay," she replied. "Still hot."

When the waitress came by, he ordered a coffee, black. They would work up to the harder questions, and he didn't want her to run away. He already sensed her resistance when he had asked her before why she let them do things to her. They were just kids, wanting to know something. He wanted to know her. Still, part of him worried that she wasn't being kind to herself. After some more small talk, he tried asking the same question again. She shrugged, pushing her coffee a little farther away and then pulling it closer to her, nearly to the edge of the table. She made the movement twice.

"It's something to do that takes my mind off other stuff," she said at last.

"What? What other stuff?" He was thinking there were lots of things she could do, instead—go to the movies, go driving … anything.

"Home." Her voice was a hard, angry whisper. She wasn't sitting in the booth with Trevor anymore. Her mind transported her back to her room, listening to her mother's drunken bickering and the loud TV surfing through channels.

"Hey," he called her back, shattering the inner walls of her house. "You okay?"

"Sure." She lifted a corner of her mouth, which felt like it weighed a tonne.

"Tell me," he said in his soft Trevor voice.

She did. She let the words fall out of one side of her mouth, and then her whole mouth, like a broken porthole on a sinking ship with the ocean busting through her. She didn't care if he didn't understand or if she wasn't making sense. She didn't cry or yell or curse. She just told him about her reality, day after day after … and when she was done, she felt exhausted and transparent. He took her hand.

Later that night, Bonnie went home alone and, as usual, went to her room without speaking to her parents. She began packing up her things. Her mother was lying on her parents' bed, snoring, with a bottle of some liquid happiness on the night table. Her dad was slumped down in his TV chair. She went over to her dad's sleeping body and lightly kissed him on the head. She knew that if she stayed, she would go mad.

"Bye, Dad." She mouthed the words in a whisper. She felt guilty not staying for him, but he never looked to her for company anymore, either. Maybe she had been a mistake, and she was the only reason he stayed in that house. Maybe if she was gone, then he would leave too. There had to be a chance. Maybe Bonnie was dreaming; maybe this was who they were and how they would stay. Maybe it had nothing to do with her.

<hr />

Bonnie hopped on a late bus heading into the city. The night stayed outside the windows like a shadow, and she was protected by the double-paned glass and aluminum siding. The bus rumbled through the dark and she watched the lights of houses and other buildings flutter by. She wondered about who was inside these houses and buildings and if they were happy. Overworked employees dreaming of sleep or happy homeowners flipping through TV land and avoiding sleep. The last bus of the day rumbled on. When she reached the downtown sector, she was one of a handful of people left on the bus. She looked at the bus driver, an old man in his sixties, as she exited and she saw his eyes. He didn't have to shake his head in disbelief or tell her to be careful—he only had to look at her. *You're a baby*, his eyes said. She knew it, too.

"Thanks," she said and turned away from him, jumping down the steps. The last jump was hard on her soles and she stumbled forward, quickly catching herself. The bus pulled away. "Hey, lady, you got a smoke?" She looked up and saw the face of a thirteen or fourteen-year-old boy. She could tell his age by his build and nervous approach—or maybe that was just a twitch. He didn't look her in the eyes. His long hair was matted and greasy. She didn't answer him right away. When he did look at her, confused by her silence, she could see his eyes were red. Was it booze, pot, or lack of sleep? "Never mind, have a nice life," he muttered, and began to move away from her, still muttering about how no one gave him fucking anything, and how he was going to die on the street with no food or cigarettes.

"No, wait. Yeah, I got one. Hold on." She reached into her jacket and pulled out a carton of Player's. "I'm trying to quit," she said.

"Good for you," he said as she pulled out her lighter and lit the end for him. "Thanks, lady. Sorry about before."

"No problem." She shrugged and lit her own cigarette. She needed it. He nodded and strolled away, suddenly looking like he had a crisp $100 bill in his back pocket. *Lady*, she mused. She began walking in the opposite direction. She passed the brightly lit signs and scantily clad women making come-ons to the men in parked cars, and being jeered at by some in return. She thought of the late night movies she used to watch—a lone man or woman roaming around downtown after dark with their cigarettes and leather jackets. She remembered thinking, *That's what it means to be grown up—that's what you do*, and she couldn't wait to get there, to be on her own and part of something bigger than the four walls of her bedroom and the limitations of her parents' house. Now there she was, only it wasn't the same. It was as though everyone responsible for her growing up had disappeared, and she was like a fish that hatched or a bird that left the nest. Only, fish went home again, and birds built new nests.

It was cold, and she didn't know where she was going. She avoided the leering looks of men lingering on the sidewalks outside the bars. Couldn't they see she was underage? Didn't they care? No. Did she care about the boys at the ball field after school? These men could see it in the way she moved, in a way she couldn't help. She moved in a way that said, *I have no parents waiting up for me; no one knows I'm here and no one cares.* Wasn't this where she wanted to be? She had willingly gone into the lion's den, the dark streets where no one knew how to sleep.

The first night, she walked until her legs couldn't bend anymore or support her sleepless weight to take another step. She had to move towards shelter and sleep—she was hungry, lost, and frozen to the bone. She chose a direction, followed it, and was led to a bridge crossing a harbour. She saw a fairly large concrete space underneath it, and as she came closer, she could see movement. People like her, or possibly not. She was too tired to worry about her protective instincts—they were people, and that was all she cared about.

She reached the bridge and moved past the small gathering of people chattering to each other, or themselves. They seemed to be recapping the day or planning their strategy for the next day, and they didn't seem to take much notice of her. She didn't have any bedding—she hadn't thought of it—only an extra pair of jeans, underwear, and a sweater in her bag. She was realizing more and more how poorly she had planned her escape. Reluctantly, she removed her jacket and formed it into a ball to place under her head, shoving her hands under her armpits for warmth. One member of the group, a woman, approached her cautiously. Everyone seemed to be afraid of each other out there. She realized that, as far as they knew, she could be the crazy one—the one who would stab them all in their sleep and take their scraps of food and money.

"Do you want a blanket?" the street woman asked. *They* were the street people to her. She didn't belong in that group. She wasn't one of them, yet.

"Do you have an extra blanket?"

"Sure."

"Thanks."

The street woman's shadow disappeared for a brief moment and then returned with an old blanket. There was a discernible hole in it, but Bonnie turned the blanket so the hole wasn't near her feet. She curled herself into a foetal position. The woman never said goodnight; she just went back to the group. Bonnie didn't know if they were a group. She didn't know the rules or dynamics there. This place seemed like a hostel without doors, a rest spot where people maybe breezed in and out, and no one really got to know anyone. Something had changed, though; something was always altered by an act of kindness. Bonnie slept on the concrete, feeling the winter wind tugging at the end of her nose. She slept soundly, though, for the first time in a long time.

The next morning was different, a new day in her strange, chosen life. No one was under the bridge when she awoke. She didn't have a watch. She sat up and the blanket fell away. The cars above shook the foundation, and all she could think of were the people in those cars going to their jobs. She suddenly wished she had a job. Then she remembered her job was to survive. She didn't have a permanent address that she could scribble on an application so that she could earn the privilege to serve coffee to strangers or sell t-shirts to tourists. She had come from having a roof over her head and now subjected herself to the dangerous streets. Why? *It was all done in an act of self-defense*, she thought. Why? There were so many teenagers who wished their parents didn't care where they were or what they did. *They're stupid. They don't know how much love they need.*

She stood up and rubbed her face. She pulled her hair into a ponytail. *You're a baby.* She rolled her head around, bent down and touched her toes. She reached her arms up and curved her spine inwards; her mouth yawned open. Bonnie left the bridge, knowing she'd be back in the evening. The morning light was blinding, and again, she didn't know where to go. She headed back the way she came, from what she could remember. She had walked in a straight line for a long time—she knew that much. She finally stopped out-side a theatre on the corner of a street she didn't recognize. She hadn't come downtown much before. She had spent most of her evenings at the ball field, escaping with the sex-crazed boys. She had one thing to hold on to—she was still a virgin, if that meant anything. Maybe it made her more of a freak. She was seventeen and a virgin; the thought made her proud and self-doubting all at once. She had been in control then, hadn't she? Or maybe they didn't want her. Maybe she had been practice for the girls they had really wanted to kiss, and a way to know what a girl's breast felt like.

Bonnie spent half of the day sitting outside the theatre with her eyes downcast, a used coffee cup in front of her as a receptacle for spare change. She already had a few dollars in her cup, but not more than a meal's worth. She pulled her sweater close around her. A woman came by and stopped in front of her. Bonnie looked up, not sure what she would meet. The woman was fashionably dressed and tall, or maybe it was only because Bonnie was sitting on the sidewalk. Bonnie was about to utter her usual, "Spare any change?" when the woman began clucking her tongue and saying, "You poor child, how did you get here?" Bonnie wanted to tell this strange woman about her parents' neglect and the boys at the ball field and her lack of encouragement, social development, and direction, but before she could say anything, the strange woman— the first person to stop and really look at her—handed her a small, thin notebook. The cover was plain. It wasn't money and it wasn't dinner, but it was a gift.

"Write your way out," the woman said simply and then carried on down the street. Bonnie held the small notebook in her hands, thinking she didn't have a pen. The woman came back. "Almost forgot," she said and provided one. She made eye contact, and then she was gone. Her stately figure fused into the crowd. Bonnie held the pen and the notebook and tucked them into her pocket. She didn't know if she could write anything or if she wanted to. This was a challenge—an assignment sent from somewhere. Bonnie knew deep within that she would write, but how did the woman know? It was another act of kindness—another voice calling. Later, she returned to the bridge before dusk, sat against the concrete wall, hesitating, and then put her pen to the first blank page in her new notebook:

DAY ONE

I have done it. I have left home—left my dad in his chair and my mother with her bottle. I couldn't stay there; I would have gone to the bottle, too. It was like living with dead people. The only time I felt alive was at the ball field, with the boys, and even then I had to step out of myself. Now it is just me. I'm glad it is almost spring, not too cold for the street. It is still cold, though, colder than being in my bed without socks on, and cold enough that I pay attention to my thoughts. I mean, really pay attention. I acknowledge being cold—not lonely or frustrated or scared—just cold and aimless. I'm not sure what I am doing out here, what I want to do, or what I can do. I can see Trevor. At least there is somebody. Otherwise, I feel there is no one outside of myself. Not even myself, at times. I haven't written myself down before; it seems I can say things here that I could never say, not even to myself. I've only been out here one night, with a group of young people down here under the bridge. They are lost, too. No one seems to speak out here. Maybe they're afraid of their words, speaking of a past life or hopeful dream. There seems to be no future and no hope here, nothing except the past. Funny how yesterday keeps creeping in; I can't seem to escape it. At home, why did everything have to be that way? What were their stories— Mom and Dad, I mean? What were their stories about each other, or even before each other? I remember old photos with me in them, and some taken of only them; they must have cared at some point. They must have held each other long enough to imagine having me, to want to bring me into their lives. Or maybe they didn't. Maybe I was a loose cannon sperm. I can feel the warmth oozing out of my fingers and every hair on my arms.

They have booze over there, those incoherent bridge sleepers. I wonder if they will share, or if I should ask. I don't want to get stuck out here. I couldn't stay home, I just couldn't. I wasn't abused, not in a physical way, but I was dying. My bed was warm, but the imbalance of silence and volume was head-splitting. They were killing themselves and I couldn't watch. I knew I couldn't help. I tried. I'm better out here. They don't have to worry about me now, the accidental sperm that careened their lives into recklessness. I tried to help. I tried to hide Mom's bottles and kiss Dad goodnight—every night, for a long time—to talk when no one was listening. I got tired of hearing only myself. There was so much silence and resentment. Out here, well, I'm not sure what to listen for. The group at the other end of the bridge is huddling together, collecting garbage for a fire. Somebody lit a match. Maybe I'll be warmer, at least for tonight. A strange woman gave me this book today. Funny, she came just when I was starting to feel tired. I miss my books. I've never kept a diary. Somehow, it seemed counter-productive to write down negative thoughts about one day to the next. I was always afraid a diary might kill me.

It is cold out here—no one looks you in the eye. They veer around me like I'm a car stranded in the middle of the road, and they can't be bothered to stop. I'm not looking for anyone's help, though. Still, I can't help noticing how we are all moving around as though we're inside our own invisible barriers. I guess mine is just as thick and tall as anyone else's. After only one day, I'm noticing these things. I was so cold on the street, I couldn't think. And it wasn't just the weather. Maybe I was thinking too much—I just couldn't grasp hold of my thoughts. I feel like I'm alone in my room, only lonelier. I remember reading Emily Dickinson's poetry when I went to class. I sometimes wondered about those long dashes she used. It seemed like she was skipping over what she really wanted to say, or hesitating. They were like long and short breaths in her thoughts, where she was waiting for something real to happen, waiting for something to finally happen that she didn't have to conjure in her mind. I remember the teacher telling us about how she never left her room. She created a whole world, a whole romance in her mind, just watching life happen outside her window. I recall a stanza of her verse:

"I'm nobody! Who are you?
Are you nobody, too?
Then there's a pair of us—don't tell!

They'd banish us, you know."

Emily has stayed with me. In a lost language and from days gone, she knows what is current and constant. Although I can't understand all of it, there is so much mystery and possible misery to someone who covers herself away from the eyes of the world, hiding her words in a drawer in her room. She may have never been touched by a man ... but she could write as if she knew. She could conjure love out of thin air—her imaginary lovers. I might envy Emily ...

At least my life was familiar and I could choose who and where I wanted to be. I could lie on my bed, alone, in my warm room. I still can, I guess, but that room exists in my head now. Sitting by the buildings today, I could see the buses approaching out of the corner of my eye. I thought, I can jump on that bus—spend my day's earnings and travel across the city. I didn't think I could go home. I can't really do that; there is something keeping me away from there. My home, my parents' house—it is the thickest, tallest boundary. For a while, I watched the clock on the tower across the way instead and started to recognize when each bus would come. I felt like I knew something the waiting passengers didn't. I mean, sure, they had their bus schedules, but did they really know the sequence of the buses? The way they each drive their circles around town and loop around again? Or how many times the same bus came around that right corner in the afternoon? I'll go back tomorrow and see if I see the same people. Maybe I'll count how many of them I recognize and make up stories about them. Maybe they'll see me and recognize me, too—make up their own stories ...

DAY 6

One of the street women came over to talk to me yesterday. At first, she was asking for a cigarette. I didn't have one to give her, and if I had, I would have been smoking the hell out of it. I think it was an excuse for her to say something to me—it usually is. Not surprising, I've been huddled in the corner here watching them for a week. She told me I didn't look street smart. I took offense to that, like she was telling me I was soft or something. There was something in her eyes, though—something curious and full of concern. Christ, she's my age, probably. I'd say she looked like my mother, but my mother would never look at me that way. My mother wouldn't really look at me at all. I asked her what her story is, you know—how long she's been on the street, how she got here and met the others (well, I guess meeting other street people isn't too difficult). She didn't look like the street type either, except that she did, because she was so thin and dirty. She doesn't seem to be a user, though. I'm glad of that, for her sake. I don't plan to stay out here, and I don't wish for anyone else to either. This is just a transition for me. I told her that and she laughed at me. I felt like punching her. Then she started to tell me stories about her foster parents and asshole boyfriends, and how it just wasn't worth the bullshit.

WEEK TWO

There is a cold isolation in the streets—something vibrating in the bone, like a frozen toe in warm water. I've been watching the people at the same bus stop. There is a girl who serves coffee, a banker, a hippie guy, an old lady, and a student. The old lady tells the student about her day, while he's trying to read Hemingway, and the hippie is always trying to pick up the coffee girl, and the banker hangs around with his briefcase, looking like he needs to be meeting someone and is just waiting to get there. He doesn't have time for the bus stop people. The coffee girl never says more than two or three words to the hippie, while clutching her coat and rubbing her nose. The hippie doesn't seem to notice that he's going on too much about the traffic fumes and how everyone should live in a commune and embrace the colour green. The old lady continues to ask the student what time it is, because she's counting the minutes, and the student hasn't turned a page in five minutes because her banter departs from real time, and he is suddenly forced to go traveling back with the old lady twenty, forty, even sixty years. Then the bus comes and they all pile in and drive away to ... wherever they go next. I want to be each of them. I want to be the coffee girl, tired from her shift; the hippie, just pretending not to care or showing I care so much by wearing tie-dyed, environmentally-friendly clothing and conserving water because I think it makes a statement about the world I have to live in: the student with his books—opening other worlds—the old lady wanting to engage in the youth and bustle of the world she knows is slipping away too fast. I even want to be the banker, believing in the movement of people's fortune and dreams. I'm almost ready to get on that bus, too. ...

... I have become the person I would have never ventured to talk to. I am becoming too much a part of this concrete—the streets, the buildings, and the bus stop. In each passing day, I am given just enough to buy a sandwich. Maybe I've been doing something wrong. I'm not earning a handout, I know that much, and there's too many of us out here. It's crowded. It's complicated. I can't breathe. I'll stop breathing if I stay. I watch the group of street people at the bridge—watch them get thinner, duller, and angrier. Their souls are dying before they do. The only passion they fuel is anger. They smash their empty bottles of alcohol on the ground as if they are sending a message: This is all we have because this is all that you give us. I don't buy it. I don't believe in blame. I had to see this for myself, I guess. The woman who gave me the blanket on my first night is losing the light behind her eyes, the small flicker I used to see. She told me to go home. I want to tell her the same thing, but I have a sense that whatever home she came from no longer exists. She looks as though she never had an umbilical cord attached to her, almost as if she materialized out of the concrete dust. I don't want to lose my soul ...

"He ate and drank the precious words,
His spirit grew robust;
He knew no more that he was poor,
Nor that his frame was dust.
He danced along the dingy days,
And this bequest of wings
Was but a book. What liberty
A loosened spirit brings!"

Chapter 32

BONNIE

"You can crash at my house if you like, with me and my, um, dad," Trevor offered. Bonnie had phoned him and asked him to meet her at the bus stop, and he did. He had sounded concerned on the phone, and part of her liked it. She wasn't an ice float after all. Now they were seated comfortably in the same coffee shop. Bonnie didn't take the warm mug between her hands for granted. He watched as she smelled the coffee long before she tasted it and mused. What had happened to her? In the beginning, she thought she could run away from everything, including herself. She knew better now.

"I'm not being beaten at home." Bonnie assumed her old, defensive tone.

"No, ... maybe not, but you're not being taken care of, either.

"I can take care of myself."

"Sure, I know, hanging out with idiot teenage boys."

She narrowed her left eye as though she were looking at him through the target on a rifle. He put up his hands in mock surrender.

"Okay, but am I lying?"

"So, what's wrong with you, then? Why were you out there with me? Were you trying to look cool or something?"

"Like I said, I'm a teenage guy. I have no other excuse."

"... And no willpower or responsibility either."

"If all I wanted from you was a cheap feel, would I be hanging around for a cup of coffee and asking you to stay at my house?"

"Strategy ... a wolf in sheep's clothing ... not to mention you'd have better access to me across the hall from you."

"I sleep in the basement and my dad sleeps with a gun under his pillow."

She was running out of quick banter and weak excuses. She looked at him, intently, and then looked down at her hands on the table, holding the off-white coffee mug with the stain around the rim.

"What is your dad like?" she asked.

"Pretty quiet, but he'll talk to you, and he does more than just zone into the TV every night. He's usually out or working on one of his cars in the garage."

"Do you really think he wouldn't mind?"

Trevor grinned. Bonnie didn't grin back.

That night she walked in the dark to Trevor's street with him. She only had her bag with her, the one she packed to leave home. He didn't say anything when they reached his house, just took her into his arms and stroked her head.

"Come home," he said, finally.

"I don't have one." she said. He took her bag and led her into the kitchen. His dad sat at the table smoking a cigarette, and he eyed her closely. He appeared to be in his forties.

"Trev tells me you've been having trouble at home," he said indifferently, but not unkindly. She didn't bother to tell him, too, that she didn't have a home anymore.

"Do you mind if I stay for a while, sir?" she asked.

"Sir?" he looked surprised. "No, I don't mind. You can have the spare room in the back."

"Thank you." She teetered in her shoes and then moved slowly through the kitchen to her new, temporary space. He didn't seem like a man who wanted to ask her too many questions and engage in unnecessary conversation. Besides, it was late. She wasn't far from her parents' house, but they probably hadn't bothered to look for her yet. They wouldn't have known anyone to call, and her mother probably had spent the days blaming her father, and her father would have done nothing. She hoped he thought of her, but she didn't want him to worry. She hoped he would think, *She's broken free*. Maybe even smile about it.

She thought she was free, too. She didn't try going back to class. What was the point? She was only a few months away from graduation—what more did they need to tell her? She only had her final exams to look forward to, and she would likely fail them anyhow, because she hadn't been attending her classes for most of the year. Trevor had told her that he was applying for a job as a mechanic in the next town. Bonnie dreamed of waitressing and serving coffee or selling t-shirts. She thought of her new life and how she would be safe with Trevor. Maybe they could make a home somewhere, someday.

She had been staying with him and his dad for a month and, although his dad didn't say much, she felt his eyes on her from time to time. His behaviour made her nervous, and she couldn't wait to leave with Trevor. Bonnie didn't want to make a big deal of it either, at the risk of being thrown out. Instead, she decided to take it as a compliment and forced herself to give his dad an easy smile and simply bounce out of the room when she felt him looking at her in an unsavory way. It seemed she was always trying to escape.

One night, Bonnie slept fitfully and then heard some rustling at the door to her room. A sliver of light entered from the hallway and was immediately blocked by a large shadow. She felt the weight on top of her and wanted to scream, but a large, meaty hand covered her mouth.

"I won't hurt you," a deep voice said. Bonnie kicked him hard with her small, sharp knee and leaped out of bed, yelling for Trevor. She heard the banging of feet against the basement stairs, and Trevor was in the room a moment later. He was stripped to his boxers, and his slim, smooth chest was heaving noticeably.

"What—?" he began.

Bonnie ran to the other room and came back with the infamous gun from under the older man's pillow, shaking it in his direction.

"She's just a little whore," his dad said to the younger man, and grinned at her from the bed. "You told me so yourself!"

"I'm not!" She was in tears.

"Sure you are," the older man spat out.

"I'm not that girl anymore!" she yelled at him, and then fired a shot into the bed.

The blanket bled, the older man screamed in pain, and Bonnie dropped the gun.

"Nice work bringing her here for me. We'll train her," he seethed in a suddenly British accent, wincing at his bloody leg. "That was a hell of a cover, Maury—oops, I mean, Trevor."

"Goddammit, Frank," the boy replied, sounding tired and annoyed. "I already told you she would put out. She's had a rough time of it. You didn't even give me a chance to get her back on track. Why couldn't you just wait?"

"What? Trevor, what the hell is going on? What are you talking about?" Bonnie demanded. Maury approached her slowly, sighed deeply, and then grabbed her by the hair and smacked her head against the wall.

◆◆◆

When the police came to inquire about the gunshot, after receiving a call from a neighbour, Bonnie was locked in the back room, tied up, and gagged. She had come around from the blow to her head, and listened in horror as Frank told the policeman, "It was a careless accident that happened while cleaning the gun. I thought the safety lock was on."

"Grazed the skin," they said. She didn't know what it all meant. She only knew that she would never go home.

Chapter 33

EVELYN

Since the time Frank had taken Evelyn away from her Midwestern existence when she was a child, she had lived in New York, London, and Paris. Each city had opened her eyes to new possibilities, even if they weren't hers to take. She loved the people and the throbbing heartbeat of the daytime rush and sleepless nightlife. She considered London to be home, now, as she'd been there the longest, working in the Piccadilly Circus district, where the tourists convened. It was a hot spot. In New York, she had learned to answer to her name, Yvonne, and forget Evelyn, and in London she learned to sharpen her skills and senses on the street.

Essentially, she had grown up in London, and she knew the downtown streets well. She felt stronger being back, and not as though she was returning to the scene of some crime. She had returned to London on her own terms and changed enough since the time she left that she didn't have to hide in the large city. After arriving in London, she had her hair cut in a shoulder length bob and bought a black pant suit. Her makeup was soft. She looked like a professional, and no one needed to know what kind of a professional. She smiled to herself, feeling fresh and ready to take on a new life.

She had been living back in London for two months, renting a flat with a controlled entrance, near Kensington Park. Soon after she had arrived, she also started brainstorming how to emerge back into normal society and make an honest living. She tried to think of what she enjoyed and would be good at doing, and she remembered how much time she had spent on her appearance for work, for Frank, and to simply feel good. She had developed an array of escapisms, and much of it came through changing the way she looked. Frank had insisted that both Bonnie and Yvonne play different roles, portray themselves differently for various customers, and that they change their appearance for each new location where they worked.

At the age of twelve, when Frank had found her, Evelyn had been a novice and was nervous about what shade of blue to wear or how much to sweep across her eyelids. Bonnie showed her the different colours and demonstrated which ones would work, which ones wouldn't, the reasons why, and how much to put on for a certain customer. Bonnie knew everything, and over the years she taught Evelyn.

Late at night, or in the early dawn, she would show Evelyn tricks to make herself look older and more sophisticated, such as French twists and braids, and how to tease her hair up without too much back combing and with a few squirts of hairspray. That way, she wouldn't just attract the young first-timers looking for a laugh. She would attract the high rollers and keep herself out of the hot pan. During those hours, she and Bonnie would also talk.

There were few opportunities to be personal, to remember themselves and forget where they were, and not have Frank there to remind them. They talked about their likes and dislikes, their dreams, even their pasts and families, from what they knew or could remember. Bonnie had said she wanted to be a model, and Evelyn told her she would be great.

Evelyn bought a newspaper and opened it to the employment section. She thought about how easy it was now to scan the words, not separate letters, and put them together in a line that made sense to her. Bonnie had taught her how to read. Late at night, they would stay up comforting each other about their customers, and Bonnie would pull out comic books and Cosmo magazines. The comic books varied from Archie to Marvel superheroes, and Evelyn became hooked on the stories. Some of the articles in the adult magazines were so risqué, they would both roll on the mattress in fits of laughter, but Evelyn was learning to read. It took months, and Frank never knew. Evelyn pretended for a long time that she was the same naïve girl he had found in the diner, until one day when she was with him and chose a direction on the street based on a sign she read.

"How do you know where to go?" he had asked. Evelyn stopped for a moment, feeling trapped. Then she shrugged and told him Bonnie had taken her that way before and she was good at remembering her surroundings. He didn't say anything else.

Now she looked at the newspaper, with no one peering over her shoulder, and scanned the columns up and down with a filed and varnished fingernail. The world was open to her. She was no longer struggling to identify colours for marketed items in stores or to remember where certain trees and buildings were to navigate her way. She wasn't sure where she wanted to go, but she knew how she could find out. She had information. She could listen with her eyes and draw letters in her mind. The world made sense. She slowly circled an advertisement for a hairdresser position in a barber shop in Greenwich. Antoine's.

Chapter 34

EVELYN

Evelyn found Antoine's barber shop and felt encouraged by the small, welcoming *ding* that signaled her arrival as she crossed the threshold. She held a single piece of paper, her cover letter. The barber shop was small, so Antoine was already near the door when she entered.

He saw she was holding a piece of paper and assumed she was an applicant. Her hair was cut in a neat, shiny bob, and her attire was both appealing and demure. She wore a white blouse that covered her generous bosom well, and a slimming, grey, knee-length skirt. Her black patent dress shoes were heeled, but not treacherously high. She also met him with confidence and a firm, straight-look-in-the-eye handshake. He liked her immediately, and he noticed a few of his customers glanced over approvingly.

She felt their eyes on her, as well, but with a mixture of appreciation and open appraisal. After all, they were still men. She had learned from Marty that there were two kinds of men: those who knew how to restrain themselves and those who took everything without asking.

Evelyn began her new job the same week and quickly found favour with the customers, remembering their names and the way they preferred their hair cut. She was also extra flirtatious with the men who had little hair to groom, and careful about teasing the men who were very particular about the way she groomed their thick, ample locks. Sometimes, she had to bite the inside of her cheek when these men acted too much like women. Evelyn didn't fuss so much about the placement of her own hair, but she was sympathetic and made sure they were each happy with their cuts, styling, and occasional dye jobs.

Bonnie had dyed Evelyn's hair numerous times, and she paid close attention until she was able to attempt dying her own hair. In every sense, Bonnie had been her means of survival, even now, and she hoped that she might break free and begin her own life, as well. She imagined Bonnie strutting down model runways and smiled sadly.

After a few months of working for Antoine, she decided to enroll in a beauty college and take classes in the evenings. Antoine had encouraged her decision, as he noticed the risks she took in the barber shop and the suggestions she would give the men. He was not running a fashion salon, but he was aware of how much the men enjoyed the change. She wasn't pushy, either. She would make small, simple suggestions, and the men would often agree to let her try something new on their next visit. Even though the changes weren't extreme, they made a difference, and his customers commented on how their wives or girlfriends liked their new styles. Once she began taking her classes, Evelyn nervously attempted new tricks, with the consent of her customers, and she always managed brilliantly. She began putting out hair magazines in the shop and suggesting new products to Antoine, even though he mostly declined and only allowed her to order a supply of new salon shampoo.

Evelyn was swamped with regulars, and Antoine was trying to hold on to the odd loyal customer for himself, usually the older men who didn't go for the modern cuts and dye jobs. He wasn't competitive or upset, but he recognized her talent and wanted her to develop her interest and skill; perhaps she would eventually open her own beauty salon, and as much as he would hate to lose her, he respected her and was happy to see her grow in her profession.

Still, when the men were gone and she was sweeping the hair away from the chair of the last customer, she often looked sad.

"Are you alright, dear?" he asked one night. At first she was startled by the question, but then shrugged.

"Yeah, just a little tired." She didn't want to burden Antoine after he had been so decent to her. She didn't want him to know about the person that still lingered inside her. She didn't want that person to exist anymore, and she was glad to feel her fading away.

"You have been working hard and you are doing good work. I know it is a lot for you to be studying too."

She smiled at that.

"Still, you look unhappy. Sometimes when you think no one is watching or when you don't have to look happy for a customer. I've noticed it. ... If there is anything I can do..."

"Thank you, Antoine. I have been making big changes lately; I guess it is all catching up with me. I am happy."

He looked unconvinced, but shrugged. "Okay," he said simply, giving her a knowing wink, and then walked into the backroom.

MARTIN

Martin had embarked on a train heading for Germany and had been residing in Lüneburg for three months. The summer was beginning to fade, and he enjoyed his time strolling through the town square, watching the ducks swim in the central pond and catching fragments of conversations between locals seated at the outside café tables. The narrow cobble streets served as small passages between the standard yellow-painted buildings. He often took a seat at the outdoor tables and was inclined to sketch his new surroundings— the people, the streets, and the quiet fascination he held with the pigeons, to which people threw their crumbs. These birds never flew, at least not very far, and he thought about these winged creatures that were still bound to the company of humans, in spite of having the means to be elsewhere. There was an incentive to stay, mainly the food and climate. They were not beautiful birds ... not like the lone eagle that one could find in scenic areas, seated majestically on the highest branches of the evergreens on the mountain peaks in the British Columbian wilderness. The pigeon was a dull, homely, awkward creature with an agreeably bobbing head and seemed most secure in groups. Martin drew them in the square, admiring their unity, persistence, and peculiar cooing to one another as the crumbs and birdseed sprayed over them like soft rain.

One overcast afternoon while Martin was absorbed in his sketchbook in the town square, after noticing a few sparrow-sized birds taking flight from the weeping willow situated on the other side of the small pond, a young man approached him. Martin's grasp of the German language was still shaky, but it seemed the man was more genuinely interested in his drawing. He motioned to request having a look at the sketch, and Martin allowed him to. The man looked at the canvas, then across at the sparrows circling around the willow tree, and then spoke in English.

"Yes, I noticed them too. Perhaps they fly where weather is warmer?"

"Perhaps." Martin smiled. He was relaxed there. The locals were cordial and selective in their conversation, and Martin didn't feel imposed upon as a foreigner.

"You like drawing?"

"Yes, I think so," Martin replied. His answer was slightly reluctant, only because he did not take his sketches seriously.

"Would you like to come to see drawings?"

"Where?"

"I have … uh … companions. They draw and discuss things. We meet at a pub not far from here. Would you like to join us?"

"Certainly," he answered. "Tonight?"

"We can go now … it is afternoon. A good time for beer."

Martin had seen men drinking beer from vendors on the sidewalk at eight o'clock in the morning. There was no bad time to drink beer in Germany, but he didn't argue. Martin did not want to embarrass or offend his new friend. He put his sketchbook away in his knapsack, careful not to bend the corners, left a handsome tip on the café table, and followed the young man up the street. He looked behind him briefly and saw a few clouds advancing towards them. The sky was turning murky and his companion fell into Martin's quickened step as they trotted over the uneven road.

"In here," his companion said in a wheezy, excitable voice. They tumbled into the tavern, and as they were hanging up their jackets near the door, they saw the pouring rain through the window. The two men smiled at each other with exhilaration, as though they had just outrun and outsmarted a wild beast.

"The weather sometimes rushes in, doesn't it?" Martin commented.

The man smiled again and extended a hand to him, after shaking off his jacket. "Johann," he said.

"Martin."

Johann turned to the bar and ordered one bottle of blackcurrant wine, in German. "This wine is made in the North. It is one of the best I have tasted." He winked at Martin.

"North of where?" Martin asked.

"North. The Baltic states. It gets very cold up there, but the summers are wonderful," he explained. "Lots of sunshine for picking." The wine bottle came across the counter, and Johann grabbed the neck as a hunter might victoriously pick up his foul after the kill, lovingly and respectively, but still with conviction. He cradled the bottom in his other palm and presented the label to Martin, grinning. "We will celebrate this happy coincidence of being chased in by the rain."

They moved farther into the tavern, and Martin quickly took in his surroundings. The interior was rough. The walls were made of untreated wood, and there were creaking floorboards. There was an authenticity there, a baseness that left room for creativity and new ideas. There was room for thought that didn't get absorbed or lost in the ambience—simple, but not bare. Martin liked it.

The only décor on the walls was paintings of women, scantily dressed or nude, which were appropriate for the solitary men who came to drink their lonely beers. The tavern was dimly lit by the six lamps hanging in measured increments along the ceiling rafters, swinging on thin twine. The tavern was narrow with a long corridor laid out between the six large, wooden tables, each light hovering above like a mini satellite. If there had been one topic for discussion that involved the entire room, the speakers could have been split into two sides to bicker at each other, with this small corridor of a no man's land existing between them.

The tavern was called Steins. The waitresses wore the traditional bar wench dresses, and they deliberately leaned over the men when they served the beer, hoping for large tips from their drunken patrons. The younger men noticed, hooting and hollering and trying to make small talk with them. The older men wanted to care, but instead, looked pitifully at their servers; their urges gone with the drink and hopeless worrying about their angry wives at home. What good was it to notice when nothing could be done? The tavern itself had a sweet hay smell, as though it had once been a barn or blacksmith shop and the horses still haunted the chambers. It wasn't unpleasant; instead, it was soothing. This place was real and so were the people inside.

"Here are my friends," said Johann. He motioned to a table where five men were seated holding their stein mugs, freshly filled from a centerpiece pitcher of beer.

"Johann!" one of the men piped up, half-tanked. "Where have you been? Come sit! Who is your friend?"

Johann smiled broadly and began the introductions: Gunther, Tobias, Heinrich, Eugene, and Adolf. Martin stopped at the last introduction, thinking, *poor sod*, and wondering who in their right mind in postwar times would name their child after one of the most sadistic, tyrannical dictators in history. It only took the horrible doings of one person to ruin their name for everyone else who came after them. Every time Adolf's name was mentioned, the rest of the table flew up their right arms and yelled, "Hail, Adolf!" and laughed.

"Stop it!" Adolf protested, narrowing his eyes at his friends. His cheeks flushed. Johann patted Adolf on the back good-naturedly. Adolf then extended his hand to Martin, and Martin shook it.

"Martin. You can call me Marty."

"Welcome," Adolf said.

"Welcome, Marty!" the other men chimed in. Martin took a seat at the table and made a mental note, changing their names to his liking: *Gary, Toby, Henry, Gene, Aldo, and John.*

Tobias, who was seated in the corner, asked Martin directly what his ideas were on the good and evil aspects of mankind. It seemed to be a discussion they were deeply in before Johann and Martin had arrived. Martin looked at Tobias silently, and then at the other men who had ceased their side arguments to listen to a new mind, and he thought for a moment. Then he parted his lips, "I'm not sure there is really a balance between good and evil in the human spirit. We all have some good and some evil in us, whether our evil deeds are intentional or if we are even conscious of them. I'm not sure how we measure how evil or good a person is. I know I have done evil things, things that could be called evil on some level. I have done these things to myself, as well as to others. I have never murdered anyone. I have never even really broken the law. Unless ... does being an illegal alien in another country count as a felony? If so, then I am guilty.

"I have lived in complete poverty. I thought money was evil; then

I began to realize the evil I was doing to myself by allowing myself to suffer without the basic comforts of human wealth and necessity. So, with unexplainable fortune and time, I have made my way back to the everyday world that many of us are lucky enough to take for granted. However, I have hurt someone. I know I have. I cannot give you the details, for many reasons, mostly because I have only just met you. Perhaps in time, but I can tell you it has been a journey and a struggle. A deep struggle ..." He trailed off. "But, here, I am only using myself as an answer to your question. I believe good and evil is a struggle. We all have evil thoughts and sometimes commit mildly evil doings with our actions or words, or in the way we neglect to use actions and words. It is all the same. If we can strive to balance out or even overcome our evil thoughts and deeds with a goodness of heart, then we cannot be tried as evil beings."

The table was silent for a moment. Then Johann spoke, "A good answer."

Soon after, the men continued to debate the existence of men's souls—whether it was merely a brain chemical or an image of one's self that each person embodied. Martin recalled a man on the street who once told him that if he were to see his own soul, he would not recognize it. There was also a myth about witnessing your dead grandmother's ghost wearing the dress she was buried in and that it was a premonition of your own death. Instead, the men argued that the soul was a state of mind; not imaginary, but not solid. It was a debate of mind over matter. Gunther quoted Descartes' famous philosophy: "I think, therefore I am." He held steadfast. He called himself a realist and had no notion of haunting his house after he passed away.

"I will be gone," he said simply. "Gone and happy." He raised his mug in resolution.

Adolf argued that the mind controlled all action—what people do and who they are. Without the mind, there was no reason.

"But you are an artist," Johann countered.

"Your point?" asked Adolf.

"Are you saying that if you were in an accident that affected your brain, you could no longer draw?"

"Possibly, or I would draw quite differently."

"My argument is that you would have an even greater need to express yourself. Even if your brain didn't allow you to draw, would everything else inside you deny your need for drawing?"

"I don't want to think of such a hell," Adolf replied. No argument had been won, and it was clear that the question was still dubious.

"The mind stores experiences—and many of us are subject to the same experiences. We experience work, industry, marketing, politics, food, war, and life; the soul is more of an internal reflex or a pressure point. It is something more individual," said Heinrich.

"Funny how you listed life," Gunther muttered. "I think we react to these experiences through reason of the mind and form opinions."

"I believe your soul is who you are. We cope with these things through the soul, or at least try to. Your mind simply has no choice but to go along with it," Heinrich said quietly.

"So, then, how is it that when I worry, my gut hurts? My physical wellness is affected by the internal workings of my mind?" asked Adolf.

"Your mind can also work against you," said Martin.

The bottle of wine was emptying fast between Martin and Johann, as the other men gulped their beers in meditative thought. Martin eventually stood up from the table in an unbalanced fashion and muttered something about the loo. Johann pointed a vague, unsteady finger towards the back of the tavern.

"To your left," he said and turned back to the discussion the men were now having about whether Eve was really a temptress or if the whole Garden of Eden scene was a set-up created by the all-knowing God. In other words, whether evil was something innate or learned. The argument faded in Martin's ears as he stumbled towards the washroom door. These men were philosophers.

He was alarmed when he opened the door to find a middle-aged woman sitting just a fraction clear of the door's swinging radius.

She had a tray on her lap, and without looking up, she spoke in a quiet but firm voice, asking for a payment of one mark. Martin swore under his breath and began fumbling in his pockets, and during this pause, the woman cast her eyes upwards. They were grey and tired. You could have seen light there once. The shape of her eyes and the expression in them struck Martin. He quickly tossed his mark onto the tray. She never uttered a thank you. How do you thank someone for paying you to relieve himself?

Martin moved into one of the stalls near the far wall. When he came out to wash his hands, the woman had left her seat and was idly pushing a mop around the floor and around his feet. She didn't seem to take notice of him still being there. She was mechanical and silent, and it didn't seem appropriate to speak to her. Besides, she probably spoke very little English. He got a better look at her now. The growing wrinkles around her mouth and eyes. She couldn't be more than fifty, as her hair was still dark with thin streaks of grey. Yet she looked like an old woman. There was a familiarity about her, in the sharpness of her nose and the thin line of her mouth. She wore no rouge. But most of all, her grey eyes seemed to want so badly to tell her story. They spoke for themselves.

Martin left the washroom, taking one last brief look at the bent body of the washroom attendant, feeling haunted, and returned to the table where two of the men were arguing and spilling their beers and the others were laughing uproariously. He didn't say anything. He sat down with a vacant expression and swivelled the empty wine glass between his fingers, peering into the bottom as though trying to determine the colour of the table through the stem.

The men took this as a sign of him being deep in thought, whatever the thoughts were, and didn't inquire. They were beginning to gather a sense of Martin already. He would speak again when he was ready.

Chapter 35

MARTIN

After the last swig of wine was swallowed, the novice group departed with an oath to meet in the tavern the following week to continue their philosophical ramblings. Martin left Johann at a divergence in the street and meandered along a curvy line, back to his humble quarters. His landlady never heard him come in, as he was careful not to muse aloud in the stairwell or fall over the railing as he climbed to the second landing. A soft turn of his key in the lock and he was inside. He tugged his arms through the sleeves of his overcoat and successfully mounted the garment on a lone hanger swinging in the closet. His bed was a small mattress on the floor, positioned just below the window, where he could look out at the stars. He lay down near the half-open window and searched for the constellations he knew best. None were in view, except for a collection of stars that were placed too haphazardly to make any sense of them. In his mind, he tried to connect the dots, but they all led back to the same place, somewhere in the middle. He reached into his knapsack and took out a small notebook that he had bought at the train station to record his travels in and wrote:

> *The moon is a porthole*
> *with God's eye against the glass.*
> *We create the stars, looking back,*
> *a way of believing in the beyond.*
> *We, a petri dish, an ecosystem*
> *of wanderers and worriers,*
> *swish through the universe*
> *on those black seas.*

The stars soon swirled together like the last drops of wine had done in his long-stemmed, kaleidoscope glass. In the eye of the swirl, he had seen Joe on the street corner with his umbrella, the scornful eyes of the passersby, the mocked image of himself in those magnificent mirrors at the opera house, the cleaning woman in the washroom who, with one glance, had unknowingly jarred him into being again. It was the same look he had seen in the eyes of the young man on the street corner in London, the one who gave him everything he didn't want and more than he could ask for. And he saw Evelyn still lying in her dreams on the hotel bed ... always Evelyn.

Chapter 36

MARTIN

Martin continued to frequent the tavern with his newfound companions every week. In many ways, it had become a chapel for him. Within those walls, the seven men dispelled their boundaries of thought. The table bore more than just the weight of their beer and wine glasses; instead, the wood seemed to bend and splinter with the weight of questions debated for centuries. These men were seekers of truth, not pioneers, and often they became caught in the endless cycles of history and human nature, which proved to be a sticky web. Martin had seen no drawings from these men, except for Adolf's sketches, but it didn't matter. He was more interested in their ideas. They were all artists, nonetheless.

On one night, his third visit, Martin's mind wandered into the deliberation of Plato's metaphor of the cave. He had heard the men speak about the idea of the false shadows on the wall, which the unenlightened held to be true images of the world. There was the notion of leaders and followers, and how, often, the self-proclaimed leaders, who turned away from the shadows and saw the true light leading them beyond the entrance of the cave and out into the world, would be shunned by those who refused to believe and accept a new reality. And then there was the question of which reality was the truth, and if there was a mortal danger in retreating from the cave, just as there was a mortal danger in the first couple's curiosity for what dwelt beyond the walls of Eden. Was it better to live by the convictions of "what we don't know can't hurt us" and "better to stick with the devil we do know than the devil we don't"? Meanwhile, Martin watched the animation of shadows cast from the candles on each table, dancing larger than the men themselves on the dim walls behind them.

He noticed how Adolf was compelled to recreate the light and shadow in the moment, as well. Adolf pulled out a sketchbook from time to time, and this evening, he began drawing rough sketches of the other men in their animated postures, mouths open, spewing retorts, guzzling beer, and the way the shadows fell on their hair and darkened their necks. They were all half in shadow. Eugene was captured with a fierce, persuading look as he argued with Heinrich about the collective imagination. How it didn't exist. How no two people could see the same object and agree entirely on it. Heinrich slammed his hand on the table to make his point that the table was there and everyone could hear the sound of his hand against the table and see his hand slapping the table.

"Until I do the same thing with my hand, I don't know what that experience is like or if the table is even really there," Eugene smirked inside his beer mug. Heinrich groaned. Adolf moved his charcoal pencil madly against his sheet of paper, bringing all of them to life from his own imagination.

"By the way, I've renamed all of you," Martin said. The group looked at him, amused. This was a new game.

"How so?" Adolf inquired. He seemed intrigued. "What do you call me, now?"

"Aldo," Martin replied. "Is that alright with you?"

Adolf nodded. The rest of the men looked disappointed because they could no longer mock him as a false leader. Martin continued to inform the others of their new names.

"Does this bother you at all?" he asked.

"Whatever makes you feel at home," Gunther said. "I am not so attached to my name. It does not define who I am."

"I agree," said Heinrich. "What was your reason for changing our names, though? Isn't that an act of control or ownership?"

"I guess I wanted to create my own country here in this tavern. Your names, as they were, didn't seem to fit." Martin thought, *I don't know what to call home*. "I'm not changing *you*."

"We didn't name ourselves in the first place," Heinrich said with a shrug. "Our parents took control of that."

"Do you think you're creating a family here?" Gunther mused.

"The closest I have to a family, yes," Martin said. "I suppose I'm trying to fit into this new environment. You are almost imaginary to me, all of you."

"Just don't call me after last call," Gunther joked. Adolf looked grateful. His former name made him uneasy. He was shy. Perhaps Adolf the dictator had been shy when he was away from the podium and microphone and flying red swastikas, and before his rise to stardom. Adolf was an artist. The former dictator was also noted as being an artist, having drawn pictures as a child. If only he had stayed occupied and full with the beauty in the world rather than moving towards the dark and hungry side of his being. Aldo, as Martin called him, was an undeveloped Adolf and the teasing from the other men provoked him. Martin wanted to give him some reprieve.

But it was true what the men said; Martin did want to colonize this table, this company, this new territory he had found. He wanted to give them all familiar names. Otherwise, he would still feel on the outside of something. He wanted to adapt to these changing scenes, or rather have them adapt to him, on his terms. He wanted the backdrop on this stage to change to his liking. Right now, he was still a lone man—a shepherd on a busy city sidewalk.

There was another part of him that yearned for a rebuttal from the men. How could they give up so quickly, so easily, and give him such power? How could they lie down and forfeit their own names? How could he respect them? If their names didn't define them, then what did? Did they know? Were they all secure enough in their skins, their purposes? If so, why did they feel the need to ask so many questions—and be satisfied without universal answers? They didn't have a need to agree, only to question, everything.

What made them individuals, but still gave them the need to be part of a group? Martin was so accustomed to being separate, and now he was torn by his excitement of being one part of a larger whole. He wanted to achieve the wholeness that these men seemed to possess—their ability for laughter, intensity, and surrender.

As a bystander, he watched their dynamics. Who was the leader of this group? He decided it was Heinrich. Eugene was the most argumentative and passionate of the group, but Heinrich was intelligent and chewed on his answers thoughtfully. He commanded the table by solicitation, even if it was borne out of frustration and defeat in the other men's faulty reasoning. They all posed good questions, important questions. Some theories were tighter than others; most theories stemmed from the work of other philosophers the men respected and subscribed to, not usually based on their own findings. Nietzsche was a favourite and was quoted freely.

"So, how was it that you lived on the streets, Martin?" Heinrich asked.

"Not comfortably," Martin half-joked.

"You don't really seem like the type," Heinrich continued, dismissing Martin's wit.

"What type?" Martin asked. He didn't know there was a type.

"You don't seem crazy."

"Do you have to be crazy?"

"Do you have to answer everything with a question?" Heinrich retorted. The men chuckled lightly; they had all ceased their side arguments, again, to listen to this conversation. They all wanted to know. Martin didn't know why, but his back was up. He didn't band with any street people. He didn't ever consider himself a street person. He was simply someone who didn't have a set of keys on a key ring or a job waiting for him in the morning. He didn't have access to the usual places. Wait, what were the usual places? Did you have to have a roof and a boss to be sane? His single key to his temporary apartment jabbed him in the thigh as he shifted in his seat.

"I didn't mean to end up on the street," he answered, defensively, "but I guess, in some ways, I chose to be there."

"Who chooses poverty and uncertainty?" Heinrich asked.

"Monks," Martin quipped. The men chuckled softly, against Heinrich this time. This was a match of sorts.

"Monks still have other monks. What man chooses to be an island?"

"I've always been an island," Martin replied solemnly. "I didn't choose that." *I didn't know how to build a raft*, he thought. *I was an island until Evelyn came.*

"It's no good," Adolf spoke. He lifted his hand from his drawing, which had transformed into barmaids, hanging lights, and small knolls in the wood floor. He had begun to sketch the men's faces with minimal features. They were all captured in some half-finished state of being—drinking, shouting, and thinking. None of the men were safe from the tip of charcoal that smeared Adolf's page with shadows and lines, thick and thin.

"What is no good?" Martin mused.

"Being a recluse, an outsider, and living on the edge of things." The men looked into their half-drunk beers and shook their heads slowly, as though they all knew. "Those people who wander around alone, talking to themselves."

"You think investing in people is better?" Martin seethed. "Those crazy street people, as you call them, find someone to talk to, whether they are really there or not. Anything we can perceive in our minds can be real."

Heinrich pointed a knowing finger at the other men, in reference to the point he was trying to make before, about the table. Gunther shooed him away with his hand.

"They're not only talking to themselves. They are talking to people the rest of us can't see. Perhaps better company," Martin continued. He was beginning to feel trapped in this group. Why had they found him? Why did he care to be there? The men just looked at him, almost pitifully, he thought.

"What is life without people?" Eugene joined in.

"Quiet," said Martin. "Oh, it depends on which people."

"You can choose."

"Not always." Martin was not entirely moved. "Besides, who needs all of the social responsibility and pressure. There are only twenty-four hours in a day—can't we choose how we spend them without becoming robots, clones, and slaves? Can't we just be? What is wrong with just being?" He didn't trust enough.

"You are a negative animal," Heinrich said.

"I am negative because I choose to be alone and peaceful? Is society positive? Society kills people." Martin's voice grew louder.

"Everyone has a social responsibility. Some just choose to ignore it and then make themselves part of the problem." Heinrich's voice was growing louder too. "Street people feed off society like bugs on algae."

The other men watched, wary and interested, holding on to their own opinions.

"Look," Martin said. "No one invested in me; why should I be so generous?" All of the cards were down.

"Why should you be so angry?" Adolf injected.

"The angry recluse," Heinrich said under his breath.

"I've had reason to be angry. Wouldn't you be angry if you didn't fit in with the world?"

"Or maybe it is just that the world has not fitted with you," Johann said. He nudged Martin lightly in the ribs.

"What was it Nietzsche had said?" Heinrich paused while the men looked at him, at a loss. "An idea about independence and how the need for help demonstrates some kind of weakness. Wait, I know … he said that such a person is probably not only strong, but also daring to the point of recklessness. That such a person enters into a kind of maze or labyrinth and loses his way while inviting a multitude of dangers. That such a person becomes lonely and is torn by his own conscience and comes to grief because he travels so far from the companionship and sympathy of other men. He cannot go back to society or the pity of men."

The table was quiet for a minute.

"Nietzsche went mad, you know. He had trouble accepting it: this human factory we are all born into, expected to assimilate to, work in, and thrive," Martin said. "Anyhow, I'm here, aren't I?" It was true. There he sat, drinking his beer and sharing with these men. He was sharing parts of himself he hadn't confided to anyone. He had been too afraid to tell Evelyn the truth. He wasn't afraid now, only startled by this shifting of scenes.

"You have reentered," said Gunther, who had been quietly listening for most of the evening. "You have not gone so far."

"You've come down from the mountain," Adolf replied simply.

"Yes, I think I have, and the smog is choking me." Martin then took a gulp of beer that went down the wrong way and coughed violently. The men laughed. Martin laughed. He hadn't laughed in a long time.

⤜◆◗◆⤛

Martin didn't latch on to Evelyn to try to save her; he had done it to lift himself. In the end, it wasn't a true act of kindness, and that was why he left. She was always stronger than him. He was able to get her to the next level without pulling himself down, but as soon as she showed signs of dependence on him, well, he wasn't ready for it. He didn't know where *he* needed to go yet. He was beginning to face it. He was convinced he had some dark clouds over him that he couldn't shake. The money hadn't helped much, except to take him to a new place where he felt the same uncertainty as he had before.

It was his ego that made him believe he didn't need anyone. He thought he was some kind of saviour or visionary growing out of the cracks in the sidewalk like a weed, not meant to be there. He thought he didn't need saving. He thought he knew how everything worked and how everyone thought. The world was one big machine—money, material, power, and beauty. It was his ego that drew him to the room of mirrors, the one he stood in front of to pick at all his human flaws. He had stood there too long, admiring his ugliness and trying to find something perfect. He thought he was special—walking in Technicolor along a black and white street, or was it the other way around? Was he the black figure? He thought he was the only person brave enough to go against the grain, not realizing how he was being eaten by the machine. He believed he was the first person to strike out and claim some new territory called solitude, to own a thought, but he wasn't independent. He was never free.

He was shielding himself against an imaginary beast—too afraid to confront anything that might implicate him or complicate him. In essence, he had given up a fight that never really began, that was only in his head, thinking he didn't need to become a part of the ever-evolving world, a world that didn't revolve around him, but beside him. He was on the outside, feeling the cool breeze of the world as it moved by him. He convinced himself there were no openings, and the world wouldn't accommodate him or even want him. So he turned his back. He couldn't compromise, and yet he needed to be a part of it more than he cared to admit. He thought he was keeping himself safe and simple, but he knew he was dying— slowly and painfully. Now, with the help of these men, the nails were being lifted out of his coffin. *A new chance*, he thought.

At the table, as he talked with the men, he felt the clouds change from black to grey, and there was a shift in the pressure. They didn't ask anything from him except ideas and truth; they pushed back, and he liked the force they brought. These men didn't allow him to be special. Evelyn had challenged him too, in the beginning, but the energy was different. Once she let her guard down, she changed. She entered a stage where she wasn't so sure anymore. He didn't want the same to happen to him, but it was happening.

"So, I suppose you have all been coming here for years," Martin said, breaking his own thoughts. The men looked at him, surprised.

"Actually, no," Eugene said. "Not much longer than you."

"Well, how did you meet?" Martin asked.

"Johann found us." Adolf grinned. Martin turned to Johann, who looked a bit sheepish.

"It's true," he said. "I was a bit lonely in my thoughts and in my daily life. I wanted to have a group to discuss things with. All things, you know. I would have approached women too; but they have their own lives and concerns. I don't think men usually feel as free to talk the same way."

"Where did you find everyone?" Martin asked. Johann explained how he had sought out men who seemed interested in the creative life. "Eugene was reading philosophy, Gunther was reciting poetry in a cafe, Adolf was sketching in the square, and Heinrich was playing his guitar and singing his own songs in the park. I was interested in learning what each of them knew." They were all artists. Martin also learned that all of the men came from different places and fields of work. Eugene was a banker from Belgium, Johann was an architect from Finland, and Heinrich was a musician from Sweden. Adolf was a screen printer and Gunther owned a bakery and was married with a young family; both men were native to Germany.

They all had lives beyond themselves and this tavern and whatever else was important to them. Still, they didn't have to sacrifice one life for the other. They managed to keep the wheels greased in their day-to-day, hum-drum lives and still keep their inner fires lit, to give up a considerable part of themselves every day and not feel cheated. They had found the balance and the resolution of inner conflict to do what was needed. They didn't talk about their work at the tavern, because for them, it was secondary. They had created a divisional space there, where the worries and stresses of encroaching work, family stress, and mounting bills couldn't enter. This was their time to drink beer and discuss what did matter. Some of the men had longer reins, it seemed, than the others, making their artistic passions their work; still, Martin wondered if they actually did have longer leashes, as they couldn't tuck away their work in a desk drawer at night. They lived, ate, and slept with it, while the other men did their part, picked up their pay cheques, and then went home. In the end, they were free men.

"How did you know it would work?" Martin asked.

Johann smiled. "Of course we didn't," he said. "Who knows about life? You manage it, do what you can and take chances."

⟐

After a while, Martin arose from the table without speaking and headed towards the back of the tavern. He had left the table so often in the course of each meeting, the men no longer took much notice of him. One man whispered loudly to another something about Martin having a "small tank," and the rest of them smiled, nodded their heads, and continued in their respective debates.

Martin hovered near the washroom door, pretending to browse through the picked over daily papers. He watched the same washroom attendant move swiftly from one washroom to the other, pulling her bucket and mop behind her the same way he had seen travellers pull their luggage in the station or homeless people pull their carts wearily behind them. These seemed to be her possessions as well, and he wondered about her other worldly attachments and what or who she went home to each night. What was this compulsive need for him to find out? He could not find an explanation for his interest, but it was evident. She glanced at him once as she moved across the floor, trying to remain invisible to the patrons.

After the tavern closed, the men left him on the curb as they swaggered across the street, their arms around each other, shouting "*Gute Nacht*" and other sentiments. Martin watched their bodies become thin in the distance, until the night swallowed them, and a few minutes later, a bent figure in a thick duffle coat emerged from the rear of the building.

"*Gute Nacht*," he greeted the approaching figure.

She stopped, unaccustomed to seeing anyone loitering on the sidewalk after hours. She was always careful to leave a few minutes later so as not to invite any confrontations that may occur. She did not like watching the men drink or listening to their off-key songs and mindless babble. She did not like this life. She pretended to be deaf or invisible or both.

She nodded at Martin, her face firm and cautious, and moved to bypass him. However, he did the unexpected and fell into stride beside her. She pulled her coat close around her and tightened the scarf concealing her hair. Martin observed her nervous movements, but proceeded to be jaunty and disregard her lack of comfort. He began his greetings in his best, albeit broken, German and in his worst German accent, and faltered over simple, conversational phrases. Eventually, she turned to him and said, "I speak English also."

"Ah, good." He gave an embarrassed chuckle. "My name is Mart— Marty."

She acknowledged him, "Hello, Marty."

"And your name?" He knew he was being forward, but he felt compelled. She eyed him again with caution.

"Frieda."

"Very nice to make your acquaintance, Frieda."

She nodded again.

"I have not been in Lüneburg very long, and I have only been to the tavern a few times."

"Yes, I know. I mean, I have noticed you at the tavern. You are the boy who often comes to the back and stares at me."

Martin flushed in the dark night.

She continued, "I don't like to take notice of it, but I can't help it, and I wonder what you are looking for."

"I don't know either. I am sorry. I think you remind me of someone. I'm not sure of whom."

"I see. Well, we are all made up of other people, aren't we? I do not mind so much." Then she changed the subject. "Are you American?"

"No, Canadian."

"Where do you come from?"

"Vancouver."

She stopped suddenly. "Vancouver?" Then she regained her composure.

"Yes, do you know the city? Or someone who lives there?"

"I knew someone long ago from this place."

"Who?"

"Oh, I keep his name only to myself. Strange, though, you remind me a little of him. Perhaps it is just the accent."

"I don't have an accent."

"No one believes they have an accent. You do."

Chapter 37

MARTIN

Martin and Frieda walked a short distance before she turned to him and said, "This is me." She had been humming a little tune, softly, as they walked along in the night. He didn't rival her on the point she had made about his accent. She was probably right; maybe he did. He never paid much attention to the sound of his own voice. Until recently, he hadn't bothered to stretch his vocal chords much at all. He believed that if he opened his mouth too wide, he would begin to emit poisonous fumes into the air, killing the sweet sounds around him. So, that night, he kept his lips closed and listened to her song, letting her small voice circle around his ears. The tune was vaguely familiar, but he shook it off. The thought that he had heard this woman's made up song somewhere before was too ridiculous. It was only a song, composed in the dark from the sounds of a woman who was being followed home by a stranger. They were sounds to comfort her, to make the night seem normal.

She moved away from him, forgetting him as though he were no longer standing there, and went through a little gate with a narrow walkway leading up to a tall building with a few lights in the windows.

"Goodnight, Frieda."

She turned slightly, to reveal her ghost-grey eyes over her shoulder, "Yes, Marty. *Gute Nacht.*"

"*Gute Nacht.*"

—————◆◐◑◆—————

She haunted him for days. The next night he was in the tavern, she wasn't there. When he inquired about her, one of the waiters, raising an eyebrow, explained that she had the night off due to an illness. The waiter did not ask Martin why he cared, but his expression was one of curiosity and distrust. It was enough to dissuade Martin from inquiring further.

Later in the evening, when he left the tavern, he took the same route along the dimly lit street to the little gate where Frieda had entered her living quarters. He had stood in the street for a few moments after she was secure inside and noticed a little light appear in a window on the third floor. On this night, Martin was careful to lock the little gate behind him, although it was only waist high and would never keep out a determined thief. He warily cast his eyes upwards as he approached the door, imagining himself as an intruder and concerned about causing alarm from a watchful neighbor. His fears were unjustified, as he reached the entrance without duress. He did not see her first name on the list of buzzers for the separate flats, but there was a name with the first initial F. He hoped this did not stand for *Fräulein*. He pressed the buzzer and her voice drifted down through the speaker.

"*Hallo?*"

"Hello, Frieda, this is ..."

"Ah, Marty, what are you doing there?"

"Yes, it's Marty. I heard you were sick."

"Yes, I have not been feeling so well."

"I wanted to see if you were alright?" There was a long silence.

"Well, I suppose you could come in."

"*Danke*," he said. When Martin reached the top of the third landing, he saw a door down the hall left ajar. He gave a little knock and went inside.

"Hello, Frieda?"

"I am in here. In the living room, what you call it." He followed the voice, and the sound of stifled coughing, into a small sitting area. He had not noticed at first, but Frieda's voice and the coughing had overlapped at one point. In the room, he saw a young girl sitting in an armchair with a crocheted blanket over her knees, and Frieda fussing over a bowl of soup and stroking the girl's head.

"Yes, okay. I am not so sick, but my daughter is. My daughter is always sick. My boss would not understand why I have to stay home to take care of her."

"I understand; I won't say anything at the tavern."

"*Danke*." Frieda turned to the girl in the armchair and began relaying the situation to her in German; at least Martin assumed this, as he heard his name uttered once or twice. The girl nodded her head, but the expression on her face was distracted with illness.

"Ah, *hallo* Marty, I am Gretchen." Her English was slow and broken, and Martin smiled in return. Frieda spoke a few more words to her, and the girl bundled the blanket around her shoulders, said, "*Gute Nacht*," and vanished to her room.

"Will she be alright?" Martin asked with unmasked concern in his voice.

Frieda patted his hand. "I don't know. She has been ill for a long time. The doctor says it is a problem with her digestion. It takes so much life out of her, poor thing. I try to take care of her."

Martin's eyes lowered. He didn't really know about taking care of another human being. He had tried to take care of Evelyn. He had managed to rearrange the letters of her name into their forgotten places. He had put her back together like a tired looking vase that had fallen and broken but, although one could still see where the pieces were glued and it didn't look sturdy, could still hold flowers.

Martin began to take in the room. He had been in this setting for nearly ten minutes and was not aware of the contents of his surroundings. He wasn't used to making himself aware, only to focusing on his changing thoughts and the people in his space. He was beginning to emerge from his space and it felt like an invitation to the world. Perhaps he was still an uninvited guest or a stranger, but he didn't have that old, uncomfortable feeling. The way Frieda responded to him was kind, even with her curt voice, and she maintained warmth in her eyes.

She found him to be no threat and she appreciated the quietness of him.

He was a man who, yesterday, had stepped out of a manhole and greeted the world. Not for lack of wisdom or experience, but for a man adopting a new world.

Frieda's carpet was off-white from time, traffic, and neglect. It was the colour of a bride's dress collecting the years while being worn underneath her everyday clothing. The special day never disappeared, the one that happened or didn't, and the dress was never taken off. Everything had depended on the decisions of one man. Where was this man, the girl's father? The answers had diminished in the colour of the walls that bore the little portraits, landscape paintings, and mirrors. A small bookshelf was leaning in the corner with German titles. The furniture in the room was sparse, yet efficient: a loveseat, a wicker chair, and a coffee table large enough to hold a book or two, a tray, and a saucer for tea. Frieda had created her own world, and it was apparent that not many others entered.

She took the tea tray away to replace the cups and refill the pot. Then she turned around, the tray firm in her hands and asked, "Would you prefer a beer or maybe coffee instead?"

"Tea is fine." She disappeared into the kitchen and Martin rose from his chair to take in the rest of his surroundings. He noticed a small portrait on the bookshelf and moved in for a closer look. The portrait was of a young man seated on a grassy bank beside a pond, with the branches of a weeping willow tree creeping into the left side of the frame. Although he could only see the branches, they reached low to the ground. The man was on the right with his back to the photographer. This situation seemed odd, but there was the sense that the subject was aware of the lens and was not a random victim ambushed by a candid photographer. However, it may have been that way, too.

His pants were rolled up just below his knees and his feet were bare. His shoes, presumably, were coupled nearby and deliberately placed. His knees were bent and his arms, donning short sleeves, hung over them easily, with a small curve in his back bending forward. He looked relaxed, but also slightly poised with some kinetic force, as though he secretly wanted to spring forward to dive into the pond. The photograph was a grainy Technicolor with a matte finish that signified the 1950s era. The day was sunny, his hair was brown, and the pond was laced with green lily pads. What struck Martin the most was that he knew this place, even with its lack of familiar landmarks and only the back of a man's head and his orange shirt; he knew this place. Frieda returned through the doorway with fresh tea. Martin put the photograph back.

"Ah, you found my photograph," she said, sounding dismissive and half-defeated, as though there was a story she wanted to tell desperately but pretended she didn't.

"Who is he?"

"He is a ghost now."

"A ghost?"

"Well, he is a ghost for me. He is the man I told you about who has your accent," she sighed. "That photograph was taken the last summer I saw him."

"What happened? Why was that the last time?"

She gave Martin an intense look, as though searching for a good answer for herself. She did not look upset, but finally shrugged her shoulders and said, "Because there is always a last time. Now, do you take both milk and sugar?" Her hands shook a little and belied the even tone in her voice.

Chapter 38

WILLIS

Willis felt as though the world was closing its doors to him. It was too much for him to think that he had not made the effort to turn the handles. He had been accustomed to not caring, weaving his spoiled life and depending upon the wealth of his name and stature, or rather his father's. Nothing was his. Perhaps being there, back in Doctor Horowitz's office, with someone to listen was the best thing that could happen. He could feel a door opening.

Willis listened to the doctor speaking and paid attention to his fatherly tone, which seemed so foreign and so welcome. He heard words like ... *normal, rest, calm, solution.*

"Willis, how would you like to spend some time at Serenity Falls?"

"Isn't that a place for crazy people?"

"No, it is a place for people who need to find some quiet in their lives." The doctor's voice was level and soothing. Instead of the walls getting smaller, like in Sam's office, the doctor's room seemed to expand.

"I think I would like that," he finally said.

"Good. I'll make the arrangements." The doctor spoke in soothing tones, as though he was trying to calm down a criminal until the police arrived to drag him away. Willis didn't get the sense that he was being lured into a cage or talked to like a child, though. The doctor seemed genuine and fatherly.

A few days later, Willis found himself at the Serenity Falls admission desk. His doctor had offered to accompany him, and Willis did not object, so he was now discussing Willis's situation with the staff nurse. Meanwhile, Willis glanced around the room. There were a handful of clean, white nurses bustling to and fro, some with charts, others carrying bedding, blankets, and other reinforcements. The pictures on the soft, yellow walls depicted garden flowers.

"... I believe he is struggling with some depression, perhaps compulsive behavior ..." The words floated out in badly concealed whispers, and as the administrative nurse peered around the doctor's head to appraise Willis, he uncomfortably looked away.

"We have similar patients here, Doctor. I'm sure he will receive the care he needs."

"Thank you, Nurse," the doctor replied and scribbled on the chart. Willis assessed the small reception area and brightly coloured, low, circular tables: blue, red, green. He expected to see kindergarten children drawing or smearing paint on large canvases of paper. Instead, he saw adults sitting in plastic chairs—some playing with cards, others just sitting.

"Please wait here." The nurse pointed to an orange plastic chair at a red circular table. Willis slumped into it with his long legs arching out. She didn't find amusement in his situation. He supposed they were all used to the tragically comical sight of child-like adults kept indoors. A man was sitting at the other side of the red table with his gaze focused across the room. Willis followed his gaze to a television set in the far corner.

"Turn it to channel two!" the man suddenly yelled to a small cluster of patients who were melding into the retro armchair furniture around the television set. They didn't move. The man clucked his tongue, annoyed at the lack of response. "Hey, you crazy bumpkins, turn the channel!"

"What for?" one man broke away from the pack, away from the cartoons on the small screen, slightly twisting his neck.

"The news is on," the man next to Willis answered in a quieter, intense voice. Then he turned to Willis, "It is important to know what is happening."

Willis nodded in agreement. He looked around him, conspiratorially, as the other patients in the room watched the television and the nurses glided silently past the admissions desk.

"Watch this," the man said to Willis, after looking at the clock on the wall. Then a small Plexiglas window opened at the far end of the counter and the television was suddenly abandoned. The patients rose and moved trance-like to the window, in an orderly, single-file line, with no shoving. One by one, the nurse handed out small plastic cups and round pills. She called them each by his or her first name, adding a gentle, "Here you go," and, "There you are." The man at Willis' table reluctantly joined the line. This was a prison, not an escape. His turn would come soon. He would have to swallow that pill.

Willis wondered again why he was there. Was this where he belonged? Did he really need a time-out from the pressures of life? What pressures did he have? He had every privilege and every resource available to him. The man came back to the table, swallowed the last of the contents of his plastic cup, and then toyed with it in his hand before setting it down in front of him. He regarded it for a moment and then looked at Willis.

"Are you a patient or a visitor?" he asked.

Willis wasn't sure how to answer the blunt question, not quite yet. He still felt he was on the other side of the admissions desk and not a file in their cabinet yet. "Not sure," he answered, not looking at him. "We'll see." He watched the television and pretended to be interested in the happenings of the world outside, *people with real problems*, he thought. The man didn't ask anymore questions, but Willis could feel his eyes watching him, as though regarding him more closely than he did the plastic cup; the unknown substance he had willingly taken into his body was something more familiar. Willis was not familiar to him and, therefore, had to be studied more closely.

Willis chose not to indulge this stranger, but he was aware that he didn't have the urge to move away to another coloured table. There was something calming and safe about the shape and colour of the table and the smooth surface. Willis had been feeling too many sharp edges and barriers, like Sam's desk and how small and anxious he had felt sitting across from Sam. Here, if he moved his chair, he could meet this man halfway and the distance between them wouldn't be as wide, small enough to arm wrestle—for what, he didn't yet know.

"I'm Willis," he said, moving to shake hands, but then holding back. He couldn't say why, but this didn't seem the place to put on normal airs.

"Norman." The other man reached out his hand. Willis took it, a little abashed, and surveyed his new companion. Norman had sharp features, a quick eye, and a small curl at the side of his lip that could be called his smile. He was clearly humoring his environment, surveying everything around him, and writing his own charts in his head.

"Those guys don't know which way is up," he commented casually, flicking his chin towards the semicircle of heads settled back in the retro armchairs around a children's daytime show. "They don't know where they are."

"Where are they?" Willis asked, curious. He wasn't sure if Norman was an objective source of information, but he was glad for the conversation. Norman turned an eye on him, his fist near his mouth, and then darted his gaze conspicuously around the room.

"Well, it's not so bad here, to be honest. The nurses are nice, the food is okay, but ..." He leaned in a little closer, "There are a few crazies."

"Uh-huh." Willis tried to keep a stern face to gain his new friend's confidence, but secretly, he felt that he had already met one of them.

"Crazies everywhere in here." Norman flicked his wrist and sat back in the seat, irritated. Willis followed his gaze back to the afternoon TV viewers, hiding his amusement. Then the quiet nagging tugged at him again—what was *he* doing in this place? Was this how he would become? Could he really get better, or would he simply succumb to being institutionalized, forgetting the real, hard world that existed beyond the smiling nurses and routine pills? He pushed back his chair a little too abruptly, so that it squeaked on the linoleum floor, and all heads in front left the TV program and jerked around to see the commotion, including Norman.

"I just remembered something," he said awkwardly. "Sorry," he said in a slightly louder voice to his audience. Doctor Horowitz was still at the admissions desk, making small talk with the nurse. "Doctor," Willis breathed once he reached the desk. The room had felt the length of a football field to cross, and he hadn't walked too quickly in order to save himself from attracting further attention.

"Willis." The doctor turned with a mildly concerned look, also somewhat patronizing. "We've almost got you settled in."

"Yes, Doctor, thank you," Willis spoke hurriedly, "but I don't think I want to be settled in after all. I don't think I should be here, at least not in *this* place."

The doctor's eye took a cold turn—he remembered the same icy blue of Sam's glance behind his medium thick frames.

"Now, Willis, it is your choice, of course, but do you remember everything you had confided in me at my office?"

"Yes, yes I know ..." Willis began, losing confidence and feeling more and more like a fifteen-year-old boy who was being told how he should think about things. Then the nurse broke in, feeling the tension that was rising between the two men.

"If I may," she started in a quiet, yet solid, voice, "Willis ... I see you have been talking with Norman."

"Yes, interesting person," Willis replied politely, but wondering about the relevance it had to his wanting to flee out the doors.

"I think you should know that we house and treat people with various levels of mental illness—everything from anxiety or depression to patients who have more severe issues."

"Oh." Willis began to waver slightly.

"This is a common room for patients, but most of the time we keep patients limited to their floors, depending on the severity of their conditions, and often, by their own wishes. Norman is one of our more moderate patients."

"You mean he's not crazy?"

"We don't like to use that term, Willis," the nurse said. Her tone was sympathetic, but firm.

"But he's not?" Willis persisted.

The nurse sighed, "Not to the extent of some of our other patients, no."

"You see, Willis," Doctor Horowitz broke in again, amused, "I think you will be fine here, and you already have a friend." Why was the doctor continuing to talk to him like he was either fifteen or about to pull out a machine gun? Willis looked from the doctor to the nurse and then nodded.

"Willis, will you please sign here?" the nurse asked.

"Sure." Willis took the pen and scratched his indiscernible signature on the clip chart. He signed the admissions release and then met the nurse's eyes.

"The nurses will take care of you, Willis. You'll be alright here, and I will be checking in to see how you are progressing,"

"Thank you, Doctor."

"Please come with me and bring your belongings with you," the nurse twittered. Willis shook his doctor's hand and followed the nurse down the corridor behind the admissions desk, walking a few steps ahead. She had good posture and a smart step.

The nurse led Willis to the elevator and escorted him to the second floor. *The higher the floor, the crazier the patient*, Willis thought.

The hallway on the second floor contained eight rooms, four on each side. Willis was led into the second door on the left.

"This will be your living space," she said in a warm tone. She went ahead of him and opened up the closet, and Willis saw three hangers inside. The bed in the corner was narrow and neatly made, with a thick blanket folded on top. A plain covered notebook lay on the bed. There was one small window with a view of the buildings. He would have the company of pigeons and sea birds. Then she left him to his own company. Her parting words were, "The doors are automatically locked between 9:00 p.m. and 6:00 a.m."

He was a prisoner, feeling stifled and strange—not yet ready to accept these new walls. In his adjustment, he also felt the small relief that he was no longer down below, outside on the sidewalk, left to his own devices, which he could no longer trust. This room was a blanket and a comfort he hoped to soon discard. He knew he needed this place, but he resented his need. What would they be able to tell him? How would an extended time-out and further lack of responsibilities—further withdrawal from the world—help him?

After the nurse left, he sat on the corner of the bed and felt the walls close in around him. He imagined this must be how the monks lived—a few sparse comforts and the rest filled in with meditation and industry. He thought about whether he was being protected from the world or if it was the other way around. He felt safe and irritated. This wasn't real life. *I am a coward*, he thought, *still not willing to face the world and my responsibilities*. He couldn't tell if he was facing his demons now or taking a first courageous step towards healing and becoming whole.

Chapter 39

MARTIN

Martin couldn't find sleep. For the first time in months, he was shaken into wakefulness. This was a quest, and in his dreams, the vague profile of the man in the photo would turn more towards the photo taker. Martin was taking the picture. He was a little boy feeding ducks in the pond, and he could feel the fibre of the man's orange shirt against his cheek. This was a dream, a slideshow. He had his own life recorded in albums kept by his aunt in Canada. There were no photographs of his mother; he could only remember her eyes. He knew he must see Frieda again.

Martin visited her often and brought tea and secondhand books for her ailing daughter. Whenever Frieda went out of the room, he would steal glances at the photograph, willing the man to turn around. He never did, and Martin continued to be haunted.

"Was this photograph taken here in Germany?" Martin finally asked Frieda one day.

"No, that photograph was taken in England, where he lived. He gave it to me."

"England?"

"Well, don't sound so surprised. The war was long over, you know." She sounded indignant.

"No, I mean, it's only that you said he had a Canadian accent ... like me ... that he was from Vancouver."

"Well, he was ... he was a soldier, and at the end of the war, he decided to stay in England. He met a woman during that time, an English woman, and married her."

"Was he still married to her when you knew him?"

"Yes, yes he was. I was never proud of it; I never wanted it to be that way. Our time together was relatively brief... but oh, I remember him. I remember him still." Her hands trembled as she lay the tea tray down on the coffee table.

"I'm sorry it had to end," he said sincerely.

"I wish I could be sorry it ever started." She smiled sadly. They drank their tea thoughtfully—he thinking of Evelyn, she seeing her lost love through a small viewfinder on a sunny, grassy bank a long time ago. Both were photographs that would not fade.

Nothing seemed easy. It seemed that someone always had to leave. For leaving Evelyn in Paris, Martin felt a twinge of shame. He hoped she had continued on her path to being whole again and had not gone back to what might have been a familiar life; not an easy way out, but something constant. He stared into his tea cup. Frieda noticed.

"What are you thinking about?" she asked.

Martin shrugged defensively. "Just a girl."

"Ah? Not just a girl, I think."

"I left her in Paris. I said a lot of things I wanted to believe. Then I realized I didn't quite believe them yet."

"So why did you leave?"

"I figured she didn't need that—someone who wasn't sure.

She needed something more solid. I thought I was, but I'm really just cardboard."

"There are people whose homes are made out of cardboard."

Martin looked at this woman. "Have you ever tried to tear a piece of cardboard with your hands?" he asked.

"Sure."

"Then you know how it breaks apart in uneven strips."

"Life happens in uneven strips."

"Yes, I suppose it does."

"Will you find this girl?"

"I don't know. The question now is whether she'd want to be found."

"Would you like to find her?"

Martin sighed. These thick knots were beginning to fray.

"Would you like to see your English-Canadian again?" He was challenging her with a good-humoured deflection.

She leaned forward and squinted at him with a hard eye, a faint smile on her lipstick-bruised lips. Her voice cast a sharp whisper, "Very much."

Martin joined his philosopher and artisan friends at Steins most weeks and then accompanied Frieda home after her cleaning shift. When they came through the door of her apartment together, her daughter would sometimes smile politely, close her book, and quietly leave the room in an awkward fashion. However, lately, she stayed in their company longer and sometimes until Martin was the one to decidedly rise, nod, and head for the door with a soft, "*Gute Nacht.*" She was curious, a tall, not unattractive girl. A bit mousy, but only because of her quiet demeanor; however, he was not unaware of her. She held some small dignity in the few words she uttered, and she chose to communicate with her eyes. Still, she seemed weaker during each visit. One evening, she departed the room with reluctance and something like an apology in her good-night and the way she moved to her own door.

"How is she?" Martin felt a growing concern for the girl.

"Nothing can be done," Frieda breathed. "Doctor says."

Martin peered at the door as though it was the gateway to her next life, as though she could be in that room and not be sick there.

"May I ask ... where is her father?" As soon as he said the words, he felt them leave his mouth like lithe swords thrown into the room, tip down, and gently weaving back and forth in the coffee table. He could almost see them there, so innocuous and, yet, so deadly.

"The man I told you about." She didn't look at Martin at first. Then she turned to face him more bravely. "I had two children by him. He didn't know about her."

"I see." He felt small, suddenly. He wanted to swallow back his swords, but she wouldn't let him.

"No, you don't," she said easily. It was not an insult or a slight. It was the truth. She picked up the photograph for strength, but it looked heavy in her strained hands. "Our first child was a boy," she started again. "I was quite young. Well, perhaps not so young." She winked at him. She looked much older now, but he assumed this was more from hard work and worry. "I was in my twenties, but I had no money and no family nearby. Willis couldn't support us and his own family. He told me this. He said he didn't want the child to go into an orphanage. He had seen the state of the orphan-ages during the war. So had I."

Martin listened, captivated.

"He told me he had an older sister who had no children of her own. He said it was the one great sorrow of her life not to have children. I remember I cried and cried, knowing what he wanted me to do. By then, our son was already two years old. I had tried to care for him, but I couldn't keep everything together and Willis was rarely there. He could only visit a few times a year."

"So you sent your little boy away," Martin's voice was barely audible. Still, the weight of these words was clear and heavy.

"Yes, yes." She nodded. "I sent him away. I had to. It was right."

"You have not seen him since." It was not a question. It was a statement, a sentence. Frieda's mouth puckered and she shook her head mutely, violently. Martin reached over, squeezed her clasped hands, rose slowly, and let himself out. For the evening, the room could hold no more words.

Chapter 40

WILLIS

Over the course of the first week in Serenity Falls, Willis began to find routine and back down on his initial defenses. It had taken a few days to dissolve the personal barriers he clung to, distinguishing himself from the other patients, who, in his mind, were the ones who really did need help. After he had been approached by a few of the other patients, he started to realize that, for most of them, the world had just become too much to handle. You can only stretch the fabric so far before it rips free of your grasp. He knew he also wasn't ready to step back into that world. First, he had to learn how to walk again, to feel some solid ground under his feet. He needed this time to heal and reflect, whether he accepted it or not.

Willis also quickly learned that this wasn't a jail, but a place of free will. Many of the patients who remained locked in their rooms all day wanted to be there. They were locked in to give them reassurance that no one could enter unannounced and disrupt their space. These were extreme cases, patients who were paranoid, stressed, mistrusting, and had high anxiety issues when forced into social interaction. They were happy to be locked inside themselves, shut in from whatever damage the world could, and possibly would, inflict on them.

At night, Willis wrote in the journal. His first entry was a poem, of sorts. He wrote:

This island, my book. This pen, my raft. I ride the ideas and slide out. I cling to everything in ink. These calendar days are a measurement of my life.

He saw the words as his thoughts in ink, something unexpected and permanent. He didn't know where the words had come from, but they existed. They were saying something about his isolation, his counting of days, and his need for order. He believed his words. He continued to write for the need of words.

In the mornings, once the doors were unlocked, Willis would go out to the community room to find Norman. The two men had slowly become friends. Norman sat at one of the round tables with his juice glass. Coffee or tea was available, but the caffeine tended to make some of the patients more nervous and high-strung than usual. The nurses sipped their coffee cups behind the counter, and Willis routinely wandered over to where the pot was brewing. He then came over to join Norman, cup in hand.

"Morning, Norman," Willis murmured one morning.

"Hm? Oh, morning, Willis." Norman only half-acknowledged his friend. As usual, he was intent on staring at the small congregation in the chairs watching Sesame Street and shaking his head.

"Did you sleep okay?"

"I guess. No bad dreams last night," Norman replied without emotion. He had told Willis about his nightmares during one of their first conversations.

"That's good," Willis remarked, and it was. It meant that Norman's medication was working. Willis had also learned that Norman suffered from schizophrenia. He was lucid most of the time, but that also meant his medication was working.

Willis' room was situated across the hall from Norman's, and during the first night or two, he was awoken by Norman shouting, "No, no! Leave me alone!" In the morning, Norman seemed fine and Willis didn't mention it "Do you ever feel like you're being chased by someone or something?" Norman asked.

Willis wasn't quite sure how to answer. "Not really," he said honestly. "But there are times I feel like I'm chasing a part of myself."

Norman looked up at him then, intrigued. "What do you mean? How can you be chasing yourself?"

"It's hard to explain." Willis suddenly felt foolish. He was moving the conversation away from what he sensed Norman wanted to tell him.

"Try me." Norman looked at him intently. The last thing Willis wanted to do was talk about himself.

"It doesn't matter," Willis muttered.

"Yeah, it does. That doesn't make any sense to me. Chasing yourself, ..." Norman scoffed. "If you're chasing yourself, then ... then you should just be able to quit. You should know that you're chasing yourself. That's nothing to be afraid of."

"Isn't it?" Willis looked back at his friend. Both men were becoming irritated in their incomprehension of each other and their own demons. "How can you stop something when you don't understand it?"

Norman was quiet for a long time, apparently mulling the whole thing over.

"I don't know ..." Willis broke in. "My father died. I see him sometimes in dreams, day and night. I never really knew my father; he never had anything to do with me. Now, when I see him, he changes into me or I change into him. Then, in my waking hours, I feel I am him, and I don't want to be. But I am. In my dreams, when he turns into me, I'm still the one following him. I guess I'm still trying to make some connection, to catch up so that I can put an end to one of us. I just want to free myself and to understand what is happening."

Norman contemplated this for a long moment too, nodding in what appeared to be sympathy. Then he said, "You're nuts."

Willis couldn't help but break out in a surprised, genuine smile. "Thanks," he said.

"I have dreams where I'm being chased. I'll be out in some remote spot, away from my room. First, I wonder how I got there, and then I'll be trying to figure out how to get back. I don't like being outside of my room at night." Norman shot him a serious look. Willis responded by nodding accordingly and emitting the right sounds at the right times.

"Anyhow," Norman continued, distracted, "there I am, out in the middle of nowhere in the dark, dead of night, and suddenly, I see this beast in the shadows. First, I see its bright, inquisitive eyes, and then the shape of it. One limb at a time slowly advancing towards me, and as it comes nearer, those luminescent eyes narrow and set their target on me like a rifle barrel, and then its limbs move a little faster.

"Next thing I know, this beast is bounding towards me, and I can never turn to run fast enough. I'm rooted like a tree. I always forget that I'm actually dreaming. Then I find my legs and I run and run, only I feel as though I'm running through water up to my waist. I can feel its great paws on my heels, its breath on my back, and just when I'm sure it is going to pounce on me and tear me apart ... I wake up."

"Everyone has dreams like that," Willis said, assuring. "You're not nuts."

Norman smiled, still looking unconvinced. "Thanks," he said. Then he looked up and his face changed.

"What's wrong?" Willis asked, confused. Norman scraped back his chair, nearly toppling over in it. He stood up, trembling, clutching the chair.

"It's that beast ..." he said in a low, guttural voice.

Chapter 41

WILLIS

Willis requested to go to his room and be locked in. He was disturbed by his friend's visions. He wasn't frightened of Norman; instead, he was frightened for him. He wondered again, *why am I in here?* He felt like a fraud, someone hiding from the world out of cowardice, not necessity. He sat on the end of his bed and twisted himself around to look at his night table. He had put his journal in there. He reached for it and took the slim black pen out of the spine. His hand drew small, invisible figure eights above the page, and then he touched pen to paper. He wrote for himself, and Norman:

WEEK ONE

I'm shivering in the corner of the room. I feel like flying, but my feet are heavy. I'm sinking into the ground. I am absorbing the tears and the silent screams. It's my little secret. I can't think—not now, I just want to dream. I need to sleep and to dream. There is no light.

WEEK TWO

My head hurts, and I can only think of one person who has caused this. Me. Was that me speaking? I have subjected myself to an adult kindergarten, and I can't complain about it. This is where I've needed to be. Only I don't need to be here as badly as some. I look around me and I know what Norman means. For us, this is a voluntary jail. For others, it is a resort— or something that resembles home. Norman isn't crazy. He is facing his demons, slowly. I haven't met my demons yet. As far as I'm concerned, he is ahead of me in identifying how to heal himself. Perhaps my reoccurring dreams about my father are the same—perhaps he is my demon. He wants me to follow him somewhere I am reluctant to go, and still, I find myself following in his shoes no matter what I do. I have a compulsion, or a gene, that needs to be removed. He hasn't been able to reach me here, not yet. Not since the girl in the motel room. She was the last one, ever. I hope Norman can find a way to stay in the room with his demon and control him, her, or it. There is something buried deep within him, too. Someone or something has a hold on him that won't let go. Many of us have demons clinging to our ankles, weighing us down, making us second guess ourselves, an inner voice that doesn't agree with our hearts, and somehow, the voice grows stronger.

WEEK THREE

Norman hasn't come out of his room yet. At least, I haven't seen him. I've started to come out and have some of my meals in the main area. I tried voting for a channel on the shared television, but I lost to Sesame Street. Strange how the large, colourful Muppets began to make sense— talking about make-believe and how we can all make our dreams come true if we really work and try hard enough. I wonder what Norman did before he came here. It seems to me he probably had a beautiful wife, a clean home ... maybe kids? How can so much normal make someone snap or stop believing? Or believe too much? Stress can cause a distortion of what is real and create a desire to move further inwards. Are the pressures of life driving people to seek respite? Not just a vacation—but a clean breakaway, an escape or exit, and a desire to be in white rooms and prison cells where they can think and read without any interruptions? The world can be too much; it is frightening, and all the people in it want different things from us. We can't always satisfy these demands or make ourselves disappear. I know.

Our participation in the world can mean life or death: who we choose to be and how our choices affect everyone and everything. There should be an exam given to be born; at the very least, a slide show presentation of what the world is like and what the progression of our lives will entail, and then when the lights come back up, we would all be given the opportunity to decide whether or not we want to go to that place. It is a satiric proposal, like Pope's suggestion to eat babies in the face of starvation. Still, although we laugh and shoo away the idea, sometimes we have to wonder what is ludicrous and what is necessary in times of crisis. We are here. We must endure and find happiness, however fleeting or small.

In this place, they give us pills and quiet rooms so that we can stop the rat races of our brains, concentrate on the brightly-coloured furniture, and watch the world happen from a safe distance, until we are ready to rejoin it or find peace in taking our pills. Do these institutions help? Are they only built to protect the functioning insane outside of these walls from the clinically insane, or are these places actually making crazy people? Who is to say one person's reality is wrong because it doesn't match someone else's? I think of Michael and his need for peace. He left with dignity. After watching Norman, I realize he is fighting the same larger battles. I can't judge.

WEEK FOUR

I miss my friend. I'm sick of this room. I want to change the television channel. I'm almost ready to go home.

Chapter 42

MARTIN

After Martin's conversation with Frieda, he began to think more about Evelyn. He had let her slip from his mind, or at least he'd covered her up. He knew he would have been no good to her by staying, and he was not clear about everything in his own mind. Who needs a partner who still has so many questions and so much uncertainty about himself and everything in the world? He also knew he would have grown to resent her. He would have dragged her all over Europe—and felt the weight of her. They were like two feeble swimmers threatening to drown each other. He had been the one to drown and let her swim. She didn't need him, he told himself—there was strength in her. Such strength, he couldn't hold it, and he didn't want to harness her and make her think she needed him. He had given her a way out and only hoped she had continued to walk out that door into something better. She deserved to. She had her own quest. If they should meet again, then they would meet ready.

He continued along his solitary track, spending time in the local tavern with Johann and his philosophical friends. They thought they were solving the problems of the world; a small circle of flea-bitten Socratics slinging back beers and pretending to ignore the barmaids. The more beers they put away, the more they merited themselves as frontier thinkers. The waitresses left the bill, bared their ivory teeth, and rolled their eyes towards other tables. Martin knew it, but he enjoyed being a part of something. Besides, he would always wait for Frieda to finish her late shift. The other men watched him when it came close to last call, and night after night, they would stumble out in a small herd and bid him good-night. Silently, they would scratch their heads, drain their mugs, and reach for their hats. One night, Adolf spoke up.

"Marty, why do you wait for that old cleaning lady every night? There are younger girls, you know, whose breasts don't …" He swung his hands, cup-shaped at his waist.

"Adolf!" one of the older men tried to scold him, but he was unsuccessful because of the poorly stifled mirth in his own voice. Martin simply smiled and let loose a short chuckle.

"No, no Adolf, … she is just a friend. We talk." This confession stunned the men into silence. They looked at him with confused faces. Their sudden awkwardness was comical.

"Talk?" another man sputtered.

"Yes, talk. What do you think? My god, she is an old woman!" Martin laughed. His friends seemed to behave even more strangely and awkwardly at this proclamation.

"Your old woman is here!" Adolf said, slowly lifting a pointed finger. Martin instantly felt sick.

"What?" He turned around to see Frieda coming out of the shadows from the back exit.

"Yes, it is the old woman," she said, unaffected. "*Gute Nacht*, gentlemen!" She smiled at Martin, obviously amused at whatever misunderstanding had been brewing in the minds of his compan-ions. "Ah, are you coming over again tonight, Marty? My daughter will be so happy to see you!" Her eyes twinkled. She was enjoying herself, rescuing him.

"Aha, yes indeed. *Danke!*"

The men all coughed and chuckled at Martin's embarrassment. He was really only flustered because he did not expect Frieda to be so playful, and he still felt sheepish about his own comment. Once the men were far enough down the narrow road, he turned to her.

"You didn't have to do that, you know—I was explaining to them—"

"Oh, I heard you explaining." She mocked offense and then turned up the corner of her mouth. "You needn't worry, Marty. I *am* an old woman—too old for anything their dirty minds could conjure up!"

"You're not so old," Martin said.

"Ah well, I meant it, though. My daughter will be very glad to see you." She paused. "I am glad, too."

Chapter 43

WILLIS

Willis was deprived of Norman's company for a few weeks after his friend's outburst in the community room. Norman had begun flipping over chairs and yelling, "Get it away from me!" while Willis watched from a relatively safe distance, feeling helpless. A few attendants came racing into the room, as though they were freshly trained and waiting for this to happen. *This was a drill, this wasn't real*, he thought. Norman would take a bow at the end of the dramatic scene and the attendants would all pat each other on the back and stop their stop-watches, wiping their foreheads with relief. No, this *was* real. The attendants grabbed Norman, his friend, and pulled him around the corner. Norman seemed to be clinging to the attendants for support, rather than struggling to get away from them. Willis sat in his chair, motionless. The whole event had occurred in under a minute.

A nurse had been watching Willis from her station. She had

sounded the alarm for the attendants, and now she approached Willis. She walked over to him slowly.

"He'll be okay," she said gently.

"How do you know?" Willis asked. It was a simple question that he believed couldn't be answered so simply. How did she have the answer? How did anyone know his friend would be okay?

"They have wonderful technology."

"What kind?"

"Tranquilizers, electric shock treatment—oh, it's amazing what they can do now."

"What? That's what they're doing to Norman?"

"Well, yes. It's for his own safety, so he is made calm and doesn't hurt himself."

"That's not helpful to him," Willis said bluntly. "How do you make the beast go away?"

The nurse moved away from him. She didn't know what he was talking about. It was something his friend had confided to him and only him. Willis looked around at all of the staff in white with their pills, needles, and electrical equipment. He was sitting in Frankenstein's laboratory, holding a number.

The days went by and Willis missed his friend. He realized with bitterness that this was a new kind of empty. He felt it much more keenly this time because he had gained much more from his camaraderie with Norman than any other person he had met. The walls seemed duller now, and the heads that were propped up in their congregation of armchairs in the corner, worshipping the faint buzz of the television set, made an eerie kind of sense. That was what you did there—you tuned out your own world and transfixed yourself on another one—a world outside yourself. Willis felt truly depressed because he was concerned about something more than himself, a novel occurrence. He was concerned about his friend.

Norman was in lockdown. He had been given a mild sedative and his usual medication, and was not treated roughly for his seemingly violent behaviour. No electric shock therapy, the nurses had assured him. Willis could see that the staff in white only acted in genuine concern for Norman's safety and only took the necessary precautions against him hurting himself. He also learned that Norman had requested the lockdown. The next day, an older woman and young girl entered the community room, walking briskly towards the admissions booth. The older woman had a mixture of deep concern, self-assurance, and purpose about her. The young girl who trailed closely behind looked anxious and miserable. The nurse in the booth, the same young nurse who had helped Willis settle in, sensed their approach long before they arrived in her presence. She received the two women with a professional yet slightly casual air, greeting them before looking up entirely to give her full attention.

"Hello, Mrs. Starkey," she said with a friendly tone, but there was an edge of tiredness.

"Hello, Julie."

"Hello, Sandra." Nurse Julie acknowledged the younger woman, who nodded nervously and gave a pathetic smile.

"We're here to see Norman," said Mrs. Starkey.

"You know the rules," said Nurse Julie.

"I'm his mother, for God's sake."

"He's requested lockdown. This isn't a good time."

"Can you tell him we're here?"

"Of course." Nurse Julie put aside her papers, closed the protective glass to the booth, and quietly went into the back hallway. She disappeared for only a few minutes, but in that short time, the two women stood closer together, muttering reassuringly to each other and acting twitchy, while keeping a discreet eye on the other patients in the room. Sandra caught Willis' eye and then jerked her head away, distractedly, pretending to be absorbed in the bulletin board mounted on the wall. Nurse Julie returned looking resigned. She sat down and reopened the panel of Plexiglas.

"I am sorry. He doesn't want any visitors just yet."

"We've made an hour's trip in the car—he won't see his own mother or his poor wife?"

"Mrs. Starkey, please try to understand. We are all here to help your son. We respect the needs of all our patients. This is meant to be a safe place for him. He doesn't feel safe right now and we don't want to cause him any further upset." Nurse Julie laid down her authoritative weapons and spoke gently to the two women. "Please try to understand. Go home and call us in a week or so."

"His own mother and wife—and we can't help him," Mrs. Starkey said quietly. She nodded, then said, "Okay, thank you, Julie. We'll go."

"Please tell him we love him," young Sandra piped up for the first time, and she held her one small hand in the other, as though she didn't trust or couldn't find any better use for them.

"I surely will."

As the two women turned and began to leave the room, heading for the small exit door, the younger woman caught Willis' eye again, deliberately. Obviously, she could sense how intently he had been watching, and she must have also sensed he had some vested interest, because she gave him a slight acknowledgment with her eyes. He nodded to her, reassuringly in response. Her eyes, he thought, were also telling him to give Norman the message.

This was a place to hide—not forever and not from everyone and everything—but well, and long enough. The patients were given enough time to recognize themselves again and to be okay or know enough to not be okay with whatever was happening inside them, whatever voices, thoughts, visions, or dreams came. Whatever they considered real was real. Reality never had to come in contact in the same way with another being—human, animal, or insect. The nurses kept the patients safe from their own bubbles, those stretched and fragile membranes were so thin, like liquid. One thoughtless poke and a world could collapse.

A few days later, Norman emerged from his sanctuary. He

was quieter than usual and a little more wary, but he seemed to have recovered.

"Norman," Willis greeted him in the community room with the brightly-coloured circular tables.

"How are you today?" He almost asked, "How are you *feeling*," but thought better of it. Feelings were too complex and real, too scary to understand or tell honestly.

Norman shrugged. "Hey, Willis. Oh, you know. I thought I'd come out and make sure the place hadn't fallen apart."

"Missed you, Norman," Willis muttered awkwardly.

Norman managed a smile. "Thanks, mate." That was feeling enough, and Norman slapped him on the back to let him know he was most of the way back. Maybe they both were.

"Hey, Norman," Willis shuffled his feet a bit. "Sometimes I think I see the beast too."

"You do?" Norman's eyes widened.

"Yeah, only I think mine looks different from yours."

Norman nodded. "Yeah," he said. "That makes sense. Brain thing, I guess." They didn't say anything for more than a minute.

"Your mum was here," Willis started again, "with your wife."

"Yeah, I know. Nurse Julie told me."

"She looks really nice—your wife," Willis said.

Norman smiled.

"Did the nurse tell you what your wife said?" Willis asked hesitantly.

Norman started, "No, what?" Those feelings again.

"She said they love you, chap." Willis watched his friend manage a strangled smile. "You're lucky to have that."

"Yeah. Yeah, I know."

Chapter 44

MARTIN

Martin felt perverse in his need to see Frieda. What drove him? What drew him to her? Especially after the confrontation from his comrades—he wondered, was this so unusual? What must Frieda be thinking about his constant visits? Perhaps she thought he was sweet on her daughter. She was lovely, in a fragile way. He looked upon her as he would a timid, inquisitive mouse, and he did feel strangely protective of her chronic condition, but there was nothing more.

"My daughter will be very glad to see you," she had said. He didn't wish to give the wrong impression to either of them. They were very kind to him. He felt sickly, as though past the pangs of hunger and sleep. A chill was in him, like bone grating on steel. What was it? He had urgency in him. He vaguely knew what it was, but was afraid to manifest the words into sound and make it real.

He had been raised by his aunt and uncle, but never knew the care of a real mother. His aunt was already in her early forties when he was born. She never seemed happy around him. Whenever she reached to hold him, it was as though he had sharp thorns on his body. But what did any of it have to do with Frieda? His skin was uncomfortable, as though those invisible thorns were growing inwards, poking at his vital organs. Still, he went to her.

"Oh. Hello, Marty!" Frieda opened the door to her small, modest flat. "We weren't expecting you tonight." She grinned broadly.

"Frieda, you don't need to pretend—"

"Pretend?" Instead of her usual mock hurt, she looked genuinely confused.

"I am here, yes," Martin shuffled. "I'm just not sure if I should be." He hadn't seen her for two days. He had tried to break himself of whatever compulsion he had.

"What do you mean? Of course you are welcome here, Marty."

"I know. Thank you, Frieda."

"Do you not want to be friends any further?" Her voice dropped a chord. His heart was stretched. *Poke it and it will either burst or implode*, he thought dimly. "I don't know what I want to be. ... I don't know what I am looking for."

"Come in," she said simply. "My daughter is sleeping now." Martin stepped inside, uncertain of what would happen between those walls.

"Sit down." She was stern, as only a mother's compassion and guidance could be. She directed him to a chair and then disappeared into her hovel kitchen. She reappeared with a tea tray and biscuits, as always.

"The photo of your friend ... the Canadian ..." Martin's voice trailed off. He was sorely afraid of causing a reenactment of that painful night when he had made her remember and then speak the words aloud.

"Yes?" She looked practiced at seeming complacent.

"Do you have a better photograph of him? A head and shoulders shot, I mean, in which you can see his face?" She looked at him for a long moment. Then she went to a chest of drawers in the far corner and deftly opened the top drawer. She carefully lifted out a photo with no frame; it floated on slender fingertips. She held the photo as if she was having a silent conversation with the subject, and then she touched it briefly and brought it over to Martin. "This is him," she said. "This is my Willis." Frieda's eyes were like large dams with small cracks forming. She put her hand to her mouth in trepidation. This could be Pandora's box opened and with no one to shut the lid again. It was clear, though, that Willis had never been completely shut away. Martin turned his eyes to the photo and nearly dropped it. He looked at Frieda, searching. She looked back at him with some strange confirmation on her face. "You see it?" she asked, her voice a ghost whisper, hoarse and unsure.

"You knew?"

"I don't know. I still don't."

"This is why."

"Why what?"

"Why I have to come here," he replied, a chilling thrill in his voice.

Chapter 45

MARTIN

The man in the photograph peered back at Martin with a glint of humour in his steady, inquisitive, blue eyes. There was a faint smile resting on his lips, a slightly uneven line drawn under the short line of his nose, small nostrils, and narrow bridge, mirroring Martin's own marked features. This man was hiding another world beneath his skin too. A strong, half-cynical front thinly covered a greater depth of vulnerable thoughts and insecure actions. Martin imagined this man could also talk his way out of things, when put on spikes. Maybe he talked his way out of himself, too—right out of his desired life. Could this really be him? Could this be the man Martin thought he needed to find, the man he thought he would never know?

He had asked his aunt a few childish but important questions when he was younger, and she always seemed uncomfortable and near tears. Most likely, she didn't want to be reminded that he hadn't been truly hers from the start. She would only say, "Your mother is gone. Must you always bring back ghosts?" Gone, not dead; he remembered that now. He was told that his father was gone, too. He had remained quiet for years, but never quiet in his thoughts. He always felt there was something more to know. He looked at Frieda, a near apparition to him now, as though she had floated out of the wall with an urgent message from the other side of the grave. Instead, she was very real, and she appeared to be looking at him with the same thoughts.

"The song you hum," he began, cautiously, "when you are cleaning."

"Yes, I used to—"

"I know, I vaguely remember it. Some warm, tender humming in the night …"

"When Willis wasn't there. When it was just you and I …" Her voice trailed off.

"Something in your eyes when I first saw you …" he started.

"I didn't dare to think it, but you reminded me so much of …" She broke to tears, not daring to move, and not yet allowing herself to welcome him again as her estranged—she couldn't even conceive the word in her mind, let alone utter it. Son. A rising force.

Chapter 46

FRIEDA

Frieda stood by the couch with one hand on her pregnant belly. Three months gone. She was torn between sitting and standing, not to mention keeping her distance and running to the man on the other side of the room.

"This wasn't supposed to happen," he said. He took a long drag from his cigarette and let the smoke escape from between his lips. He had been in her bedroom when she told him the news. Now he was dressed and pacing in her living room, and smoking furiously.

"Willis ... I didn't do this by myself," she said, her lip quivering. He snubbed out his cigarette in the ashtray, strode quickly to her side and laid gentle, yet urgent, hands on her shoulders.

"I know, darling, I'm not blaming you." He stepped back and rubbed the hair away from his temple. "I just don't know what I can do."

"I'm not asking you for anything," she said. She was lying, of course, but she wanted to stay strong. She wanted him, but she wanted their baby, too. "I'm keeping it!"

"You have to, and I never thought otherwise. I don't want you to lose it." He had tears standing on his bottom lashes. "I just can't leave everything. I have a family." He wasn't trying to be hurtful; he was simply trying to sort it all out.

"I know you do." There was no malice in her voice. There was nothing there except understanding, compassion, and defeat.

"I love you," he said emphatically.

"I know that, too." She smiled weakly.

This was the first scene of Martin's existence. Like many unplanned pregnancies, there was joy and panic; only his sudden emergence was greeted with another complication. His mother was his father's mistress—still common, but a hard and unpleasant situation. Frieda was twenty. Willis was a few years older, with a wife and young son. He had opted to stay with his family and cover up his second life, the life he wanted more.

Their son was born and Willis continued to make his frequent "business trips" to visit both mother and baby in Germany. For two years he doted on his would-be family, until the tension at home became too thick. His wife was growing more and more suspicious of him and desperate for him to be at home. She didn't throw herself across the front door, preventing him from leaving, but she chopped the vegetables in such a way that he was sure she knew. He was too miserable to continue, and he hated his deception. His wife and son didn't deserve the life he had given them, and neither did Frieda and their child. He tried to compensate his lack of attendance at home by providing them with a comfortable living, as though it might be a distraction for them, and that they would forget about him, bedazzled by new clothes, toys, furniture, and kitchen appliances. It wasn't working. They wanted him. He should have been happy about it, but he wasn't. Even if he left Frieda, he knew, darkly, that he would never be able to stay at home in that life again.

Frieda was in her living room one day when he arrived without warning. She had not expected to see him for another three weeks. She sat on the couch while their young son played nearby. She surprised him, though, by speaking first. Her shoulders slumped as she whispered violently, "I don't think I can do this anymore." He wasn't sure what she meant by *this*. She moved away from the couch and stood beside him, looking at their little boy. Then she leaned into him and covered her face in his shirt, sobbing.

"I can't handle the responsibility all on my own," she cried.

"What do you mean? I give you enough money to provide for you both ..." he started.

"I know you have your family, Willis... but I need you here. I need you to help me raise our son. He barely knows you."

"He's two years old, Frieda," he argued.

"That doesn't matter. He'll know, and he'll learn to miss you and to have disappointments." She was tired and growing angry. She was angry at him and at their situation. How did he think he could keep this going?

"What do you plan to do?" His voice was solemn. She hadn't fully expected this response from him. She was hoping it might be enough to make him reconsider.

"I— I don't know."

She sounded feeble. He sighed audibly and restrained too much emotion from his voice. "I have one idea," he said, and he sounded so calm it almost frightened her. "I confess that I thought of it when I first learned you were pregnant."

"What idea?" She was stunned that he had ideas he hadn't shared with her, but then she expected there were likely many of them.

"I have a sister who moved over to England after the war. I think she wanted to be closer to me, but we rarely see each other. She lives in London, but I don't think she plans to stay there long— perhaps a few years. She has talked about wanting to move back to Canada. I'm not sure where." He was tap dancing, spinning his words into a soft landing. "She can't have children."

"Would she provide a good home?" Frieda couldn't believe she was uttering those words; she was making it real.

"Yes, she has a well-to-do husband, and she is also educated," he assured her.

"You would always have access to your son then. What about me?"

He wanted to tell her that he would be losing his son too. "This is the only solution I can think of," he said flatly. "And ... I don't want to put anymore salt in the wound, but she would probably also want to change his name."

Frieda had insisted on naming their son Willis, and he didn't have the heart to tell her it was also the name of his other son. She never asked about his family—when he was with her, his other life and all the people in it disappeared. To his relief, Frieda only nodded dumbly.

"Yes, I suppose she would," she said.

"Listen to me, Frieda; do you want to give him up or not? I am only asking you this because I cannot leave my family."

He was so dejected, it pained her. How had it come to this? She was being asked to give up both the man she loved and the one part of him that would forever remind her of him. She knew she couldn't manage with her son on her own. She had to work, and she had so much growing to do. She hated being isolated with him all day, every day, without a husband to help her. Her friends had all moved away from her, as they pursued their courses and jobs and went dancing on Friday nights. She didn't have Willis, and she was losing herself all at once.

"Alright," she said, tears streaming down her cheeks. "Alright."

Chapter 47

WILLIS

Norman was more subdued and less judgmental of the TV congregation. He seemed not to see them anymore, and instead, he slowly became part of the plastic chairs and Formica tables. He was not leaving, not as long as the beast came back, which was less and less. Still, he walked slowly and checked around corners frequently. The more Willis watched his friend give into his daytime nightmare, the more he realized that his own condition could not be credited as serious. His own problems may have needed some counseling, but not anti-hallucinogenic pills. His problems were selfish and self-inflicted by displaced anger and accusation and not having enough accountability for his own actions, or lack of action. He was still a little boy in a man's body, feeling the loneliness of neglect and disappointment. He wasn't mentally ill. He was angry and withdrawn and, therefore, an emotionally dysfunctional adult. Meanwhile, he was watching his friend fight and lose his battles, and the only conqueror was a symphony of drugs to calm the beast.

When Willis' mother came to see him, he allowed the visit. He was in his room when the nurse notified him that he had a guest. Willis didn't need to ask who it was. He felt a mixture of humility and annoyance at his mother's seeming concern for his welfare.

"Oh, Willis," she exclaimed when she saw him, and she gave him a warm, maternal hug. Willis thought her affectionate display was only for the nurses' benefit, but he immediately chided himself for thinking so. After all, she was his mother, and for many years she had carried the burden of the role of two parents. She had a right to be concerned, not that any of it was her fault or responsibility.

"Willis, how are you?"

"I'm better, Mother. I am taking it day by day."

"What, here?" She looked confused and a little embarrassed. "Son, why don't you come home with me? I spoke to your doctor. I …"

"You what?"

"Now, don't get upset. He wouldn't tell me anything. Bloody confidentiality." She ruffled slightly. "But I'm asking you. What is it? What's wrong? Are you not feeling quite right in the head?" She had lowered her voice to a conspiratorial whisper.

Willis straightened his back and shifted in his shoes. "It's a little more complicated than all that, Mother," he said, feeling a sharp, irritable pang.

She searched his eyes, trying to dig into him. There had to be some weak spot in his foundation, something to chisel.

What she didn't realize was that he was made of soft clay, and she didn't know how to mould clay.

Instead, she wanted to cut with scissors and erase with correction tape, burn everything down into ash. She didn't know how to skillfully bend something without breaking it, or to acknowledge what already existed and work with it rather than against. She only knew how to destroy and rebuild.

Willis may have been soft clay, but he was already dry and glazed. He was near done. She pursed her lips tightly, holding back an onslaught of questions, pointless drivel, accusations, guilt, and, finally, sympathy.

He looked back at her, exhausted, not wanting to explain to her what he was still trying to understand for himself. *She is a wall of hollow bricks*, he thought, and he couldn't fill her. He had tried since childhood, but she was too preoccupied with the absence of his father. Even when he was there, he was absent. Willis began to move away from her, desperate to get back to his room and be in the comfort of solitude, where he could rest and think and not be intruded upon.

"Wait," his mother uttered, like a kitten first finding its voice—a sharp, pathetic sound. She didn't look at him directly. "Take this. Let me know when you need to talk." She held out a folded paper. "Take this," she said again. He realized that she was incapable of other words, and the surface of his clay suffered a small fault line.

⎯⎯◆◗◆⎯⎯

Willis left his mother and went back to his room. He sat heavily on his bed, unfolded the letter, and began to read her words:

Dear Son,

I don't presume to know what you are going through, but I'll venture as far to say that I believe I have some small idea. I was there too, remember? But I wasn't there for you, and enough years have gone by that you should know why.

I was young when I had you—and your father was a dashing young soldier. You should know I was in love with him. I tried to fill him with everything I had, without ever being renewed of this endless giving. He was ambitious, with no room for family. I was giving too much of myself to the wrong person and only existing from day to day, making sure you were fed properly, clothed, educated, and well-mannered—but I didn't make sure you were loved enough. Really loved, heart and soul loved. It may be too little too late, but I am sorry.

I wasn't loved by him, so I couldn't give it to you. Not in the way I was supposed to. We both loved you, Willis—just not enough. We were too wrapped up in our own stories, our own misdealt hands and shortcomings. The one thing I need to stress upon you is that he did love you, no matter how poorly he showed you.

There were other reasons he was moving away from us so slowly and definitely, and for so long. The early days were my fault. I never could just let him come to me in his own time, to have space and rest to sort out the life that was thrust upon him—oh no, I had to thrust myself upon him, harder, trying to rid myself of my own confusion and insecurity. I drove him from us, I think. Yes, I am sure of it. After all these years, if you need to blame someone, then blame me. I am still here and capable of talking with you. I am not defending him. I am only saying there are reasons that I have been forced to acknowledge—for both our shortcomings—reasons I didn't become aware of until much later.

I know that you sensed your father cheated on me, on us, from the time of your childhood. The excuses become flimsy after a while, don't they? Like the same piece of Saran wrap used over and over again to contain soggy leftovers. Pretty soon, nobody wants it. You weren't deaf and blind. I was, though. I didn't want to hear or see the truth about his constant business trips. In the beginning, I believe that they were business trips. I believe he shrouded himself in work to better provide for you and to avoid me. The truth is that he was never a family man; he was a businessman.

You remember how depressed I was when he was away? How I used to stay in the bedroom, sleeping and crying? I wasn't a strong person then. The worst part of all is to drive yourself mad with wondering and never knowing whether or not to believe the stories that manifest, almost three-dimensionally, in your head. The not knowing can kill a person. I know. I also knew he had a sister. You never met her, because they were estranged for reasons he never shared with me. I was so desperate to have some small piece of him, some part of his life that preexisted you and me—to try and know him and to understand something. I'm still not sure of what I was looking for, but I found the unexpected when I decided to visit her. Luckily, she still lived in England at that time. She moved to Canada shortly after

I met her. I thought that was a trifle strange, too. She has lived over there for twenty years now.

Her name is Ivy. She was wary of me at first. She said Willis had sent her pictures of us over the years, but she was asked not to send any in return. Of course, I thought it was all very strange, until I met her son.

My son, it pains me to reveal this part to you. Her son was about three years old at the time (you would have been six or so), and I could see your father's eyes in him—so many similarities in his small face. His name is Martin, but they called him Marty. He was quiet and calculating, a fraction too polite for a three-year-old boy when I made his acquaintance. Son, that little boy had your father's eyes. I didn't know how it was possible. I wondered if he detected in me the pulsing desire to flee from the small, firm squeeze of his hand. I tried to cover my surprise and awkwardness. I never did have a proper talk with your Aunt Ivy—strange to call her that, as she is such a stranger to us. Instead, I muttered something about family connections and how hard it was with Willis gone half of the time. She smiled and patted my arm. "They are men," she said in a patronizing way. "It is no good for them to stay safe indoors at home—they are destined to see the world and conquer what part of it they can." Although I wrote her words down as a reminder, I found no comfort in them and only thought of my own sacrifices—my own battles fought and lost. I left knowing only one thing— your father was lost, and no child or woman could save him. I stopped trying then, and I stopped wondering … perhaps I stopped living, too. None of it was fair to you, but how could I reveal such a terrible secret without knowing all of the circumstances? Your Aunt Ivy was barren, that much I did know. I couldn't explain your father, and you, being in this child, but I knew it was so. I wrote to Ivy soon after your father's passing and she responded. It seemed your father's restrictions had been lifted from her with his death. I asked nothing of Marty, other than his wellbeing—there would be no point in making everything difficult, even now, and despite my own anger, I didn't want to upset the boy's life with inconsequential truths. I was his aunt, and that was all. She offered that he had gone a bit wayward and was living in London. She had not heard from him, and she placed single quotations around 'living.' Again, I didn't ask. I hope you *can forgive me for these things I kept. There seemed no point in telling you. When you came to visit me that day at my flat, you seemed lost, too. I saw more of your father in you than I had before. I was startled by your erratic behaviour and your insistence of things being a certain way that you could never control. I feared for your lack of direction, and I have for some time. There is no predetermined destination—there is only a journey where you decide on the roads. There are many crossroads, and you can't listen to the first scarecrow you meet. He won't help you anyhow. Maybe none of this is helpful, but you've only had one man to follow, one who lost his own way years ago. It is important you know that. You are your own man with your own compass. You have parents who led you into a dark place, but that was long ago. You can lead yourself out. You always could. You also have a mother, if you want her.*

With love, Mom

The next morning, after little sleep, Willis checked himself out. He had the beginning of an answer.

Chapter 48

ELLIE

She violently cut the vegetables while her son watched television in the next room, preparing the meal to the accompaniment of bells, whistles, wisecracks, and sledge hammer cartoon noises. Her husband walked through the door with his heavy suitcase. She stopped cutting.

"Willis. You're home early," she said with the knife floating in her hand, her shoulder taut and her elbow a well-greased hinge. He didn't respond right away. Instead, he shoved his luggage into the hallway, out of the way of the door.

"We finished sooner. I thought I would surprise you," he said. His voice was flat and tired. There was no spark left in their relationship. She turned her attention back to dinner, chopping off the bad ends of the vegetables and then breaking down the rest into smaller, bite-size, manageable pieces. This was her marriage.

"Sam always keeps you working for one reason or another—he has his claws in you. You expect me to believe he simply told you,

'The job's over; go home and enjoy your family?'" she sneered, and he didn't like it.

Sam may as well wear my wedding ring, she thought dismally.

"I'm home. Can I enjoy being home? Please?" He stalked out of the hallway, and she could hear him asking their son, Willis, about his cartoon program. The conversation didn't last long, which was predictable. She knew he wasn't really interested. She sighed. *Willis Jr. is too young to notice his father's failure to interact with him*, she thought. She let her son stay in front of the television, immersed in that other world. He seemed happy there, happy and oblivious.

She began cutting the onions, wiping her eye as she went. Once the vegetables were done, she scraped them into the boiling pot, replaced the lid, turned the heat down to simmer, and went into the bedroom, where she found her husband.

"I talked to Sam," he said, his back turned to her as he perused the closet for his casual slacks. "I won't be going on any business trips for the rest of the year."

"It's March," she said.

"Yes. What does that matter?"

"You mean you're going to be home for nine months?"

"Yes. That's what I said—the rest of the year." He sounded irritable. She didn't know how to respond. He hadn't been home for more than four consecutive months during their entire married life.

"You're going to be home," she said again, unable to stop her stunned repetition.

"Do you want to check the stove?" he asked. He was afraid he might crack. He wasn't home for ten minutes and already he was regretting his act of self-incarceration. He was trying to be loyal and noble.

"Sure," she said, turning towards the door. No, she didn't want to check on dinner. She wanted to lock the bedroom door, to lock them both in and find out what the hell was really happening. For so long she had wanted him to be home and to be a stable father and husband in their household. She had cried herself to sleep missing him, hating him, fabricating runaway imaginings of where he might be and with whom. All of it was unfounded, but very real in her mind. She had grown used to this—this martyrdom of wifely duty and her role as a single parent.

She knew Sam better than to accept that he had freed her husband of any upcoming business ventures, out of the kindness of his heart. She couldn't ever envision Sam thinking of family first. It simply wasn't in his vocabulary. There was something else keeping her husband home, and he didn't seem happy about it. Then again, maybe it was her fault for assaulting him at the front door. She didn't want to cause waves now, or push him farther away and out of their lives again. She couldn't do that to her son. Still, part of her didn't want him to be home anymore. For too long he had been somewhere else that he never shared with her. To her horror, she realized that she didn't trust him. He was like an animal gone from the herd and returning with a different scent on him. Most herds would kill the suspect beast. She went back to the stove and finished making his dinner.

⊰⧫⊱

He kept his word, although he still worked late in the evenings. He was a mainstay in their lives for the rest of the year and for a few years after. Then, one day, he came home and announced, "I have to go away for a bit—a week-long trip. Sam needs me to help him pull through a business deal in France."

"Okay," she said, and went to the closet to pull out his suitcase and collect any shirts that needed ironing. She had become so accustomed to having him around, the security of him. In his absence, the cartoons in the living room seemed amplified; everything did. She could hear the grating of her kitchen knife against raw vegetable and the clean breakage. There was an echo in the house again, or perhaps it was only between her ears. The absence of his voice was deafening. She could never say how much she loved him, not to him, and not even to herself. She often worried that he yearned to return to Canada, his home country, but he seemed content to call England home.

She felt isolated now, as if she was the one living in a foreign place. She had Willis Jr. with her, and she kept him close. In many ways, she had conditioned him to not be social or acknowledge anything beyond her. She had knowledge of her husband's sister living in London, and she knew that she had a young child. Her husband was a successful businessman, a tycoon of sorts. Maybe she would sympathize, or at least provide some female companionship and family connection. She never understood why their families didn't mix before. Ellie decided to contact her.

She found her sister-in-law in the phone book, took the phone out of the carriage, and began dialing the rotary numbers. There was a sharp buzz in the phone before the voice on the other end recited the numbers back to her.

"Yes, hello, Ivy?" she began. "This is Ellie, Willis' wife."

"Ellie—oh, Ellie, yes," the woman's voice started. She sounded flustered. A rehearsed, almost forced sweetness in her voice with a cooler edge.

Ellie Hancocks found her confidence. "Yes, hello," she said. "You must think it strange that I am calling you now ..."

"No, no," the other woman interrupted her. "Actually, I am surprised you hadn't called sooner."

"Why is that?" This conversation was becoming strange indeed. Why hadn't she called Ellie, then? Was she eager to talk to her or had she been dreading that day? There was a hesitation on the other end.

"No particular reason," Ivy replied, sweetly, "only that we are so close in proximity." Her highbrow speak for "neighbours," but they weren't really. Her sister-in-law lived across the city. Five stops on the Tube.

"I'd like to meet you," Ellie said, trying to put an end to the rambling of strangers trying to make niceties.

"Is Willis out of town?"

"Yes. He has gone away on business for a week."

"Then let's meet."

Chapter 49

MARTIN

Martin wasn't sure what to do with this new information. He had always sensed a piece of the puzzle was missing. He couldn't see the picture in full view, so he was never sure where the missing piece belonged. Now he held this puzzle piece between his thumb and forefinger, still not sure of where it belonged. Frieda seemed to be at a loss as well. This new relationship lay between them like a chess game, and they had lost track of whose turn it was. Inexplicably, he sensed it was his. He felt that, somehow, she waited for him to unravel the secret, all the while afraid of his intuition, his ability to read her heart. She was relieved and anxious, all at once.

Martin thought of his half-sister. He had never had a sibling, and he wanted to begin making up for lost time. He wanted to help take care of her and to give her his friendship. He felt that she had warmed up to him, trusted him as a regular visitor and friend of her mother. He wanted to be involved in their lives, and to belong. ... Perhaps he could also work at the tavern or somewhere close by to earn his keep. Maybe he could go to school. He planned to give money to Frieda and her daughter to cover their medical bills and living expenses, but he also wanted to do something honest—to participate in doing real work—for his new mother and sister.

His mother and sister; the thought jolted him as though he were being pulled out of himself. He looked over at the empty chair in the corner where Frieda's daughter usually sat. Perhaps the gift of money was not a curse, but a challenge set for him. What would he do with it? Would he continue in a life of no responsibility or sense of consequence, or would he allow himself to be altered and let others in? He realized how separate from the world he had been. He had not allowed himself to connect with anyone. He had been living in his head, wrapped inside his ego like an embryo. He had something to learn from these people, and maybe that was his hardest lesson. He couldn't face the fact that he had nothing to offer back, let alone anything he needed to learn. How arrogant he had been. How blind and arrogant he was to not see a world around him.

"My aunt took good care of me," Martin offered. At this, Frieda allowed a tear to escape and slide freely down her face. She didn't move to banish it from her cheek.

"I'm glad," she said simply. A smile broke on her lips and another tear escaped her bright, grey eyes. This time she gave a short, embarrassed laugh as she smoothed the wet emotion off her cheeks. He understood. The tears were not for his loss and return, but for his generosity of words. Her worst fear was that he would reject her. His few kind words meant there was a chance—not for starting again, but for continuing their friendship on a new track, a gateway to another destination.

"I'll stay," he said.

Chapter 50

WILLIS

During their last visit, before Willis went into the hospital, his mother was abrasive. Now he realized that although she meant every word, she was also covering up more vulnerable emotions. She was not so hard, but she had learned to be hardened. Inside, she was as lost as him. She didn't want to play the victim. Her husband was dead, she was free, and the past couldn't be changed. She was determined to build a new beginning, starting by mending her relationship with Willis. He understood now.

Before Willis checked out, he wanted to say goodbye to Norman. Unfortunately, he'd had a violent relapse and was in voluntary lockdown again. Willis left a message for his friend, telling him that he would outrun the beast someday. He wasn't sure what it meant, except that he wished his friend to be well again. He felt that Norman would make sense of it. Willis tried to imagine the beast chasing Norman—what it looked like and how quickly it moved. The fact that the beast was still pursuing Norman convinced

Willis it was time to leave. The only beast Willis had found was the one he saw in the mirror.

He was his own worst demon, and that didn't mean he was psychotic. No drugs could take away his self-absorbed behaviour. His mother had seen the seeds of his father growing in him, an uncertain and reckless attitude that could lead to nothing except self-loathing and escapism. The persona of his wealthy, confident, cold-hearted father was a facade, one he bought into. Then he modeled a set of rules built on this fallacy. He had not understood his mother or father, or ever stopped to wonder what drove them into themselves. He was too busy lamenting their failure to him. Weren't children supposed to demand love and attention? Weren't they only meant to receive?

He had also made himself a victim long ago. But what could he have done differently? How could he communicate his sense of disappointment and confusion, especially when his disappointments were telegraphed or relayed through the means of someone outside the family? His father's friend and barrister, Sam, came to mind. How could he reach out past such a definitive voice, a gateway, past the solid, punctuated periods and excuses as dense as his father's last terms, offerings, and wishes? He could start talking, though, to his mother, his surviving relative, whose blood was still warm and who could suture the gaps long left open to fester.

When Willis walked out into the morning, the sky was cloudy enough to remind him of a thin layer of grey. There were still issues to settle, but he decided to enjoy this knowledge, knowing he had problems to solve before racing ahead to start solving them. The knowledge of it and the opportunity was enough of a break in the clouds, for now. The nurse at the admissions booth had told him, "Good luck." He carried it with him, feeling its potential. There was a chance for good luck, and it lay in his actions. He needed this time to absorb the world again and assimilate himself back into it as a valuable, purposeful citizen and human being. The cool air bristled on his exposed neck and hands, unlike the poorly circulated air in the hospital's community room. Willis was free in more ways than one.

No one on the sidewalk looked at him strangely; it was only on the inside that he felt like an outsider. He moved out of the hospital entranceway, his prison, and turned right, towards the subway. He was moving slowly back into a different institution and one with no guaranteed lockdown. He couldn't completely shut out this world.

The traffic on the London sidewalks had not thinned and the sounds had not changed, but everything seemed amplified. Stranger still, he did not feel stressed or anxious. Instead, he was newly embraced by the sights, sounds, and people. This was his home, his life. He strolled rather than bustled along with the fast-paced crowd, walking among them, but not yet falling into their stride.

The subway was full of morning commuters traveling across London to their various offices and cubicle spaces with coffee and Danish in hand. He knew he had an office, a physical office, but he didn't want to go back there. He wanted to veer away from his father's footprints. He could be anything, perhaps work in a coffee shop where he could chat with customers all day. He didn't want to argue for people's lives anymore; he just wanted to live. He wanted to do something uncorrupted and be happy and eager when he woke in the mornings. Willis knew this world existed, although he'd never been a part of it before. It would be a healthy way to spend his time and would put his mind on something other than himself—whatever it took to start living a normal and productive life. Once again, Willis felt free. For so long, he had existed by treading stagnant water. These new plans were his and not his father's.

He moved forward on the subway, saying more and listening more to people whom he never thought he would be sharing his day. The entire class system crumbled for him on that morning, as he held more respect for the man who sold him his newspaper and the store clerk he shared a conversation with on the Tube. He immersed himself in their stories and humanity.

Soon, a woman stepped into their car, and Willis looked up from his conversation with a city worker; this man, coffee in hand, was heading to a worksite in the outskirts of London. She flew in the door, with long legs and a distracted look. Her chin-length, cropped hair covered half of her face, and she turned away from the possible stares of other passengers. She was like a tall person, so painfully aware of their height they did anything to hide, cover, or bend lower to vanish into the crowd. Usually, it wasn't possible. A presence was a presence. He was struck by her jerky, shy movements, and then realized she looked familiar to him. He continued his conversation with the city worker, sneaking glances that were not yet perceived. He waited for her stop, but it didn't come, and soon it was the city worker's stop. After saying goodbye, he left his seat, cautious as a cat crawling towards something interesting but foreign, and potentially dangerous. She was not facing him, and her arms were tightly crossed with a purse string hanging precariously over her right shoulder. He moved into the seat beside her, and even then she did not become aware of him right away, until he spoke.

"Excuse me, I think I know you," he said, his voice lofting above a whisper.

"Lots of people know me," she answered, tired. She heard herself say the words, so tired and practiced. She shook her head as if trying to shake loose something. "I'm sorry." How her old ways worked to impede her. She was not that "I'm whoever you want me to be" girl anymore.

He waited for her to collect her thoughts. He was sure lots of people did know her.

"Where do you think you know me from?" It was an attempt to start over. He felt himself relax.

"I'm not sure." He felt awkward again, as though he should have an answer and a story prepared for this woman. After all, he had encroached upon her space, her time, and possibly her life, all in this moment. She was looking at him, anticipating something, probably trying to place *him*.

She felt he was just one of many men who thought they knew her, but only knew one part of her—the part she kept trying to forget. Damn him, here he was insisting on reminding her.

"I haven't been in London for very long," she offered. "I've just come back from Paris."

"Come back? How long were you away?" Willis asked hopefully.

"A few months," she answered breezily. "Perhaps a little more."

"I see," he said. "Why were you in Paris? Do you work there?"

She almost choked, as the air was sucked into her throat strangely. He seemed confused and concerned by her involuntary response and said, "It's okay if it's personal. You don't have to tell me about it."

"Thank you, I don't know you, so I don't think I will." A careful answer that gave nothing away, except the depth of discomfort and secrecy. She was a secret.

"That's fine," he said. She switched her long legs in the seat and he suddenly remembered her. Then he understood. He wasn't sure if he should say anything about it to this young woman who had stolen his lucky franc on that unlucky day. Fortune worked in strange ways.

"What is your name?" he asked, keeping any hint of familiarity out of his voice. He was careful not to look at her with narrow, searching eyes. She breathed in, slower, "Evelyn," she said quietly, and then more assured, "Evelyn."

"Evelyn," he repeated. He vaguely remembered an "Ev" sound.

"My stop is coming up," she said. He could feel her moving away.

"Wait, would you like to join me for lunch?"

She contemplated this a moment, as though it were a weighty decision. He was asking her for lunch. She had to eat.

"Sure, why not?" Evelyn heard herself say. The announcer came over the loud speaker, her voice muffled, announcing the name of the next stop, which was Earl's Court, and reminding passengers to "mind the gap." The train stopped and the jaw-like doors opened. Evelyn and Willis bounced out. "Where should we eat?"

He remembered that she had only just returned from Paris, but he thought she would have a better idea for finding the most appetizing local establishments. He was not used to this part of London. This was her territory, wasn't it? Maybe she had picked this stop to simply lose him, and he had confused her with his invitation.

"Isn't this your part of town?" He asked before he could stop his thoughts from escaping his mouth. She looked at him, embarrassed and out-of-sorts.

"Not really, no," she said without further explanation. Her accent was a bit muddled, but he figured it was because she had spent so much time in France. He didn't know why he had assumed she was from that part of town because she got off the train there. It was completely unfounded. "Why do you think I live here?" She turned towards him, allowing his comment to register. It had seemed so innocent, but it was intrusive.

"I don't know," he said honestly. "Ah, here's a pub." He was losing the upper hand, not that he ever really had it.

"Great, another pub," she spoke out of the corner of her mouth. Pubs started things she didn't want to get started.

"You don't fancy the pub?" He looked even more uncomfortable. "We can go somewhere else if you prefer."

"No, no." She waved her hand, distracted. "It's fine." None of it was fine. She had a strange familiarity about this man. "I'm sorry," she started, "I didn't ask your name."

"Wil— Willis," he said. She smiled, a wave of nostalgia washing over her. She gave him an approving look.

"Nice threads, Willis." She lightly touched his sleeve. He had changed back into the day clothes he wore on the day he checked into the hospital. He smiled. She didn't have to know. They walked into the pub and found a table beside the window. A perky waitress took their orders, two pints of beer and two fish and chips. The pints came first, and as she took a couple of swigs from her glass, she peered out the window, as though it was a new place to her. He didn't want to admit it, but he was just as fascinated with the passersby and grey streets. They had both been away for a significant period of time. Her gaze was different, though. She saw past the people and streets. He decided to go out on a limb.

"Who is he?" he asked, trying to suppress the turned up corners of his mouth. He took another swig to hide his amusement. It didn't occur to him that he could be wrong and make an ass out of himself. He felt too sure, and her facial expression was too incredulous.

"Pardon?" She, in turn, tried to sound cool and abrasive.

"Your boyfriend," he said, gaining confidence. "Who is he?"

She looked out the window again. "He wasn't my boyfriend," she volunteered. He didn't really expect her to, so he wasn't sure what to do with this information. Then he realized, if she was the same woman he thought she was, then there would probably be no boyfriend; bad for business. "I'm not even really sure who he was."

"You miss him." Willis surmised that he was not much older than this girl, and he didn't want to be too involved, but something moved him to take on a brotherly role.

"Everyone has to move along." She sounded unconvincing. She sloughed off the question, if that's what it was. More than anything, it was another intrusion.

"You miss him," Willis said with conviction. He didn't really care either way. He just wanted to be right. Her indifference and uncomfortable gestures confirmed this for him. She was silent for a minute.

"Yeah, okay." She bent her neck forward as though she were carrying an enormous weight. "He came in so unexpectedly and then left too quickly, but I understood."

"How did you meet him?"

She eyed him carefully. How much was she willing to reveal? "On the train to Paris," she said. "We shared a carriage. I didn't want to go to Paris." She wasn't sure why she had confessed that. Perhaps it was because she knew she was so far out of the clutches of Frank. She could just talk.

"Why? Who doesn't want to go to Paris?"

"Well, I wasn't exactly sightseeing." Why was she telling him all of this? She couldn't stop herself from talking, and she wasn't feeling shy or ashamed or confused. If anything, she felt tired and angry. She wanted to exorcise that part of her, and maybe she could do that as a strange kind of confessional to this near-stranger. Somehow, he felt safe and still oddly familiar.

"What were you doing there?"

"Meeting people I didn't want to meet." She brought back her jagged voice and then paused. "Except Marty ... I didn't know I would meet him."

"Marty?" Willis had a sharp moment of recognition. Martin was not a common name, and he was searching his mind for where he had heard it before. Then he remembered his mother's letter and the young man on the sidewalk. Could they be the same person? He kept his poker face, although he was sure his mouth had pulled slightly. The secrets were building under his tongue.

"Yeah, Marty. Short for Martin. He was my Paris." Her face lighted, and it warmed him to see it.

"So, what was his story?"

"I don't really know. He tried to pan off some cockamamie story to me about why he was traveling to Paris. He was coming from London, obviously, but he had come all the way from Canada."

"All in one go?" Willis' curiosity was growing stronger.

"No, no. Well, I don't know for sure. He had picked up a slight lilt in his accent. He had a load of money, but he didn't seem like a wealthy person." She looked like she was playing a tape recording in her head, trying to bring back every word, every touch, every-thing he had given her, a picture of his face. "He didn't give much of his identity away, but I knew him."

"How do you mean he didn't look wealthy?" Willis tried not to sound too intense, but her description of this Martin was becoming more intriguing to him.

"I don't really know—it's a hard thing to explain. He was clean, but scruffy; in control, but lost. He didn't seem to have much in the way of material attachments." She shrugged her shoulders and smiled helplessly. That was Martin; that's what she knew. He was someone who held a universe inside of him, just like her. Maybe he was also confessing himself to someone now. She hoped he wouldn't carry any burdens. Willis nodded, looking satisfied with her description, but there was something else in his posture. A tension had grown in his shoulders, and the skin around his knuckles stretched a little tighter. She didn't say anything.

"Canadian, ..." he repeated to himself. "Where in Canada?"

"British Columbia," she mused.

"Ah, the west coast, I've heard it is beautiful there. Actually, my father is from Vancouver, but I've never been." Now it was his turn to taper off from the conversation and swim in his own thoughts of why and if. ... He forgot she was there for a moment. Silently, he wondered if this was all such a coincidence, this chance meeting with one of the women he had once used for his own gratification, and how much she was connecting pieces for him and bringing questions to answers. He was enjoying his pint and simply sitting with her. They were able to expose themselves there, safely, in the afternoon in the real world, sitting among everyday people. They weren't admitting themselves to each other, but they were sharing themselves in fragments. In these moments, the world was changing for both of them. He had a thought—he recognized her, so why shouldn't she vaguely recognize him? It was possible. Was she so numb that she could erase every face that came next to hers? Sitting there, talking to her as though none of it existed, their body histories. He didn't believe so.

"Are you in a hurry to go anywhere?" he asked her.

"No," she mused. "Not especially."

"Will you take a walk with me?" They were both suspended in this day, having touched down from an uncertain place. They finished their pints. She smiled to herself, entertaining a memory of another day she had accepted to go for a walk and spent an hour in sunshine. This was grey, but it didn't matter. There was a sun behind the curtain.

They walked to a nearby park and sat on a park bench. He looked out at the grey clouds with a look of contentment.

"It is good to be outside," he said. She wasn't sure what he meant, but she knew what it meant for her.

"Yes," she agreed. "And to be alone in it ..." She stopped and gave him a sharp look. "I didn't mean ... I mean, I like this, ..." she stammered, wanting to stuff the grey clouds into her mouth.

"It's alright," he assured her. "I know exactly what you mean."

"You do?"

He sighed; he was going to cross over. "I've been locked inside and feeling crowded for a while now, in every sense," he paused. "I've had some treatment recently."

"What were you treated for?"

"Anxiety, depression, feeling confused and out of sorts, in general. I wasn't coping." There was a silence beside him, and he hoped she wasn't registering clinical words like "psychotic" and "shrink." She turned to him.

"Thank you for telling me something so personal about yourself." Her voice was as smooth as caramel. She seemed subdued and thoughtful, her head bent.

"What is the matter?"

"Why were you out of sorts, do you think?"

"Long story—I don't want to detain you," he said. There was something in his voice that wanted her to tug a little harder.

"I don't need to go anywhere—not yet," she urged.

He chuckled, a little unnerved, as he was being made to show his cards, "Well, to start with, I didn't have much of a relationship with my father—classic case, right? He was not around much when I was growing up. Instead, he was away growing money trees." He felt as though he should be lying on a leather couch rather than leaning back on a park bench with a strange woman. But was it all so strange, really? Wasn't he orchestrating this experience—a last stage of his treatment, the confessional? Hadn't he chosen her on the Tube? He knew it would eventually come to this. He wanted it to, even if he didn't feel ready.

She interjected, "I can relate, I think … I was messed up in my family life."

His long frame relaxed, as he didn't feel so guarded after her words—these small gifts. It was refreshing to have honesty.

"Marty—he never opened up completely. He was there, but he gave more of his energy to keep me standing. He never let himself lean on me. He was more concerned for *my* welfare, but there was more going on inside of him." She was placing puzzle pieces in her mind. "That's why he had to go after he made sure I was alright." This was not a preconceived statement; this came from her lips as a revelation. She ran her hands through her hair, roughly. Martin had cared about her. She knew that, in some vague sense; she'd liked having a man there to protect her from the outside world and herself. He was never worried about her fragility, though. If anything, he was constantly trying to push her out of her comfort zones and to confront the big, scary picture. She was living on the other side of the thin layer that separated her from her power to be her own guardian, a layer that distorted the world for her and made her believe she could never cross over.

She had felt the sweet pang of Marty's leaving while on the rooftop, lying under the stars. She knew he was out there. Still, it hit her more deeply now because she hadn't thought so much about his destiny, only that his time with her had to end. Why, she couldn't say—only that she never expected someone to stay for good reason. She was away from Frank and feeling stronger, and he didn't want her to lean so much on him that he became another Frank to her—someone who hampered her growth. She was away from all the Franks in the world now, and as she spoke to Willis, she felt another freedom starting to uncoil inside of her. She was shedding an old skin there.

"Marty sounds like a decent man," Willis said. He was glad to know that this man, who he believed to be his half-brother, had helped her.

"I don't know too many of them," she replied.

He didn't want to pry too deep into her life. It wasn't necessary to open any wounds, barely healed, but she kept talking.

"Luckily, my father wasn't my real father," she continued. "No real father would have treated me the way he did."

"You don't have to tell me," he said. He wanted to stop her from exposing herself again. He didn't want to know. He just wanted to sit there, hold her hand if she let him, and let the world be silent for a short time. She didn't say anymore, and he felt it wasn't because he had stifled her. Maybe she was relieved and she didn't want to puncture holes in the dead stars to show that they didn't really exist anymore. She just wanted to let everything be. Still, she said, "He took something away from me ... something I haven't been able to get back. Not until now." She sounded defiant.

"What did he take from you?"

"Everything a little girl should not be asked to give away. He took my innocence. I can't have it back completely, but I can redefine it. I have been innocent—no, ignorant—of not understanding true contentment and being whole, and now I can start to find it." She smiled and let out a little breath.

"I believe you will," he said softly. He could have told her that he knew her secret, but he didn't. How he had collided with her once before—before either of them were ready or willing to look at the way they had fed on each other's misery. The malicious, selfish Willis he had once been was finally exorcised, the one who wanted to make everyone bleed as much as him, if not more. Instead, he was struggling to give something back to her. He felt helpless, but he knew it didn't matter. He wasn't trying to control anything this time. Their shoulders were touching, instinctively, and that was enough. He had come full circle with her—this woman he had victimized less than a year before, and now they were two humans sharing a portion of the afternoon. This was what he needed and what had been lacking for him. Simple human contact—it didn't have to stem from his father, his parents, but that was where he had learned to not expect it. Then the world had become a place of solitude and rejection for him, and he had clung to his facade of highbrow ideals and his father's money, knowing all the while it wouldn't be enough. He had even tried following in his father's footsteps, a gravitational pull. It was bound to collapse, and it did. All he needed was this, her—not to keep, but for this time. Then he could go back to his life, the one he had yet to recreate. They were both teetering on a new brink of self. The overcast sky was moving away from them, revealing glimpses of a sun slipping past noon. She anxiously smoothed her hands over her knee-length skirt, covering the tops of her knees.

"I think I should go," she said. She felt that she had spent enough time leaning on this man, too. She didn't want to fall over or backward into a dependency situation, allowing someone else to take too much of her, to look inside and determine the workings of her. She rose from the bench, slow and diplomatic.

"Okay," he said. "There is a whole afternoon to conquer. We better not miss it." He smiled easily as they parted. He looked back once to watch her unshackled step and her head floating above her shoulders. Then he turned back around and placed his hands in his pockets, felt his slim wallet with a few small pound notes inside—enough for a coffee—and gravitated back towards the city's core.

CPSIA information can be obtained at www.ICGtesting.com
Printed in the USA
LVOW06s1943291015

460296LV00008B/1097/P